徐薇

教你懂 新多益
文法
NEW TOEIC

- ◎ 徐薇老師
  精彩解說

- ◎ 多益考點
  精確掌握

眞練習＋文法解析，多益必考重點一次搞定！

徐薇教你懂新多益文法 --- 序

　　從事英語教學二十多年，我深刻了解學習者在學英文和參加英文考試時會遇到的困難。尤其是年齡愈大的學習者，想要學好英文或是應考備戰，最需要的就是「快速而有效的方法」，這正是我們推出《徐薇教你懂新多益文法》的目的，期望透過我一直推動的「徐薇 UP 學」，幫助眾多想挑戰多益測驗及加強英文能力的學習者，以最有效的方式學好英文，英文成績不斷 UP、UP、UP ！

　　《徐薇教你懂新多益文法》一書共有十四個單元，前十二個單元所整理出的文法重點皆是新多益測驗情境中最常出現的文法概念，以精簡易懂的方式將所有常考觀念做有系統的條列式整理歸納，不同於坊間文法書的龐雜瑣碎，《徐薇教你懂新多益文法》希望能幫讀者快速抓重點，用最有效快速的方式掌握新多益測驗的文法命題方向！第十三以及第十四個單元為新多益測驗常出現的片語總整理，讀者可以在最短時間熟悉最常考的詞彙，以達到事半功倍的效果！

　　每單元一開始會有徐薇老師針對不同文法主題所作的重點提醒，搭配例句的解說使讀者更容易融會貫通；此外，每單元結束前皆附有實力挑戰題，讀者可以將每單元所學到的文法觀念再做更進一步的練習。並附上詳細完整的題目解析，即使讀者在家自學也很方便。

　　其實新多益測驗所考的文法多為實用的文法觀念，不會有過於艱深冷僻的文法題，所以只要讀者多做題目、多熟悉單字片語，必定能在新多益測驗中拿到高分。

預祝各位學習者

征戰考場，無往不利！

徐薇

目錄

Unit ❶ 時態

 徐薇老師小叮嚀　🎧 MP3:Unit1

常見的英文時態包括：

	過去式	現在式	未來式
簡單式	過去簡單式	現在簡單式	未來簡單式
進行式	過去進行式	現在進行式	未來進行式
完成式	過去完成式	現在完成式	未來完成式

在多益的文法測驗中，常考的時態不外乎有下列幾種：

(1) 現在簡單式：用來表示「現在的事實、狀態、習慣或動作」以及「不變的事實、真理或格言」等，常搭配表現在的時間副詞 now、every day、daily 或頻率副詞 sometimes、always 等。

例1：My supervisor _____ an inventory of the warehouse daily.
(A) made
(B) makes
(C) has made
(D) will make

(2) 表時間或條件的副詞子句要用現在簡單式代替未來式，主要子句還是要用未來式。

例2：When all the board members _____, the meeting will commence.
(A) arrived
(B) will arrive
(C) has arrived
(D) arrive

(3) 現在完成式：動詞形式為「have/has + p.p.」。表示剛完成的動作、經驗以及從過去某一時間點持續到現在的動作或狀態。

例 3：The financial error _____ unnoticed for the last three quarters.
(A) has gone
(B) went
(C) is going
(D) will go

(4) 現在完成進行式：動詞形式為「have/has + been + V-ing」。現在完成進行式和現在完成式同樣都可以用來表從過去持續至今的動作。

例 4：She _____ one thousand dollars each week for five years.
(A) has been saving
(B) had saved
(C) will save
(D) saves

(5) 過去完成式：動詞形式為「had + p.p.」。過去完成式用來表示比過去簡單式更早發生的動作或經驗。

例 5：The tech giant _____ to release their new tablet before the market tanked.
(A) plans
(B) had planned
(C) has planned
(D) will plan

(6) 未來完成式：動詞形式為「will + have + p.p.」。表示到未來某時已經完成的動作或持續至未來某時為止已經持續一段時間的動作或狀態。

例 6：The study _____ by the time you return from your trip abroad.
(A) will finish
(B) finished
(C) finishes
(D) will have finished

時態重點整理

重點1

表時間或表條件的副詞子句，用現在代替未來，主要子句仍用未來式。

$$
\left.\begin{array}{l}
\text{When/Before/After} \\
\text{As soon as/Until} \\
\text{If/Unless/As long as}
\end{array}\right\} + \text{S.} + 現在式動詞 \sim ， \text{S.} + \text{will} + 原形動詞 \ldots
$$

例 : If the typhoon <u>approaches</u> tomorrow, the workshop <u>will adjourn</u>.
　　　　　　　現在式　　　　　　　　　　　　　　　　　　未來式
（如果明天颱風接近的話，研討會就會延期。）

重點2

現在完成式常考句型 (1)：

$$
\text{S.} + \text{have/has} + \text{p.p.} \sim + \left\{\begin{array}{l}
\text{for} + 一段時間 \\
\text{since} + 一段時間 + \text{ago} \\
\text{since} + 過去某時間點 \\
\text{since} + \text{S.} + 過去式動詞
\end{array}\right.
$$

例1 : The accountant has been on sick leave <u>for five days</u>.
（會計已經請五天病假了。）

例2 : This bridge has been under construction <u>since a month ago</u>.
（這座橋自從一個月前就在施工了。）

例3 : I have worked for this company <u>since 1998</u>.
（自從 1998 年起我就一直在這家公司工作。）

例4 : Ten people have been laid off <u>since</u> the new manager <u>took office</u>.
（自從新經理上任之後，已經有十個人被裁員了。）

重點3

現在完成式常考句型 (2)：

$$S. + have/has + p.p.\sim + \begin{Bmatrix} in \\ for \\ over \\ during \end{Bmatrix} + the + past/last + 一段時間$$

★ 此句型的現在完成式也可以用現在完成進行式，強調動作到現在仍一直在持續。

例1：The yen has depreciated by 25% <u>over the past ten days</u>.
（在過去的十天以來，日圓已貶值了百分之二十五。）

例2：David has been working on the project <u>for the last two weeks</u>.
（過去的兩星期以來，David 一直在忙著這個企畫案。）

重點4

過去完成式的使用時機：

發生於過去的兩個動作，
先發生的用過去完成式 (had + p.p.)，後發生的用過去簡單式 (V-ed)。

例1：All the flights <u>had been booked</u> before he <u>decided</u> to fly home.
（在他決定要搭飛機回家前，所有的班機早就都被預訂了。）

例2：By the time the police <u>were</u> on the scene, the kidnapper <u>had already fled</u>.
（在警方抵達現場時，綁匪早已經逃走了。）

連續發生的短暫動作，如有連接詞 before, after, as soon as 等明顯標示出先後，則兩動作皆可用過去簡單式 (V-ed)。

例3：Before Eric <u>left</u> the office, he <u>had turned off</u> the air conditioner.
= Before Eric <u>left</u> the office, he <u>turned off</u> the air conditioner.
（Eric 離開辦公室之前先關掉了冷氣。）

重點5

未來完成式的使用時機：

① 到未來某時間點時已經完成的動作
② 未來某動作之前已經完成的動作
③ 持續至未來某時為止已經持續一段時間的動作或狀態
④ 至未來某時為止的經驗

例1 ： I <u>will have gotten</u> the financial report done <u>by</u> this time tomorrow.
（明天這個時候我將已經完成財務報告。）

例2 ： When you come back, I <u>will have finished</u> mopping the floor.
（你回來時，我將已經拖完地了。）

例3 ： She <u>will have worked</u> as the editor-in-chief of the China Post for twenty years <u>by</u> next year.
（到明年為止，她將已經擔任中國郵報的主編有二十年了。）

例4 ： You <u>will have watched</u> this movie six times if you watch it again.
（如果你再看一次，你這部電影就看了六遍了。）

Give it a try! 實力挑戰題

1 When all the board members _____, the meeting will commence.
(A) arrived
(B) will arrive
(C) has arrived
(D) arrive
Ⓐ Ⓑ Ⓒ Ⓓ

2 She _____ one thousand dollars each week for five years.
(A) has been saving
(B) had saved
(C) will save
(D) saves
Ⓐ Ⓑ Ⓒ Ⓓ

3 The politician _____ before the agents tackled the gunman.
(A) has been shot
(B) will have shot
(C) had been shot
(D) had shot
Ⓐ Ⓑ Ⓒ Ⓓ

4 Before the night comes to an end, we _____ the lifetime achievement award.
(A) have presented
(B) will present
(C) had presented
(D) present
Ⓐ Ⓑ Ⓒ Ⓓ

5 Ellen had hosted the last ten dinner parties before Regina _____ to host this one.
(A) agreed
(B) agrees
(C) will agree
(D) had agreed
Ⓐ Ⓑ Ⓒ Ⓓ

6 Your son _____ from senior high school by the time you receive your Ph.D.

(A) will graduate

(B) has graduated

(C) will have graduated

(D) graduates

Ⓐ Ⓑ Ⓒ Ⓓ

7 As long as the temperature _____ mild, our family reunion will take place at the park.

(A) was

(B) is

(C) has been

(D) will be

Ⓐ Ⓑ Ⓒ Ⓓ

8 Mark has been employed by this firm since he _____ from law school.

(A) graduates

(B) has graduated

(C) graduated

(D) will graduate

Ⓐ Ⓑ Ⓒ Ⓓ

9 The study _____ by the time you return from your trip abroad.

(A) will finish

(B) will have finished

(C) finishes

(D) finished

Ⓐ Ⓑ Ⓒ Ⓓ

10 The financial error has gone unnoticed _____.

(A) for the last three quarters

(B) since you are on board

(C) since three quarters

(D) since he takes over as manager

Ⓐ Ⓑ Ⓒ Ⓓ

11 Brian _____ an elaborate backyard garden over the past five years.
(A) had been constructing
(B) will have constructed
(C) has been constructing
(D) is constructing   Ⓐ Ⓑ Ⓒ Ⓓ

12 Dallas, Texas has just recently become one of the most popular places to host international events _____.
(A) in the past three years
(B) for three years ago
(C) among the last three years
(D) since three years   Ⓐ Ⓑ Ⓒ Ⓓ

13 The financial report had already been released before the CFO _____ the numbers had been inflated.
(A) realizes
(B) will realize
(C) has realized
(D) realized   Ⓐ Ⓑ Ⓒ Ⓓ

14 You _____ over two million dollars by the time you retire if you keep up this pace.
(A) have saved
(B) had saved
(C) will have saved
(D) saved   Ⓐ Ⓑ Ⓒ Ⓓ

15 The tech giant _____ to release their new tablet before the market tanked.
(A) plans
(B) had planned
(C) has planned
(D) will plan   Ⓐ Ⓑ Ⓒ Ⓓ

16 It _____ that the regional manager has been embezzling money since 1998.
(A) has been unearthed
(B) have been unearthed
(C) has unearthed
(D) will have been unearthed Ⓐ Ⓑ Ⓒ Ⓓ

17 As long as everyone _____ in, we will be able to open the shop in under one week.
(A) will pitch
(B) pitches
(C) will have pitched
(D) pitched Ⓐ Ⓑ Ⓒ Ⓓ

18 The stream _____ for five years by the corrupt chemical company.
(A) have polluted
(B) has been polluted
(C) was polluted
(D) had polluted Ⓐ Ⓑ Ⓒ Ⓓ

19 All of Rick's dreams had been realized before he _____ thirty years old.
(A) had been
(B) is
(C) was
(D) will be Ⓐ Ⓑ Ⓒ Ⓓ

20 Our stock has shot up in value _____ the past two weeks.
(A) since
(B) at
(C) within
(D) over Ⓐ Ⓑ Ⓒ Ⓓ

Unit ② 假設語氣

徐薇老師小叮嚀　　　🎧 MP3:Unit2

在多益的文法測驗中，假設語氣的相關文法雖算不上是高頻率出現的題型，但因為句型的種類繁多及其特殊性，還是要稍加留意。

(1) 和現在事實相反的假設句型：條件子句用過去簡單式，主要句一律用 would/should/could/might + 原形動詞

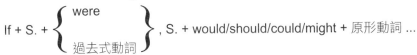

If + S. + { were / 過去式動詞 }, S. + would/should/could/might + 原形動詞 ...

例 1：If I _____ you, I would continue to argue with your insurance company until they compromise.
(A) am
(B) were
(C) had
(D) will be

(2) 和過去事實相反的假設句型：條件子句用過去完成式，主要句一律用 would/should/could/might + have + p.p.

例 2：If you _____ the presentation, you would have gotten a better grasp of how the new software works.
(A) attended
(B) attends
(C) had attended
(D) will attend

(3) 表「要求、命令、堅持、建議」的句型：此四大類動詞後所接的 that 子句中要用助動詞 should，而且 should 常常被省略掉，留下後方的原形動詞。

例 3：My boss demanded that I _____ working on such a pointless project.
(A) ceased
(B) to cease
(C) ceasing
(D) cease

(4) 表「做 ... 是必要或較好的」特殊句型：此句型的結構為 It is + 表必要或較好的形容詞 + that + S. + (should) + 原形動詞……。

例 4 : It is vital that Angela _____ the server tonight while we do some web site maintenance.

(A) monitors
(B) monitored
(C) had monitored
(D) monitor

假設語氣重點整理

重點1

和現在事實相反的假設句型

$$If + S. + \begin{cases} were \\ 過去式動詞 \end{cases}, S. + would/should/could/might + 原形動詞 ...$$

例 1 : If I <u>were</u> a member of the board, I <u>would oppose</u> some of the conditions in the contract.

(如果我是董事會成員的話，我會反對合約中的一些條款。)

例 2 : If he <u>had</u> enough capital, he <u>might expand</u> his business by opening more branches.

(如果他有足夠的資金，他可能會藉由開設更多分店來拓展業務。)

重點2

和過去事實相反的假設句型

If + S. + had p.p.~ , S. + would/should/could/might + have + p.p....

例1 : If we <u>had left</u> earlier this morning, we <u>could have made</u> it to get to the airport in time.

（如果我們今早早點離開的話，我們就可以及時抵達機場了。）

例2 : If the product <u>had been advertised</u> then, this company <u>would have racked up</u> more profits.

（如果當時這產品有打廣告的話，這家公司就會獲利更多了。）

重點3

混和型假設

> If + S. + <u>had p.p.~</u> , S. + <u>would/should/could/might + 原形動詞</u> ....
>   和過去相反　　　　　　　　　和現在相反

例1 : If you <u>had attended</u> the training seminar last week, you <u>would not encounter</u> so many difficulties now.

（假如你上週有參加訓練研習的話，你現在就不會遭遇如此多的困難了。）

例2 : If my parents <u>hadn't encouraged</u> me to submit my writing to publishing companies five years ago, I <u>wouldn't be</u> here to receive this award.

（如果我父母親在五年前沒有鼓勵我向出版社投稿的話，我現在就不會在這兒接受這個獎。）

重點4

表「萬一」的假設

> If + S. + should + 原形動詞 ~ , { S. + would/should/could/might + V.
>   S. + will/can/may/should + V.
>   祈使句
>
> ★ 此句型中的 should 表「萬一」

例1 : If it <u>should rain</u> tomorrow, the job fair <u>would be postponed</u>.

（假如明天下雨的話，就業博覽會就會延期。）

例2 : If he <u>should change</u> his mind, please <u>let</u> me know.
(萬一他改變心意，請讓我知道。)

重點5

if 的省略

① If + S. + were~, S. + would/should/could/might + 原形動詞
= Were + S. ~, S. + would/should/could/might + 原形動詞
② If + S. + had p.p.~, S. + would/should/could/might + have p.p....
= Had + S.+ p.p. ~, S. + would/should/could/might + have p.p....
③ If + S. + should + 原形動詞 ~ ⎫   ⎧ S. + would/should/could/might + V.
                                  ⎬ , ⎨ S. + will/can/may/should + V.
= Should + S. + 原形動詞 ~   ⎭   ⎩ 祈使句

例1 : If <u>I were</u> you, I wouldn't accept the job offer.
= <u>Were I</u> you, I wouldn't accept the job offer.
(如果我是你，我不會接受這份工作。)

例2 : If <u>Marvin hadn't violated</u> the department rules, he wouldn't have been demoted.
= <u>Hadn't Marvin violated</u> the department rules, he wouldn't have been demoted.
(如果 Marvin 沒有違反部門規定的話，他就不會被降職了。)

例3 : If <u>you should</u> need my help, don't hesitate to call me at any time.
= <u>Should you</u> need my help, don't hesitate to call me at any time.
(萬一你需要我幫忙，馬上打電話給我。)

重點6

wish 的假設句型

$$S. + wish + (that) + \begin{cases} S. + were/\ 過去式動詞\ ....(\ 和現在事實相反\ ) \\ S. + had\ p.p................(\ 和過去事實相反\ ) \end{cases}$$

例1 : I wish I <u>were</u> a bit taller.
(但願我可以再高一點。)

例2 : The legislator wishes that he <u>hadn't gotten involved</u> in the scandal.
(那位立委真希望自己沒有捲入這宗醜聞中。)

重點7

表「若非；要不是」的假設句型

(1) 和現在事實相反的表達法：

① But for
　 Without
　 If it were not for
　 Were it not for
$\Big\}$ + N., S. + would/should/could/might + 原形動詞

② But that + S. + 現在式動詞 , S. + would/should/could/might + 原形動詞

(2) 和過去事實相反的表達法：

① But for
　 Without
　 If it had not been for
　 Had it not been for
$\Big\}$ + N., S. + would/should/could/might + have p.p...

② But that + S. + 過去式動詞 ., S. + would/should/could/might + have p.p.

例1 : But for your sponsorship, the exhibition wouldn't be held as scheduled.

= Without your sponsorship, the exhibition wouldn't be held as scheduled.

= If it were not for your sponsorship, the exhibition wouldn't be held as scheduled.

= Were it not for your sponsorship, the exhibition wouldn't be held as scheduled.

= But that you sponsor the exhibition, it wouldn't be held as scheduled.

(要不是有你的贊助，展覽就無法如期舉行了。)

例2 : But for your encouragement, I might have given up then.

= Without your encouragement, I might have given up then.

= If it had not been for your encouragement, I might have given up then.

= Had it not been for your encouragement, I might have given up then.

= But that you encouraged me, I might have given up then.

(要不是有你的鼓勵，我當時可能早就放棄了。)

重點8

It is + adj.+ that + S. + (should) + 原形動詞 的假設句型

It is + 表必要或較好的形容詞 + that + S. + (should) + 原形動詞……

⇨ 此句型通常是表說話者認為做某事是「必要或較好」的主觀意見

⇨ 常用於此句型的形容詞主要有：

① 重要的：important, vital, crucial

② 必須必要的：necessary, essential, imperative

③ 適當的：appropriate, proper

④ 其他：better (比較好的)，advisable (明智的)，natural (自然的)，desirable (合意的)，preferable (更好的、更合意的)

例1 : It is necessary that you (should) keep regular hours if you want to be healthy.
（如果你想要身體健康的話，你有必要養成規律的作息。）

例2 : It is better that you (should) stay here and wait until further instructions.
（你待在這兒等候進一步指示是比較好的。）

重點9

表「該是做～的時候了」的假設句型

It is (high/right/about) time +
{
that + S. + 過去式動詞 ....
that + S. + should + 原形動詞 ...
for + sb. + to 原形動詞 ....
}

例1 : It is time that you <u>had</u> your hair cut.
= It is time that you <u>should have</u> your hair cut.
= It is time for you <u>to have</u> your hair cut.
（該是你去剪頭髮的時候了。）

重點10

表「要命堅建」的假設句型

S. + 要命堅建動詞 + that + S. + (should) + (not) + 原形動詞
⇨ 適用於此句型的動詞主要有以下幾大類：
① 要求：ask, demand, require, request
② 命令：order, command
③ 堅持：insist, maintain
④ 建議：advise, move, propose, recommend, suggest

例1 : The doctor suggested that my father (should) abstain from smoking.
（醫生建議我父親應該要戒菸。）

例2 : David insisted that we (should) go Dutch.
（大衛堅持我們應該各付各的。）

Give it a try! 實力挑戰題

1 If I _____ you, I would continue to argue with your insurance company until they compromise.
(A) am
(B) were
(C) had
(D) will be
Ⓐ Ⓑ Ⓒ Ⓓ

2 If you _____ the presentation, you would have gotten a better grasp of how the new software works.
(A) attended
(B) attends
(C) had attended
(D) will attend
Ⓐ Ⓑ Ⓒ Ⓓ

3 If you should run into a problem with logging in, you _____ the help desk.
(A) called
(B) had called
(C) should call
(D) have called
Ⓐ Ⓑ Ⓒ Ⓓ

4 If you hadn't given me that stock tip last year, I _____ so well off financially now.
(A) wouldn't be
(B) will not be
(C) wouldn't have been
(D) would be
Ⓐ Ⓑ Ⓒ Ⓓ

5 If I _____ that this truck was going to break down so often, I would not have bought it.

(A) have known

(B) had known

(C) knew

(D) know
Ⓐ Ⓑ Ⓒ Ⓓ

6 Sally wishes she _____ the time and money to play golf once a week now.

(A) had

(B) has

(C) had had

(D) have
Ⓐ Ⓑ Ⓒ Ⓓ

7 _____ you created your profile, the company would never have recruited you.

(A) If

(B) Hadn't

(C) Should

(D) Were
Ⓐ Ⓑ Ⓒ Ⓓ

8 It is natural that you _____ so many questions as you are a new employee.

(A) asked

(B) had asked

(C) should ask

(D) to ask
Ⓐ Ⓑ Ⓒ Ⓓ

9 My boss demanded that I _____ working on such a pointless project.

(A) ceased

(B) to cease

(C) ceasing

(D) cease
Ⓐ Ⓑ Ⓒ Ⓓ

10 Becky advised that her husband _____ his job until he finds a new one.

(A) not quit

(B) not to quit

(C) quit not

(D) should quit ⒶⒷⒸⒹ

11 It is about time that you _____ your back examined by a chiropractor.

(A) have

(B) to have

(C) had

(D) had had ⒶⒷⒸⒹ

12 If I _____ business instead of literature, I might have obtained employment more quickly.

(A) studied

(B) should study

(C) had studied

(D) study ⒶⒷⒸⒹ

13 If I _____ a reliable car, I would not have to take public transportation every day.

(A) were

(B) had

(C) have

(D) had had ⒶⒷⒸⒹ

14 _____ Ken's generosity, the museum wouldn't have had the funding to stay open.

(A) But for

(B) But that

(C) Were it for

(D) With ⒶⒷⒸⒹ

15 But that you _____ me, I might not have pursued engineering as my major in the first place.

(A) encouraged

(B) encouragement

(C) had encouraged

(D) have encouraged ⒶⒷⒸⒹ

- ▶

16 It is vital that Angela _____ the server tonight while we do some web site maintenance.

(A) monitors

(B) monitored

(C) had monitored

(D) monitor ⒶⒷⒸⒹ

- ▶

17 If you _____ sick, you might want to try this newly approved medicine that I brought back from Europe.

(A) had felt

(B) feel

(C) should feel

(D) are feeling ⒶⒷⒸⒹ

- ▶

18 If you were as talented as Bobby, you _____ an athletic scholarship to any university you wanted.

(A) can get

(B) could get

(C) could have gotten

(D) should have gotten ⒶⒷⒸⒹ

- ▶

19 I wish I _____ a better understanding of computer operating systems.

(A) have

(B) will have

(C) had

(D) have had ⒶⒷⒸⒹ

20 If our company had relocated our factories to Vietnam, we _____ so many issues with government regulations now.

(A) wouldn't have

(B) wouldn't have had

(C) had

(D) won't have

Ⓐ Ⓑ Ⓒ Ⓓ

Unit ③ 不定詞與動名詞

徐薇老師小叮嚀　🎧 MP3:Unit3

(1) 動名詞形式為 V-ing，不定詞形式為 to V，否定則是 not to V；動名詞和不定詞都可以當句子的主詞、受詞或主詞補語，若動名詞或不定詞當主詞時，後方動詞記得一定要用單數。

例1：To predict technology trends several months in advance _____ risky.
(A) is
(B) are
(C) have
(D) has

(2) 只能接動名詞當受詞的動詞有：spend、finish、practice、keep、enjoy、admit、deny、delay 等；只能接不定詞當受詞的動詞有：want、decide、hope、afford、attempt、hesitate、intend 等。

例2：If you attempt _____ your cell phone service before the two-year agreement expires, you will incur a significant fine.
(A) to cancel
(B) canceling
(C) to canceling
(D) canceled

例3：The marketing department has delayed _____ out their new campaign.
(A) to roll
(B) to rolling
(C) rolling
(D) rolled

(3) 有些片語中的 to 為介系詞，所以後方的動詞要改為動名詞，不可以接原形動詞。常考的有：look forward to（期待）、object to（反對）、be dedicated to（致力於）... 等等。

> **例 4**：I am looking forward _____ our 25-year class reunion.
> (A) to attend
> (B) of attending
> (C) in attending
> (D) to attending

(4) wh- + 不定詞 形成「名詞片語」，可以當作句子的主詞或受詞。

> **例 4**：If you have any question about _____ a deal, Sean is the person who can give you some advice.
> (A) how to close
> (B) how closing
> (C) if to close
> (D) to close

不定詞與動名詞重點整理

重點1

不定詞當主詞

> <u>To + 原形動詞 ~</u> + 單數動詞 ......
>   主詞
> = <u>It</u> + 單數動詞 .....+ <u>to + 原形動詞 ~</u>
> 虛主詞   真主詞

> **例 1**：<u>To travel around the world</u> is my dream.
> = It is my dream to travel around the world.
> (環遊世界是我的夢想。)

> **例 2**：<u>To deal with customers' complaints carefully</u> is of great importance.
> = It is of great importance to deal with customers' complaints carefully.
> (小心處理客戶投訴是很重要的。)

重點2

不定詞當受詞

句型：
S. + Vt. + <u>to + 原形動詞</u> ....
　　　　　　受詞

例1：I <u>would like to say</u> thanks to those who participated in this significant event.

（我想要向所有參加這個有意義活動的人說聲謝謝。）

例2：If you do not <u>wish to receive</u> our catalog, we will exclude you from our mailing list.

（如果你不想收到我們的目錄，我們會將您從郵寄名單中刪除。）

必須接不定詞作受詞的動詞有：

agree （同意）	aim （旨在）	aspire （渴望）	appear （似乎）
afford （負擔的起）	attempt （企圖）	choose （選擇）	consent （同意）
decide （決定）	determine （決定）	desire （渴望）	decline （婉拒）
expect （期待）	endeavor （努力）	fail （未能）	guarantee （保證）
hesitate （猶豫）	hope （希望）	intend （打算）	long （渴望）
manage （設法做到）	mean （有意）	need （需要）	offer （提議；主動提出）
plan （計畫）	promise （答應）	pretend （假裝）	refuse （拒絕）
resolve （決定）	seem （似乎）	swear （發誓）	volunteer （自願）
want （想要）	would like （想要）	would love （想要）	wish （希望）

重點3

不定詞當受詞補語

句型：S. + Vt. + O. + (not)+ <u>to + 原形動詞</u> ....
　　　　　　　　　　　　　 受詞補語

例1 : The manager <u>encouraged</u> all interns <u>to attend</u> the training workshop.
（經理鼓勵所有實習工讀生參加訓練研討會。）

例2 : My father <u>advised</u> me <u>not to criticize</u> my former employer in the job interview.
（我父親建議我不要在求職面試中批評前雇主。）

必須接不定詞當受詞補語的動詞有：

ask （要求）	allow （允許）	advise （建議）	cause （致使）
compel （強迫）	command （命令）	convince （說服）	enable （使能夠）
encourage （鼓勵）	expect （期待）	force （強迫）	forbid （禁止）
instruct （命令；指導）	inspire （激發）	order （命令）	permit （允許）
persuade （說服）	pressure （施加壓力）	remind （提醒）	request （要求）
require （要求）	teach （教導）	tell （告訴）	tempt （引誘）
urge （催促）	warn （警告）	want （想要）	wish （希望）
would like （想要）	prompt （促使）		

重點4

不定詞當形容詞

> 句型：N.+ to + 原形動詞 ....
> 　　　　　 形容詞
> 注意：若不定詞的動詞為不及物動詞，則後面要接介系詞。

例1： I have nothing to say.
（我無話可說。）

⇨ to say 修飾 nothing

例2： He needs someone to talk to.
（他需要聊天的對象。）

⇨ to talk to 修飾 someone。
talk 為不及物動詞，所以後方要接介系詞 to。

重點5

不定詞表「目的」

> 句型：S. + V. ......+ to + 原形動詞 ....
> 　　　　　　　　 副詞
> 　　 = To + 原形動詞 ...., S. + V..............
> 注意：表目的的不定詞亦可以置於句首。

例1： All the design staff worked overtime to meet the deadline.
= To meet the deadline, all the design staff worked overtime.
（所有設計團隊的人都加班是為了趕上截止期限。）

例2： The assistant put up a notice to inform all the employees of the cancellation of the presentation.
= To inform all the employees of the cancellation of the presentation, the assistant put up a notice.
（助理張貼了告示以通知所有員工演講取消的消息。）

📖 其他表「目的」的句型：

① S. + V. ~ + in order to Vr. ......= S. + V. ~ + so as to Vr.........
   = In order to Vr........, S. + V.~ = S. + V. ~ + in an effort to Vr. ......

   例：He went to the U.S. <u>in order to pursue</u> his interests.
   　　　= He went to the U.S. <u>so as to pursue</u> his interests.
   　　　= <u>In order to pursue</u> his interests, he went to the U.S.
   　　　= He went to the U.S. <u>in an effort to pursue</u> his interests.
   　　　(為了追求興趣，他去了美國。)

   注意：so as to 不可以移至句首

② S. + V. ~ + so that + S. + V...........
   = S. + V. ~ + in order that + S. + V...........

   例：He went to the U.S. <u>so that</u> he could pursue his interests.
   　　　= He went to the U.S. <u>in order that</u> he could pursue his
   　　　　interests.
   　　　(為了追求興趣，他去了美國。)

③ S. + V. ~ + with a view to + V-ing......
   = S. + V. ~ + with an eye to + V-ing......
   = S. + V. ~ + for the purpose of + V-ing......

   例：He went to the U.S. <u>with a view to pursuing</u> his interests.
   　　　= He went to the U.S. <u>with an eye to pursuing</u> his interests.
   　　　= He went to the U.S. <u>for the purpose of pursuing</u> his interests.
   　　　(為了追求興趣，他去了美國。)

重點6

動名詞當主詞

<u>V-ing~</u> + 單數動詞 ......
主詞

　　例 1：<u>Working on the project alone</u> helps to improve my efficiency.
　　　　　(獨自做這個企劃案有助於改善我的效率。)
　　例 2：<u>Advertising a new product</u> is costly, but it is really worth it.
　　　　　(替新商品打廣告雖然所費不貲，但卻是值得的。)

重點7

動名詞當受詞

句型：
S. + Vt. + <u>V-ing........</u>
　　　　　　　受詞

例1：The accountant <u>admitted</u> <u>tampering with the financial report</u>.
（會計承認竄改財務報告。）

例2：It is said that the board <u>is considering</u> <u>merging these two departments</u>.
（據說董事會正在考慮將這兩個部門合併。）

必須接動名詞當受詞的動詞有：

admit （承認）	acknowledge （承認）	avoid （避免）	allow （允許）
appreciate （感激）	anticipate （期待）	burst out （突然）	consider （考慮）
commence （開始）	carry on （繼續）	can't help （忍不住）	delay （延期）
deny （否認）	defer （延期）	enjoy （喜愛）	escape （倖免）
finish （完成）	fancy （想像）	feel like （想要）	give up （放棄）
imagine （想像）	involve （牽涉；包含）	keep （持續）	loathe （厭惡）
mind （介意）	miss （錯過）	oppose （反對）	practice （練習）
put off （延期）	picture （想像）	postpone （延期）	quit （停止）
risk （冒險）	resist （抗拒）	suggest （建議）	take to （開始養成習慣做~）

重點8

動名詞的常考句型

(1) It is no use + V-ing (做…是沒有用處的)
(2) There is no + V-ing (不可能…)
(3) cannot help + V-ing (忍不住…)
    = cannot help but + 原形動詞
    = cannot but + 原形動詞
(4) have + trouble/difficulty/a problem/a hard time + V-ing
    (做…有困難)
(5) have + fun/a good time + V-ing (做…很開心)
(6) be busy + V-ing (忙著做…)

例1 : It is no use crying over spilt milk.
(覆水難收。)

例2 : There is no denying that this new marketing strategy does boost sales.
(無可否認這個新的行銷策略真的提高了銷售量。)

例3 : I couldn't help crying when I saw this picture of my mother.
(看到我母親的這張照片時,我忍不住哭了。)

例4 : I have difficulty adapting myself to the pace of life here.
(我對於適應這兒的生活步調有困難。)

例5 : I had a good time chatting with you.
(跟你聊天我很開心。)

例6 : Jenny is busy rehearsing for the recital.
(Jenny 正忙著為獨奏會排練。)

重點9

to 當介系詞，後面要接名詞或動名詞的常考片語

(1) look forward to (盼望)

(2) object to (反對) = be opposed to = oppose

(3) $\begin{Bmatrix} be \\ become \\ get \end{Bmatrix}$ + $\begin{Bmatrix} used \\ accustomed \end{Bmatrix}$ + to (現在習慣…)

(4) adapt oneself to (適應…) = be adapted to

(5) be addicted to (沉迷於…)

(6) in addition to (除了…之外) = besides = aside from = apart from

(7) when it comes to + N./V-ing, …(一談到…)

(8) devote/dedicate + oneself/N. + to + N./V-ing (致力於…)

　= be devoted/dedicated to + N./V-ing

例1 : I am <u>looking forward to</u> <u>attending</u> your wedding.
（ 我很期待參加你的婚禮。）

例2 : Most of the residents in this village <u>object to</u> <u>construction</u> of the nuclear power plant.
（ 這個村莊大部分居民都反對核電廠的興建。）

例3 : I <u>am not used to</u> <u>getting up</u> so early.
（ 我不習慣這麼早起。）

例4 : It took the newcomer a long time to <u>adapt himself to</u> the working environment.
（ 這位新手花了很多時間才適應這個工作環境。）

例5 : My sister <u>is addicted to</u> <u>watching</u> Korean soap operas.
（ 我姐姐很迷韓劇。）

例6 : <u>In addition to</u> <u>swimming</u>, I work out twice a week.
（ 除了游泳之外，我一星期健身兩次。）

例7 : <u>When it comes to</u> <u>cooking</u>, my mother is an expert.
（ 談到烹飪，我母親可是位專家。）

例8 : This non-profit organization <u>is dedicated to</u> <u>providing</u> relief supplies for hunger-stricken people in Africa.
（ 這個非營利組織致力於提供救援物資給非洲飽受飢荒之苦的人們。）

Give it a try! 實力挑戰題

1 It is the duty of this department _____ our finances accurately.
(A) audit
(B) to audit
(C) to auditing
(D) will audit   Ⓐ Ⓑ Ⓒ Ⓓ

2 Tom aims _____ the conflict with his neighbors by erecting a fence around his yard.
(A) to resolve
(B) to resolving
(C) resolving
(D) resolved   Ⓐ Ⓑ Ⓒ Ⓓ

3 You always urge me _____ close attention to all the details before signing a contract.
(A) pay
(B) to paying
(C) paid
(D) to pay   Ⓐ Ⓑ Ⓒ Ⓓ

4 She joined an athletic club with an eye to _____ ten kilograms.
(A) losing
(B) lose
(C) lost
(D) loss   Ⓐ Ⓑ Ⓒ Ⓓ

5 If you attempt _____ your cell phone service before the two-year agreement expires, you will incur a significant fine.
(A) to cancel
(B) canceling
(C) to canceling
(D) canceled   Ⓐ Ⓑ Ⓒ Ⓓ

6 The salesman tempted me _____ the highest quality smart phone in the shop.

(A) purchasing

(B) to purchase

(C) to purchasing

(D) purchase   Ⓐ Ⓑ Ⓒ Ⓓ

----

7 My sister bought a sleek luxury car _____ off her wealth to everyone.

(A) showing

(B) to showing

(C) to show

(D) for showing   Ⓐ Ⓑ Ⓒ Ⓓ

----

8 The sign warns park patrons _____.

(A) not to litter

(B) to not litter

(C) not litter

(D) not littering   Ⓐ Ⓑ Ⓒ Ⓓ

----

9 _____ child obesity, the mayor lobbied for the construction of a new community recreation center.

(A) So as to combat

(B) To combatting

(C) With a view to combat

(D) To combat   Ⓐ Ⓑ Ⓒ Ⓓ

----

10 You finally persuaded me _____ my house on the market.

(A) to putting

(B) to put

(C) putting

(D) put   Ⓐ Ⓑ Ⓒ Ⓓ

11 _____ peace with our neighboring countries is the political aim of my administration.

(A) To making

(B) Make

(C) Made

(D) To make Ⓐ Ⓑ Ⓒ Ⓓ

12 The city government refuses _____ recycling pickup more frequently than once a week.

(A) to offer

(B) to offering

(C) offer

(D) offering Ⓐ Ⓑ Ⓒ Ⓓ

13 The secretary recorded a new voice mail greeting _____ a list of the office's holiday hours.

(A) providing

(B) to provide

(C) to providing

(D) provided Ⓐ Ⓑ Ⓒ Ⓓ

14 Kevin took the family out to a high-end restaurant _____ the special occasion of his big job promotion.

(A) to mark

(B) marking

(C) as to mark

(D) in order to marking Ⓐ Ⓑ Ⓒ Ⓓ

15 It is the vision of our nonprofit organization _____ all children with access to great after-school programs.

(A) providing

(B) to provide

(C) to providing

(D) provided Ⓐ Ⓑ Ⓒ Ⓓ

16 I would like _____ my gratitude to you for covering for me when I was out sick with the flu.

(A) expressing

(B) to expressing

(C) to express

(D) express

Ⓐ Ⓑ Ⓒ Ⓓ

17 _____ technology trends several months in advance is risky.

(A) Predict

(B) To predicting

(C) Predicted

(D) To predict

Ⓐ Ⓑ Ⓒ Ⓓ

18 He took classes _____ upgrade his skill set and improve his job prospects.

(A) so as to

(B) as to

(C) so that

(D) with a view to

Ⓐ Ⓑ Ⓒ Ⓓ

19 The tension between these two countries caused oil prices _____ sharply.

(A) rise

(B) to rise

(C) rising

(D) to rising

Ⓐ Ⓑ Ⓒ Ⓓ

20 My mentor taught me _____ to know a customer before I try to recommend anything to him or her.

(A) to getting

(B) getting

(C) to get

(D) get

Ⓐ Ⓑ Ⓒ Ⓓ

21 _____ new software allows me _____ up with the newest trends in the field of graphic design.

(A) Purchasing; to keep

(B) Purchasing; keeping

(C) To purchase; keeping

(D) Purchase; keep

Ⓐ Ⓑ Ⓒ Ⓓ

22 The marketing department has delayed _____ out their new campaign.

(A) to roll

(B) to rolling

(C) rolling

(D) rolled

Ⓐ Ⓑ Ⓒ Ⓓ

23 It is no use _____ the truth in light of the new evidence.

(A) to deny

(B) to denying

(C) of denying

(D) denying

Ⓐ Ⓑ Ⓒ Ⓓ

24 We couldn't help _____ why the policy remains unchanged.

(A) wondering

(B) wonder

(C) but wondering

(D) but to wonder

Ⓐ Ⓑ Ⓒ Ⓓ

25 I have a hard time _____ that Gary got the manager position and not me.

(A) to accept

(B) accepting

(C) to accepting

(D) accepted

Ⓐ Ⓑ Ⓒ Ⓓ

26 When it comes to _____ the best products, this Japanese company has no equal.
(A) innovate
(B) innovating
(C) innovation
(D) innovated　　　　　　　　　　ⒶⒷⒸⒹ

27 The new private school is devoted to _____ students the best education money can buy.
(A) giving
(B) give
(C) gave
(D) given　　　　　　　　　　ⒶⒷⒸⒹ

28 _____ the report was time-consuming, but it was vital for every employee _____ the current status of the company.
(A) Preparing; understanding
(B) To prepare; understanding
(C) Prepare; to understand
(D) Preparing; to understand　　　　　　　　　　ⒶⒷⒸⒹ

29 The news editor opposed _____ the scandalous story to the public.
(A) to release
(B) to releasing
(C) releasing
(D) being released　　　　　　　　　　ⒶⒷⒸⒹ

30 I have become accustomed to _____ in this college town.
(A) living
(B) live
(C) lived
(D) being lived　　　　　　　　　　ⒶⒷⒸⒹ

31 I have become a vegetarian in addition to _____ my daily calorie intake.
(A) lower
(B) lowering
(C) lowered
(D) being lowered   Ⓐ Ⓑ Ⓒ Ⓓ

---

32 _____ when Mr. Andrews will make a decision.
(A) There is not second-guessing
(B) It is impossible second-guessing
(C) It is no second-guessing
(D) There is no second-guessing   Ⓐ Ⓑ Ⓒ Ⓓ

---

33 I am busy _____ my car's engine and can't come to the party.
(A) repairing
(B) to repair
(C) with repairing
(D) to repairing   Ⓐ Ⓑ Ⓒ Ⓓ

---

34 It is common for overworked, stressed out employees to get addicted to _____ drinks which contain caffeine.
(A) have
(B) having
(C) had
(D) have had   Ⓐ Ⓑ Ⓒ Ⓓ

---

35 I am looking forward _____ our 25-year class reunion.
(A) to attend
(B) of attending
(C) in attending
(D) to attending   Ⓐ Ⓑ Ⓒ Ⓓ

36 _____ the most efficient way to produce microchips is essential to our business.

(A) Research

(B) To researching

(C) Researching

(D) Researched   Ⓐ Ⓑ Ⓒ Ⓓ

37 I have a problem _____ Charles as a creative genius.

(A) imagining

(B) to imagine

(C) to imagining

(D) with imagining   Ⓐ Ⓑ Ⓒ Ⓓ

38 Granting employees an hour-long lunch break _____ them re-energize for the afternoon rush.

(A) lets

(B) make

(C) have

(D) get   Ⓐ Ⓑ Ⓒ Ⓓ

39 I couldn't help _____ depressed when I learned that we might need to make job cuts to avoid bankruptcy.

(A) but to feel

(B) but feeling

(C) feeling

(D) felt   Ⓐ Ⓑ Ⓒ Ⓓ

40 _____ that our main competitor's product is superior to ours.

(A) It is not denying

(B) There is no denying

(C) It is not impossible denying

(D) It is no denying   Ⓐ Ⓑ Ⓒ Ⓓ

Unit ❹ 分詞

徐薇老師小叮嚀　　🎧 MP3:Unit4

在多益的文法測驗中，分詞的相關文法算是高頻率常出現的題型，包括了分詞構句、分詞片語、情緒分詞的用法，這些都是要特別注意的題型。

(1) 分詞構句：分詞構句由副詞子句簡化而來，當副詞子句與主要子句主詞相同時，主詞則去掉，不相同時則保留，接下來再將動詞改為分詞，主動改為現在分詞，被動則保留過去分詞。連接詞除了表因果關係的 because 之外，其餘皆可保留喔！

例1 : _____ the lifetime achievement award, he couldn't help but weep.
(A) Receiving
(B) To receive
(C) Received
(D) Receipt

(2) 分詞片語：分詞片語是來自主格關代引導的形容詞子句，所以同樣放置在所修飾的名詞後方。

例2 : The movie _____ 500 million US dollars will be released on DVD this week.
(A) made
(B) which making
(C) which make
(D) making

(3) 情緒動詞的現在分詞通常修飾事物，情緒動詞的過去分詞修飾人。

例3 : The conflicting reports made our executives _____ about the direction of the company.
(A) confusing
(B) confuse
(C) confused
(D) confusion

分詞重點整理

重點1

分詞當形容詞

> 分詞 + N. (分詞當形容詞修飾後方的名詞)
> ⇨ 現在分詞表「主動或進行」
> ⇨ 過去分詞表「被動或完成」

例1 : He tiptoed out of the room for fear of waking up the sleeping baby.
(他踮著腳尖走出房間以免吵醒正在睡覺的嬰兒。)
⇨ sleeping 修飾 baby，表「正在睡覺的」

例2 : Fallen leaves lay scattered all over the floor.
(地板上到處都是落葉。)
⇨ fallen 修飾 leaves，表「已經掉落的」

重點2

分詞片語

> N. + 分詞片語 (分詞片語當形容詞修飾前方的名詞)
> ⇨ 分詞片語是由主格關代的形容詞子句簡化而成的
> ⇨ 主格關代形容詞子句簡化成分詞片語兩大步驟：
> ① 去掉主格關代
> ② 將動詞改為分詞，主動改為現在分詞；被動用過去分詞。

例1 : All participants who register by next Monday will be given some coupons.
= All participants registering by next Monday will be given some coupons.
(所有在下星期一前登記的人將可以獲得一些折價券。)

例2 : Any drivers who park illegally will be fined.
= Any drivers parking illegally will be fined.
(任何違規停車的人都會被罰款。)

例 3 : The product <u>which was designed</u> to meet elderly people's needs caused a sensation as soon as it came on the market.

= The product <u>designed</u> to meet elderly people's needs caused a sensation as soon as it came on the market.

（那個專為老人設計的產品一上市之後立刻造成轟動。）

重點3

對等子句簡化的分詞構句

(1) 兩邊句子主詞相同時，步驟如下：
  step 1 ：先去掉連接詞 and
  step 2 ：再去掉 and 子句的主詞
  step 3 ：再將動詞改為分詞（主動改為現在分詞，被動則用過去分詞）
(2) 兩邊句子主詞不相同時，步驟如下：
  step 1 ：先去掉連接詞 and
  step 2 ：保留 and 子句的主詞
  step 3 ：再將動詞改為分詞（主動改為現在分詞，被動則用過去分詞）

例 1 : My sister lay on the sofa, and she was reading a novel.

step 1 step 2

⇨ My sister lay on the sofa, and she <u>was reading</u> a novel.

step 3

⇨ My sister lay on the sofa, <u>reading</u> a novel.

（主動改為現在分詞）

⇨ My sister lay on the sofa, reading a novel.

（我妹妹躺在沙發上，看著小說。）

例 2 : David looked up in silence, <u>and he was lost</u> in thought.

⇨ David looked up in silence, <u>lost</u> in thought.

（大衛沉默地往上看，想到忘我的地步。）

例 3 : Marvin knelt down before his girlfriend, and tears streamed down his face.

　　　主詞 1　　　　　　　　　　　　　　　　　　　　　主詞 2 ／（主動改為現在分詞）

　　⇨ Marvin knelt down before his girlfriend, tears streaming down his face.
　　(Marvin 跪在他女友面前，淚流滿面。)

例 4 : He stood silently in front of me, and his arms were folded.
　　⇨ He stood silently in front of me, his arms folded.
　　(他沉默地站在我面前，手臂交叉著。)

重點4

副詞子句簡化的分詞構句

(1) 副詞子句主詞與主要子句主詞相同時，步驟如下：
　　step 1：先去掉連接詞 (除了表原因的連接詞外，其他的可以保留)
　　step 2：再去掉副詞子句的主詞
　　step 3：再將動詞改為分詞 (主動改為現在分詞，被動則用過去分詞)
(2) 副詞子句主詞與主要子句主詞不同時，步驟如下：
　　step 1：先去掉連接詞 (除了表原因的連接詞外，其他的可以保留)
　　step 2：保留副詞子句的主詞
　　step 3：再將動詞改為分詞 (主動改為現在分詞，被動則用過去分詞)
(3) 否定副詞子句形成的分詞構句也為否定，否定字要放在分詞前方。

例 1 : Because John was late, he took a taxi to work.
　　　　　　step 1　step 2
　　⇨ Because John was late, he took a taxi to work.
　　　　　　　　step 3
　　　　　　→ Being late, John took a taxi to work.
　　　　　(主動改為現在分詞) (代名詞改為人名)

　　⇨ Being late, John took a taxi to work.
　　(John 因為遲到了就搭計程車上班。)

例2 ： While I was walking my dog in the park, I saw a man rob an old lady of her purse.

⇨ (While) Walking my dog in the park, I saw a man rob an old lady of her purse.

(當我正在公園遛狗時，我看到一個男子搶一位老婦人的錢包。)

例3 ： Because this company is faced with mounting debts, it has decided to declare bankruptcy.

⇨ Faced with mounting debts, this company has decided to declare bankruptcy.

(因為這家公司面臨龐大債務，所以它決定要宣布破產。)

例4 ： After his work had been finished, he let out a sigh of relief.

主詞1　　　　　　　　　　　　　　主詞2

⇨ (After) His work having been finished, he let out a sigh of relief.

(在他工作完成之後，他放心地嘆了一口氣。)

例5 ： Because the elevator was out of order, we had no choice but to walk up the stairs.

⇨ The elevator being out of order, we had no choice but to walk up the stairs.

(因為電梯故障了，我們不得不走樓梯。)

例6 ： Because she didn't feel well, she took a day off yesterday.

⇨ Not feeling well, she took a day off yesterday.

(因為她身體不適，她昨天請了一天假。)

重點6

情緒動詞的分詞

「情緒動詞」之分詞：
(1) 現在分詞：表「令人…的」，常修飾事。
(2) 過去分詞：表「感到…的」，必修飾人。

例 1 : The disappointing profit figures make all the board members depressed.

(令人失望的財報數字使得所有董事會成員很沮喪。)

⇨ disappointing (令人失望的) 修飾 profit figures (財報數字)
depressed (感到沮喪的) 修飾 all the board members (全體董事會成員)

例 2 : Anyone who is interested in this job should send a résumé and three letters of reference to David Whitman, Director of Human Resources.

(任何對這工作感興趣的人應該將履歷及三封推薦信寄給人資部主管 David Whitman。)

⇨ interested (感興趣的) 修飾 anyone (任何人)

常見的情緒分詞有：

情緒動詞的現在分詞		情緒動詞的過去分詞	
interesting	令人覺得有趣的	interested	感到有趣的
boring	令人覺得無聊的	bored	感到無聊的
confusing	令人困惑的	confused	感到困惑的
disappointing	令人失望的	disappointed	感到失望的
exciting	令人興奮的	excited	感到興奮的
surprising	令人驚訝的	surprised	感到驚訝的
shocking	令人震驚的	shocked	感到震驚的
tiring	令人疲倦的	tired	感到疲倦的
satisfying	令人滿意的	satisfied	感到滿意的
delighting	令人愉悅的	delighted	感到高興的
puzzling	令人困惑的	puzzled	感到困惑的
frustrating	令人受挫的	frustrated	感到挫折的
depressing	令人沮喪的	depressed	感到沮喪的

Give it a try! 實力挑戰題

1 The _____ food commercial successfully appeals to many housewives.
(A) freeze
(B) frozen
(C) freezing
(D) froze   Ⓐ Ⓑ Ⓒ Ⓓ

2 The _____ cars were all mashed into a pile on the icy road.
(A) wrecking
(B) wreck
(C) wrecked
(D) wreckage   Ⓐ Ⓑ Ⓒ Ⓓ

3 The movie _____ 500 million US dollars will be released on DVD this week.
(A) made
(B) which making
(C) which make
(D) making   Ⓐ Ⓑ Ⓒ Ⓓ

4 He focused intently on the money as it was being counted, _____ by greed.
(A) consumed
(B) consuming
(C) to consume
(D) having consumed   Ⓐ Ⓑ Ⓒ Ⓓ

5 _____ the lifetime achievement award, he couldn't help but weep.

(A) Receiving
(B) To receive
(C) Received
(D) Receipt

Ⓐ Ⓑ Ⓒ Ⓓ

6 Watching the football team's _____ comeback victory left me galvanized, and I decided to play sports again.

(A) inspired
(B) inspire
(C) inspiring
(D) inspiration

Ⓐ Ⓑ Ⓒ Ⓓ

7 _____ by the customer, Harold hung up the phone in disgust.

(A) To scold
(B) Scolding
(C) Scold
(D) Scolded

Ⓐ Ⓑ Ⓒ Ⓓ

8 _____ at having sent out so many résumés with no response, I got an uplifting call for a job interview.

(A) Frustrating
(B) Frustrated
(C) To frustrate
(D) Frustration

Ⓐ Ⓑ Ⓒ Ⓓ

9 The shopkeeper glared at the noisy student, her eyes _____.

(A) burning
(B) burned
(C) burn
(D) be burned

Ⓐ Ⓑ Ⓒ Ⓓ

10 Any dollar bills _____ a special blue watermark on the back can be considered counterfeit.

(A) which not have

(B) not had

(C) which not having

(D) not having   Ⓐ Ⓑ Ⓒ Ⓓ

11 The conflicting reports made our executives _____ about the direction of the company.

(A) confusing

(B) confuse

(C) confused

(D) confusion   Ⓐ Ⓑ Ⓒ Ⓓ

12 All customers _____ before 8 AM will be sent directly to a voice mailbox.

(A) calling

(B) called

(C) who calling

(D) which call   Ⓐ Ⓑ Ⓒ Ⓓ

13 _____ that the company would need to take drastic measures to avoid a collapse, the president took a deep breath and sighed.

(A) Concluded

(B) Concluding

(C) To conclude

(D) Conclusion   Ⓐ Ⓑ Ⓒ Ⓓ

14 Witnessing such a traumatizing event as the fatal car crash made Carol feel _____.

(A) satisfying

(B) depressing

(C) delighted

(D) shocked Ⓐ Ⓑ Ⓒ Ⓓ

. . . . ▶

15 Bradley was hired as an executive for the firm right after _____ his Ph.D.

(A) getting

(B) he getting

(C) he gets

(D) gotten Ⓐ Ⓑ Ⓒ Ⓓ

. . . . ▶

16 Most employees are unhappy about the new policy _____ each employee to give three weeks' notice for vacation requests.

(A) to require

(B) which requiring

(C) requiring

(D) that require Ⓐ Ⓑ Ⓒ Ⓓ

. . . . ▶

17 If you fail to abide by the policies _____ in our agreement, we might switch to other contractors.

(A) which outlined

(B) outlined

(C) outlining

(D) which outlining Ⓐ Ⓑ Ⓒ Ⓓ

18 The accusations _____ by the whistleblower did damage the reputation of our company.

(A) brought forth

(B) which brought forth

(C) bringing forth

(D) which was brought forth   Ⓐ Ⓑ Ⓒ Ⓓ

---

19 You had better do a thorough assessment of the new fast food chain before _____ to sign a franchise agreement.

(A) agreed

(B) agreeing

(C) you agreeing

(D) agree   Ⓐ Ⓑ Ⓒ Ⓓ

---

20 The carbon dioxide _____ by this factory has exceeded the standard amount.

(A) which emitted

(B) emitting

(C) which emits

(D) emitted   Ⓐ Ⓑ Ⓒ Ⓓ

Unit ⑤ 連接詞

徐薇老師小叮嚀　🎧 MP3:Unit5

多益的文法考題中雖很常出現考連接詞的題目，但多半都是考基本觀念，例如：對等連接詞用來連接地位相等的單字片語或子句，而從屬連接詞用來連接兩個完整句子，不會出現太艱深的題目，甚至很多題目因為四個選項皆為連接詞，所以都只是在考語意的判斷。

(1) 常考對等連接詞包括：and、but、or、either ~ or ~、both ~ and ~。

例1：This advertisement caused fierce controversy because it was awful and _____.
(A) blood
(B) bloody
(C) bleed
(D) bleeding

(2) though / although 和 but 都是「但是、雖然」的意思，表轉折語氣，但兩個句子只能用一個連接詞，因此 though 和 but 不可連用。另外要注意的是，while 除了可以表「當」之外，也可以表「雖然」。

例2：_____ the city has built many centers to provide job training to the poor, very few residents have taken advantage of these resources.
(A) Because
(B) Although
(C) When
(D) As soon as

(3) 從上下文判斷轉承副詞 (連接性副詞)，例如前後語氣轉折時用 however (然而)，前後出現因果關係時用 consequently 或 therefore (因此)，前後語氣是要表額外資訊時要用 furthermore 或 additionally (此外)。

例3：The retirement package for this position is excellent; _____, it has flexible scheduling.
(A) in addition to
(B) as a result
(C) to begin with
(D) additionally

連接詞重點整理

重點1

對等連接詞

> 對等連接詞連接身分地位對等的單字、片語或子句
> (1) both A and B (A 和 B 都)
> (2) not only A but also B (不僅 A 還有 B)
> (3) A + as well as + B (A 以及 B)
> (4) either A or B (不是 A 就是 B)
> (5) neither A nor B (既不是 A 也不是 B)
> (6) not A but B (不是 A 而是 B)

例1 : Both the CEO and the general manager were present at yesterday's new product launch.
(執行長以及總經理都出席了昨天的新品發表會。)

⇨ both ~and ~ 連 接 了 兩 個 名 詞 the CEO 和 the general manager

例2 : Because of his great performance, George got not only the promotion but also a raise.
(因為表現優異，George 不僅升官了而且還加薪了。)

⇨ not only ~but also ~ 連接了兩個名詞 the promotion 和 a raise

例3 : That newcomer is intelligent as well as diligent.
(那位新進員工聰明又認真。)

⇨ as well as 連接了兩個形容詞 intelligent 和 diligent

例4 : Either Greg or Tom has to take the blame if anything goes wrong.
(如果出問題，不是 Greg 就是 Tom 要負責。)

⇨ either ~or ~ 連接 Greg 和 Tom

例5 : His assistant neither called nor sent an e-mail.
(他的助理既沒有打電話來也沒有寄電子郵件來。)

⇨ neither ~nor ~ 連接兩個動詞 called 和 sent

例 6 : His problem lies <u>not</u> in lack of intelligence <u>but</u> in lack of patience.

(他的問題不是在於缺乏聰明才智而是在於缺乏耐心。)

⇨ not ~ but ~ 連接兩個片語 in lack of intelligence 和 in lack of patience

重點2

對等連接詞連接主詞時動詞的單複數

(1) A + as well as + B + V-A
⇨ as well as 連接兩個主詞時，動詞單複數恆由前面的主詞決定
(2) A or B
either A or B
neither A nor B
not only A but also B
not A but B
⇨ 動詞單複數由最靠近的主詞決定

例 1 : The coach as well as the players <u>is</u> happy about the result.
(教練以及球員們都對結果感到滿意。)

⇨ 動詞 is 是由 the coach 決定的

例 2 : Neither visitors nor <u>employees</u> <u>are</u> allowed to park in the red area.
(訪客和員工都不可以停在紅色區域。)

⇨ 動詞 are 是由 employees 決定的

重點3

表「時間」的從屬連接詞

When (當)
While (當)
As (當)
Before (在 ~ 之前)
After (在 ~ 之後)
As soon as (一 ~ 就 ...)
+ S. + V.~ , S. + V...

例1 : When I am out of town, Vincent will take my place.
（當我出城時，Vincent 會暫代我的位置。）

例2 : While we were discussing the effects that the new product has on the environment, an earthquake broke out.
（當我們正在討論新產品對環境造成的影響時，突然發生了地震。）

例3 : As soon as my sister heard the clearance sale offers, she rushed to the outlet mall without delay.
（我姐姐一得知清倉大拍賣的消息時，她就立刻衝到那個購物中心。）

重點4

表「原因」的從屬連接詞

$$\left\{\begin{array}{l} \text{Because(因為)} \\ \text{Since(因為)} \\ \text{As(因為)} \end{array}\right\} + \text{S. + V.\~ , S. + V...}$$

= S. + V..., so (所以) + S. + V. ~

= S. + V..., for (因為) + S. + V.~

★ because 和 so 不可以同時使用

例1 : Because there is an ongoing large-scale strike, the delivery of all merchandise is postponed.
（因為大規模的罷工持續進行中，貨物的遞送都延後了。）

= There is an ongoing large-scale strike, so the delivery of all merchandise is postponed.

= The delivery of all merchandise is postponed, for there is an ongoing large-scale strike.

例2 : Because the Ebola epidemic is getting out of control, all the flights to Guinea, Sierra Leone and Liberia are cancelled.
（因為伊波拉疫情失控，所有飛往幾內亞、獅子山以及賴比瑞亞的航班都取消了。）

= The Ebola epidemic is getting out of control, so all the flights to Guinea, Sierra Leone and Liberia are cancelled.

= All the flights to Guinea, Sierra Leone and Liberia are cancelled, for the Ebola epidemic is getting out of control.

其他表「因為」的介系詞片語：

because of = as a result of = on account of = owing to = due to
= thanks to

例1 : <u>Because of</u> the rising oil prices, more and more people are using public transport instead of driving.

(因為油價持續上漲，越來越多人使用大眾運輸而不是自己開車。)

例2 : <u>Due to</u> the construction of the bridge, traffic congestion should be expected.

(因為橋樑的施工，交通阻塞是可以預期的。)

例3 : <u>Owing to</u> the ongoing renovation of the boardroom, the board meeting has to be rescheduled.

(因為董事會會議室正在進行整修，董事會議必須改期。)

重點5

表「雖然 ... 但是 ...」的從屬連接詞

$$\left\{ \begin{array}{l} \text{Although} \\ \text{Though} \\ \text{Even though} \\ \text{While} \end{array} \right\} + S. + V.\sim , S. + V...$$

= S. + V..., but + S. + V. ~

★ although/though 和 but 不可以同時使用

例1 : <u>Although</u> Tony doesn't have enough experience for this job, the manager is willing to give him a chance because of his passion and determination.

(雖然 Tony 沒有做這工作足夠的經驗，但是因為他熱情又堅定，經理願意給他一次機會試試。)

= Tony doesn't have enough experience for this job<u>, but</u> the manager is willing to give him a chance because of his passion and determination.

例2 : Though this shop sells clothes at competitive prices, its business is slack because of poor quality and bad management.

(雖然這家服飾店賣的衣服價格低廉，但是因為品質不佳及經營不善，生意還是很清淡。)

= This shop sells clothes at competitive prices, but its business is slack because of poor quality and bad management.

📖 其他表「雖然」的介系詞或介系詞片語：

despite = in spite of = for all = with all

例 : Despite repeated efforts to apologize for his misconduct, he has no choice but to resign as director.

(儘管他為自己的失職一再道歉，但是他還是不得不辭去董事職位。)

重點6

表「不論」的從屬連接詞

No matter + wh- + S. + V.~, S. + V...
= Wh-ever + S. + V.~, S. + V...
★no matter 後方一定要緊接 wh- 開頭的疑問詞

例1 : No matter who you are, you have to wear formal business attire in the office.

(不論你是誰，在辦公室都必須穿著正式商業服裝。)

= Whoever you are, you have to wear formal business attire in the office.

例2 : No matter how hard I try, I never seem to live up to the supervisor's expectations.

= However hard I try, I never seem to live up to the supervisor's expectations.

(不論我再怎麼努力，我似乎都沒辦法達到主管的期望。)

重點7

連接性副詞 (轉承副詞)

連接性副詞實際上是副詞,不是連接詞,功能是在語意上連接兩個句子,但因為只是副詞,所以前方應放分號或句號。常考連接性副詞有:
(1) 然而:however, nonetheless, nevertheless
(2) 而且:in addition, furthermore, moreover, what's more, additionally
(3) 因此:therefore, thus, hence, consequently, accordingly, as a result
(4) 例如:for example, for instance
(5) 否則:otherwise
(6) 首先:first, in the first place, to begin with, first of all
(7) 最後:finally, in the end, last but not least
(8) 總之:to sum up, to summarize, in conclusion

例1 : Sales this year exceeded the previous year; however, there was a drop in profit.
(今年的銷售量超越前一年;然而,利潤卻是下降了。)

例2 : The location is perfect; moreover, the rent is low.
(地點很棒;而且,租金又低。)

例3 : Wendy failed to return the borrowed books by the due date; therefore, she was charged a late fee.
(Wendy 未能在截止日前歸還借閱的書籍;因此,她被收取了滯納金。)

例4 : This new product has many design flaws; for example, it is too heavy.
(這個新產品有很多設計缺陷;例如,它太重了。)

例5 : Don't be late again; otherwise, you might be subject to loss of pay next time.
(別再遲到了;否則你下次可能會被扣薪水。)

例6 : This advertisement is awful; to begin with, it is too bloody.
(這廣告很糟;首先,它太血腥了。)

例7 : There was opposition to the budget proposal in the beginning, but in the end it was approved.
(雖然這預算案一開始遭到反對,但是最後它還是獲准了。)

Give it a try! 實力挑戰題

1 Being gifted _____ self-motivated, Melissa had no problem ascending the corporate ladder at an accelerating rate.

(A) but

(B) as well as

(C) or

(D) but also

Ⓐ Ⓑ Ⓒ Ⓓ

2 The family reunion will take place in _____ a public park or a restaurant.

(A) as well as

(B) neither

(C) either

(D) not only

Ⓐ Ⓑ Ⓒ Ⓓ

3 Tom's failure in college was not for lack of effort, _____ for lack of financial support.

(A) but also

(B) and

(C) but

(D) as well as

Ⓐ Ⓑ Ⓒ Ⓓ

4 The athletic director as well as I _____ concerned about cuts in funding to the sports programs at our school.

(A) is

(B) are

(C) am

(D) has

Ⓐ Ⓑ Ⓒ Ⓓ

5 Neither we nor Ken _____ found any evidence of wrongdoing at the government agency.

(A) have

(B) are

(C) is

(D) has Ⓐ Ⓑ Ⓒ Ⓓ

---

6 _____ our database administrator is on vacation this week, no significant issues in the IT department can be dealt with.

(A) Since

(B) Although

(C) No matter

(D) For Ⓐ Ⓑ Ⓒ Ⓓ

---

7 _____ the stressful office environment, we have had high turnover of staff these past few years.

(A) Because

(B) Despite

(C) As a result

(D) As a result of Ⓐ Ⓑ Ⓒ Ⓓ

---

8 _____ the city has built many centers to provide job training to the poor, very few residents have taken advantage of these resources.

(A) Because

(B) Although

(C) When

(D) As soon as Ⓐ Ⓑ Ⓒ Ⓓ

---

9 _____ the suspension of all trading on the stock market, we were able to mitigate some of our losses.

(A) Instead of

(B) In addition to

(C) Thanks to

(D) Compared with Ⓐ Ⓑ Ⓒ Ⓓ

10 _____ the approaching winter storm, schools and businesses announced that they would not open the following day.

(A) Since

(B) On account of

(C) In spite of

(D) Thanks for   Ⓐ Ⓑ Ⓒ Ⓓ

11 _____ this bar has perfect equipment and facilities, the location is not ideal.

(A) When

(B) With all

(C) Because

(D) Even though   Ⓐ Ⓑ Ⓒ Ⓓ

12 _____ the effort he has gone through to solicit funds, the non-profit company still went belly up in the end.

(A) For all

(B) As a result of

(C) In comparison with

(D) Owing to   Ⓐ Ⓑ Ⓒ Ⓓ

13 _____ how many sales calls I made, I still could not close the deal with enough customers.

(A) Although

(B) As

(C) No matter

(D) Despite   Ⓐ Ⓑ Ⓒ Ⓓ

14 _____ repairs we attempted to make, the server would still no longer function exactly right.

(A) However

(B) Whatever

(C) No matter

(D) Although   Ⓐ Ⓑ Ⓒ Ⓓ

15 Your business plan is so ambitious that it's unrealistic; _____, you are projecting fifty million dollars in sales in just your first year!

(A) in addition

(B) therefore

(C) for example

(D) however   Ⓐ Ⓑ Ⓒ Ⓓ

16 There were so many disappointing aspects to this presentation; _____, it was depressing to watch.

(A) to sum up

(B) instead

(C) otherwise

(D) last but not least   Ⓐ Ⓑ Ⓒ Ⓓ

17 _____ the professor was explaining the problem in another way, the students rudely began to get up and leave the classroom.

(A) As long as

(B) Until

(C) While

(D) Since   Ⓐ Ⓑ Ⓒ Ⓓ

18 _____ Kingston met the client for lunch, he went to the dentist to have his teeth professionally whitened.

(A) When

(B) Before

(C) Because of

(D) In spite of   Ⓐ Ⓑ Ⓒ Ⓓ

19 The retirement package for this position is excellent; _____, it has flexible scheduling.

(A) in addition to

(B) as a result

(C) to begin with

(D) moreover Ⓐ Ⓑ Ⓒ Ⓓ

20 My responsibility is to double check every order _____ it ships out.

(A) since

(B) because

(C) before

(D) although Ⓐ Ⓑ Ⓒ Ⓓ

Unit ⑥ 名詞子句

徐薇老師小叮嚀　🎧 MP3:Unit6

(1) 連接詞 that 引導的名詞子句可做句子的主詞、受詞或主詞補語。

例1：That this operating system will soon be replaced _____ a relief to all my co-workers.

(A) is

(B) has

(C) are

(D) were

(2) 若題目為疑問詞引導的名詞子句時，注意名詞子句句型不可倒裝，即形式為：

S1 + V1 + wh- 疑問詞 + S2 + V2

例2：When you get the chance, would you mind describing _____ the advertising campaign will look like?

(A) what

(B) that

(C) if

(D) when

(3) whether 表示「是否」時，引導的名詞子句表不確定的事情，子句後方可加 or not。

例3：_____ the boss will grant Joe some time off or not depends on how busy he thinks we will be during the holidays.

(A) If

(B) That

(C) What

(D) Whether

名詞子句重點整理

重點1

名詞子句的結構

名詞子句有下列三種結構：
(1) that + S. + V…
(2) whether (是否) + S. + V…
(3) wh- + S. + V…(wh- 引導的名詞子句即為間接問句)

例1 : That the economy will fall into recession causes panic among investors.
(經濟會衰退的消息引發投資人的恐慌。)
⇨ That the economy will fall into recession 為名詞子句，當句子主詞。

例2 : I wonder whether we will be able to get the project done on schedule.
(我在想我們是否能夠如期完成這專案。)
⇨ whether we will be able to get the project done on schedule 為名詞子句，當動詞 wonder 的受詞。

例3 : I am curious about where the new power plant will be built.
(我很好奇新的發電廠會興建在何處。)
⇨ where the new power plant will be built 為名詞子句，當介系詞 about 的受詞。

重點2

that 子句的功能

that 子句有下列四種功能：
(1) 當主詞：That + S. + V...+ 單數動詞 ~
(2) 當動詞的受詞：S. + V. + that + S. + V...
(3) 當主詞補語：S. + beV. + that + S. + V...
(4) 當同位語：the + N. + that + S. + V...

例1 ：<u>That the two banks aim to merge</u> surprises everyone.
（這兩家銀行打算合併的消息讓大家很驚訝。）

➡ That the two banks aim to merge 為名詞子句，當句子主詞，動詞一定要是單數 (surprises)。

例2 ：I am pleased to announce <u>that Dave has just been promoted to manager</u>.
（我很高興向大家宣布 Dave 剛剛被升為經理了。）

➡ that Dave has just been promoted to manager 為名詞子句，當動詞 announce 的受詞，此時 that 可以省略。

例3 ：The website you designed is fantastic; the only problem is <u>that your charge is way too high.</u>
（你設計的網站很棒；唯一的問題是你收費實在是太高了。）

➡ that your charge is way too high 為名詞子句，放在 is 後方當主詞補語。

例4 ：Despite the fact <u>that he would earn less in the new position,</u> he took the job offer because he wanted to have better quality time with his family.
（儘管他新工作賺得較少，但是因為他想要有更好的優質時間陪伴家人，所以他接受了這份工作。）

➡ that he would earn less in the new position 為名詞子句，當作名詞 fact 的同位語。

3. whether 子句的功能

whether 子句有下列四種功能：
(1) 當主詞：Whether + S. + V...+ 單數動詞 ~
(2) 當動詞的受詞：S. + V. + whether + S. + V...
(3) 當介系詞的受詞：S. + V. + prep. + whether + S. + V...
(4) 當主詞補語：S. + beV. + whether + S. + V...

例1 : <u>Whether Mr. Smith will succeed Mr. Johnson as CEO</u> remains to be seen.

(Smith 先生是否會繼 Johnson 先生後擔任執行長現在尚未確定。)

⇨ Whether Mr. Smith will succeed Mr. Johnson as CEO 為名詞子句，當句子主詞，動詞一定是單數 (remains)。

⇨ whether 當「是否」引導名詞子句當主詞時，不可以用 if 代替 whether。

例2 : I doubt <u>whether the project will be a success (or not)</u>.
= I doubt <u>if the project will be a success</u>.

(我懷疑這案子是否會成功。)

⇨ whether the project will be a success 為名詞子句，當動詞 doubt 的受詞。

⇨ 只有在 whether 當「是否」引導名詞子句當動詞的受詞時，可以用 if 代替 whether；但 if 通常用於口語或非正式情境，而 whether 可以搭配 or not。

例3 : I am curious about <u>whether the CFO will resign because of the financial misconduct</u>.

(我很好奇財務長是否會因財務管理不善而辭職。)

⇨ whether the CFO will resign because of the financial misconduct 為名詞子句，當介系詞 about 的受詞。

⇨ whether 當「是否」引導名詞子句當介系詞受詞時，不可以用 if 代替 whether。

例 4 : The problem is <u>whether your idea can be put into practice</u>.
（問題是你的想法是否可以被執行。）

⇨ whether your idea can be put into practice 為名詞子句，
當主詞補語。

⇨ whether 當「是否」引導名詞子句當主詞補語時，不可以
用 if 代替 whether。

4. wh- 子句的功能

> wh- 子句有下列種功能：
> (1) 當主詞：Wh- + S. + V...+ 單數動詞 ~
> (2) 當動詞的受詞：S. + V. + wh- + S. + V...
> (3) 當介系詞的受詞： S. + V. + prep. + wh- + S. + V...
> (4) 當主詞補語：S. + beV. + wh- + S. + V...

例 1 : <u>When the reconstruction of the auditorium will begin</u> is
unknown.

（沒有人知道禮堂的重建工程何時要開始。）

⇨ When the reconstruction of the auditorium will begin 為名
詞子句，當句子主詞，動詞一定是單數 (is)。

例 2 : Although Eric was busy, he took the trouble to explain <u>how
the system worked to me.</u>

（雖然 Eric 很忙，但是他依舊不厭其煩跟我說明系統是如何運
作的。）

⇨ how the system worked 為名詞子句，當動詞 explain 的受
詞。

例 3 : I am not interested in <u>what he said at all.</u>
（我對他說的話一點都不感興趣。）

⇨ what he said 為名詞子句，當介系詞 in 的受詞。

例 4 : My only doubt is <u>how effective the drug is.</u>
（我唯一的疑惑是這種藥有多有效。）

⇨ how effective the drug is 為名詞子句，當主詞補語。

Give it a try! 實力挑戰題

1 That this operating system will soon be replaced _____ a relief to all my co-workers.

(A) is

(B) has

(C) are

(D) were

Ⓐ Ⓑ Ⓒ Ⓓ

2 I doubt _____ all these old files will be saved when we move to the new building.

(A) this

(B) what

(C) whether

(D) that

Ⓐ Ⓑ Ⓒ Ⓓ

3 The congressman debriefed us all on _____ was in the new bill proposed by the President.

(A) that

(B) how

(C) whether

(D) what

Ⓐ Ⓑ Ⓒ Ⓓ

4 I doubt _____ we will have enough funds to finish this project.

(A) that

(B) what

(C) why

(D) whether

Ⓐ Ⓑ Ⓒ Ⓓ

5 When you get the chance, would you mind describing _____ the advertising campaign will look like?

(A) what

(B) that

(C) if

(D) when

Ⓐ Ⓑ Ⓒ Ⓓ

6 Ken is worried about _____ we have tested the new software enough before releasing it.

(A) that

(B) what

(C) whether

(D) it

Ⓐ Ⓑ Ⓒ Ⓓ

7 _____ the boss will grant Joe some time off or not depends on how busy he thinks we will be during the holidays.

(A) If

(B) That

(C) What

(D) Whether

Ⓐ Ⓑ Ⓒ Ⓓ

8 _____ the fourth quarter report exceeded expectations encouraged all the company employees.

(A) What

(B) That

(C) If

(D) Whether

Ⓐ Ⓑ Ⓒ Ⓓ

9 We are debating _____ customers should be charged an extra fee for next-day shipping.

(A) that

(B) whether

(C) what

(D) this

Ⓐ Ⓑ Ⓒ Ⓓ

10 The matter under discussion is _____ we can regain the trust of our customers.

(A) that

(B) what

(C) why

(D) how

Ⓐ Ⓑ Ⓒ Ⓓ

11 I have to acknowledge the fact _____ his idea is more innovative than mine.
(A) whether
(B) if
(C) that
(D) why   Ⓐ Ⓑ Ⓒ Ⓓ

12 I want to underline the fact _____ safety is our major concern when it comes to making a new product.
(A) that
(B) when
(C) whether
(D) where   Ⓐ Ⓑ Ⓒ Ⓓ

13 The results of the survey show _____ consumers think the quality of a product is more important than its price.
(A) whether
(B) that
(C) if
(D) when   Ⓐ Ⓑ Ⓒ Ⓓ

14 Since our boss is quite demanding, I don't know _____ your performance lived up to his expectations.
(A) that
(B) if
(C) why
(D) where   Ⓐ Ⓑ Ⓒ Ⓓ

15 It is predicted _____ 70 percent of manual jobs will be taken over by robots in the near future.
(A) what
(B) whether
(C) if
(D) that   Ⓐ Ⓑ Ⓒ Ⓓ

16 Since most people now get their news from the Internet, it is no surprise _____ our print division will be closed.

(A) that

(B) whether

(C) if

(D) what   Ⓐ Ⓑ Ⓒ Ⓓ

17 The problem with your proposal is _____ it is too impractical.

(A) why

(B) that

(C) if

(D) whether   Ⓐ Ⓑ Ⓒ Ⓓ

18 We take pride in the fact _____ our company has an extremely diverse work force.

(A) when

(B) if

(C) what

(D) that   Ⓐ Ⓑ Ⓒ Ⓓ

19 Alice only has two weeks of training, so I don't think _____ she is able to handle this on her own.

(A) whether

(B) when

(C) that

(D) where   Ⓐ Ⓑ Ⓒ Ⓓ

20 _____ Lawrence had been dismissed from his duties as supervisor was shocking to his wife.

(A) That

(B) Whether

(C) If

(D) When   Ⓐ Ⓑ Ⓒ Ⓓ

Unit ❼ 代名詞

徐薇老師小叮嚀　　🎧 MP3:Unit7

代名詞在多益的測驗中算是高頻率出現的文法，測驗的都是基本的觀念，像是主格、受格、所有格的使用時機，另外反身代名詞也是要注意的重點。

(1) 主詞用主格，動詞或介系詞的受詞用受格，表所有時用所有格。

例1：I couldn't believe that _____ ideas were adopted instead of theirs.
(A) myself
(B) I
(C) me
(D) my

(2) 當主詞和受詞為同一人時，受詞要用反身代名詞。

例2：I often lose _____ in a daydream during one of our boring conference calls.
(A) me
(B) myself
(C) my
(D) ourselves

(3) 注意代名詞單複數和動詞的搭配是否一致。

例3：One of my colleagues _____ registered for the upcoming seminar.
(A) have
(B) has
(C) is
(D) was

例4：Few of the warnings regarding our financial insolvency _____ heeded.
(A) have
(B) were
(C) is
(D) has

 **代名詞重點整理**

重點1

人稱代名詞的格與功用

人稱	數	主格	受格	所有格	所有代名詞	反身代名詞
第一人稱	單數	I	me	my	mine	myself
	複數	we	us	our	ours	ourselves
第二人稱	單數	you	you	your	yours	yourself
	複數	you	you	your	yours	yourselves
第三人稱	單數	he	him	his	his	himself
		she	her	her	hers	herself
		it	it	its	its	itself
	複數	they	them	their	theirs	themselves

(1) 句子主詞要用主格；受詞要用受格；所有格後方一定要接名詞。
(2) 所有代名詞 = 所有格 + 名詞
(3) 使用人稱代名詞時，要特別注意單複數與人稱及性別有無一致。

例1 : I should have reminded <u>you</u> that there was a meeting yesterday.
(我應該要提醒你昨天有會議的。)
⇨ I 為主詞，所以用主格。you 為動詞 remind 的受詞，所以這裡的 you 是受格。

例2 : <u>You</u> had better not make any mistake during <u>your</u> probation period.
(你最好在試用期間不要犯任何錯。)
⇨ you 為此句主詞，所以是主格；your 為 you 的所有格，後接名詞 probation period。

例3 : You deserve the award since your design is superior to <u>mine</u>.
(因為你的設計比我的好，你應得到這個獎。)
⇨ mine 為所有代名詞，在此相當於 my design。

重點2

反身代名詞的用法

(1) 當句子主詞與受詞為同一人時，受詞要用反身代名詞。
(2) 強調主詞
(3) 慣用片語：
    ① by oneself 獨自   ② enjoy oneself 玩得開心
    ③ seat oneself 就座   ④ behave oneself 行為規矩

> **例1**：Do I make <u>myself</u> clear?
> （聽清楚我說的話了嗎？）
> ⇨ 主詞和受詞都是我，所以受詞要用 myself。

> **例2**：I <u>myself</u> made an inventory of all the furniture.
> = I made an inventory of all the furniture <u>myself</u>.
> （我自己一個人盤點了所有家具。）
> ⇨ 強調主詞時，可放主詞後方也可放句尾。

> **例3**：I usually seat <u>myself</u> at the back of the room at the conference.
> （開會時我通常坐在會議室後面。）
> ⇨ 主詞和受詞都是我，所以受詞要用 myself。

重點3

指示代名詞 (this/that/these/those) 的用法

(1) this(單數)/these(複數) 指較近的事物；that(單數)/those(複數) 指較遠的事物。

(2) 在比較的句子中，所比較的名詞在第二次提到時為了避免重複，用 that 代替單數或不可數名詞；those 代替複數名詞。

(3) this/that 可用來代替前面提過的句子。

例1 : That is the girl I told you about. It is said that she is the manager's daughter.

(那就是我跟你說過的女孩。聽說她是經理的女兒。)

例2 : The memory of my computer is larger than that of yours.

(我電腦的記憶體容量比你的大。)

⇨ that 在此代替 the memory。

例3 : D&D Co., Inc. declared bankruptcy last week. This came as a surprise to many investors.

(D&D 股份有限公司於上週宣布破產，這讓很多投資人都很驚訝。)

⇨ this 在此代替 D&D Co., Inc. declared bankruptcy last week 這個句子。

重點4

不定代名詞的用法 (I)----- 單數不定代名詞

Each (每一個)
Either (兩者中任一)
Neither (兩者中無一)
Little (少到幾乎沒有)
A little (一些)
Much (很多)

} + of + the/these/those/ 所有格 + N. + 單數動詞 …

> **例1** : Each of the five candidates is overqualified for this job.
> (以這工作來說，這五位應徵者中每一位條件都太好了。)

> **例2** : Neither of the two strategies seems to work out.
> (這兩個策略似乎都不奏效。)

> **例3** : Much of his income was spent on 3C electronic products.
> (他的收入中有很多都花在 3C 電子商品了。)

重點5

不定代名詞的用法 (II)----- 複數不定代名詞

Both (兩者)
Few (少到幾乎沒有)
A few (一些)
Several (好幾個)
Many (很多)

} + of + the/these/those/ 所有格 + N. + 複數動詞 …

> **例1** : Both of the two warehouses are filled with goods.
> (這兩個倉庫都塞滿了貨物。)

> **例2** : Many of the attendees wear black suits.
> (很多出席者都穿著黑色套裝。)

重點6

不定代名詞的用法 (III)----- 單複數皆可的不定代名詞

All (三者以上全部)
Any (任何)
Some (一些) } + of + the/these/those/ 所有格 + { 複數 N. + 複數 V.
None (三者以上無一)
Most (大部分) 不可數 N. + 單數 V.

> **例1** : All of these household chemicals may lead to children's IQ drop.
> (這些家用化學品全都可能會導致小孩智商的降低。)

> **例2** : All of the furniture in the entire store is reduced by 40 percent today.
> (整間店的所有家具今天都打六折。)

> **例3** : Most of the equipment in this factory is purchased from a Germany-based supplier.
> (這間工廠大部分的設備都是購自一間總部位於德國的供應商。)

重點7

代名詞 it 的用法 (I)----- 當虛主詞

不定詞或名詞子句當主詞時，可用 it 代替，此時 it 放句首當虛主詞，不定詞或名詞子句則移至句尾。

It + 單數 V. ~ + { to Vr...
that/wh-+ S.+ V...

> **例1** : It is a pleasure to invite you to participate in the annual employee picnic.
> (能邀請您參加年度員工野餐活動真是榮幸。)
> ⇨ it 為虛主詞，代替真主詞 to participate in the annual employee picnic。

例2 : It is no surprise <u>that Jacobs was nominated as best actor</u>.
(Jacobs 被提名為最佳男演員一點都不令人意外。)

⇨ it 為虛主詞,代替真主詞 that Jacobs was nominated as best actor。

重點8

代名詞 it 的用法 (II)----- 當虛受詞

$$
S. + \begin{Bmatrix} make \\ think \\ find \end{Bmatrix} + it + adj./N. + \begin{Bmatrix} to\ Vr... \\ that/wh\text{-}+ S.+ V... \end{Bmatrix}
$$

例1 : He makes it a rule <u>to go jogging before breakfast</u>.
(他養成習慣在早餐前去慢跑。)

⇨ it 為虛受詞,代替真受詞 to go jogging before breakfast。

例2 : I find it amazing <u>that he managed to complete the project by himself</u>.
(他成功地獨自完成這項專案讓我覺得很不可思議。)

⇨ it 為虛受詞,代替真受詞 that he managed to complete the project by himself。

Give it a try! 實力挑戰題

1 She always insists that her work schedule is worse than _____.
(A) ours
(B) our
(C) us
(D) we
Ⓐ Ⓑ Ⓒ Ⓓ

2 She didn't give _____ enough time to finish the project.
(A) her own
(B) I
(C) herself
(D) hers
Ⓐ Ⓑ Ⓒ Ⓓ

3 The storage space in this warehouse is ten times bigger than _____ of what we had at our shop.
(A) this
(B) that
(C) those
(D) these
Ⓐ Ⓑ Ⓒ Ⓓ

4 Little of what Kim says _____ any real importance.
(A) have
(B) is
(C) were
(D) has
Ⓐ Ⓑ Ⓒ Ⓓ

5 Few of the warnings regarding our financial insolvency _____ heeded.
(A) have
(B) were
(C) is
(D) has
Ⓐ Ⓑ Ⓒ Ⓓ

6 Several of my colleagues _____ registered for the upcoming seminar.
(A) have
(B) has
(C) is
(D) was   Ⓐ Ⓑ Ⓒ Ⓓ

7 None of the stolen money _____ in the apartment of the suspect.
(A) were found
(B) have found
(C) has found
(D) was found   Ⓐ Ⓑ Ⓒ Ⓓ

8 Sharon makes _____ a point to keep up with all the latest technologica
developments.
(A) that
(B) this
(C) it
(D) which   Ⓐ Ⓑ Ⓒ Ⓓ

9 I couldn't believe that _____ ideas were adopted instead of theirs.
(A) myself
(B) I
(C) me
(D) my   Ⓐ Ⓑ Ⓒ Ⓓ

10 They _____ are to blame for this catastrophic failure.
(A) themselves
(B) them
(C) their
(D) theirs   Ⓐ Ⓑ Ⓒ Ⓓ

11 I often lose _____ in a daydream during one of our boring conference calls.

(A) me

(B) myself

(C) my

(D) ourselves ⒶⒷⒸⒹ

----

12 _____ file cabinets over there need all their contents to be transferred to digital files.

(A) These

(B) That

(C) Those

(D) This ⒶⒷⒸⒹ

----

13 Each of these entrées _____ like a savory choice for dinner.

(A) looks

(B) look

(C) were

(D) has ⒶⒷⒸⒹ

----

14 A few of the customers' comments _____ valid concerns, but others were ridiculous.

(A) is

(B) were

(C) has

(D) was ⒶⒷⒸⒹ

----

15 Some of the employees _____ eligible for the employee of the month award.

(A) is

(B) have

(C) has

(D) are ⒶⒷⒸⒹ

16 _____ is my wish that you attain every goal that your heart desires.

(A) It

(B) That

(C) What

(D) This

Ⓐ Ⓑ Ⓒ Ⓓ

---

17 He finds _____ useful to have majored in Japanese in college.

(A) that

(B) it

(C) this

(D) himself

Ⓐ Ⓑ Ⓒ Ⓓ

---

18 _____ was my expectation that you would finish the financial report on your own.

(A) That

(B) This

(C) It

(D) What

Ⓐ Ⓑ Ⓒ Ⓓ

---

19 We make _____ our mission to produce safe quality strollers for a fair price.

(A) that

(B) it

(C) this

(D) X

Ⓐ Ⓑ Ⓒ Ⓓ

---

20 One of the most important steps when you deal with any problem is the acceptance that _____ is real.

(A) he

(B) she

(C) they

(D) it

Ⓐ Ⓑ Ⓒ Ⓓ

Unit ⑧ 形容詞與副詞

徐薇老師小叮嚀　🎧 MP3:Unit8

(1) 形容詞修飾名詞；副詞修飾一般動詞、形容詞、副詞和句子。

例1 : Your _____ pursuit of your dream has resulted in your getting this awesome position.
(A) relented
(B) relent
(C) relentlessly
(D) relentless

例2 : I find your actions _____ reckless, and I am suspending your driver's license.
(A) shockingly
(B) shocking
(C) shocked
(D) shock

(2) 頻率副詞使用時要注意，若與 be 動詞連用時，頻率副詞要置於 be 動詞之後；若與一般動詞連用，則要置於一般動詞之前；若同句中有助動詞又有一般動詞時，則頻率副詞要置於兩者之間。

例3 : He _____ late for conference calls since he is busy placing orders for customers.
(A) usually is
(B) is ever
(C) is usually
(D) never is

(3) 表示「也～」或「也不～」的附和句時，要注意句子的動詞與時態要與前方句子一致，若為倒裝句，要以副詞 so(也) 或 neither(也不) 引導，主詞和動詞位置要對調。

例 4 : She was busy with her new business, and _____.
   (A) her brother is, too
   (B) her brother did, either
   (C) so was her brother
   (D) neither was her brother

形容詞與副詞重點整理

重點1

形容詞和副詞的基本功用

(1) 形容詞的基本功用：形容詞主要用來修飾名詞。
(2) 副詞的基本功用：
   ① 修飾一般動詞
   ② 修飾形容詞
   ③ 修飾副詞
   ④ 修飾句子

例1 : All the participants will be given a <u>complimentary</u> <u>copy</u> of this magazine.
   (所有參加者都將獲贈這本雜誌免費的一本。)
   ⇨ 形容詞 complimentary 修飾名詞 copy。

例2 : You had better <u>drive</u> <u>carefully</u> on icy roads.
   (在結冰的路面上你最好小心開車。)
   ⇨ 副詞 carefully 修飾一般動詞 drive。

例3 : If you have difficulty <u>completing</u> the form <u>accurately</u>, you can turn to Linda for help.
   (如果你不知怎樣精確地填好表格，你可以向 Linda 求助。)
   ⇨ 副詞 accurately 修飾動詞 complete。

例 4 ： I am <u>very</u> <u>grateful</u> for your support and encouragement.
（我很感激你的支持與鼓勵。）

⇨ 副詞 very 修飾形容詞 grateful。

例 5 ： Having lived in the U.S. for five years, she now speaks English <u>very</u> <u>fluently</u>.

（她已經住在美國五年了，所以她現在英語說得很流利。）

⇨ 副詞 very 修飾副詞 fluently。

例 6 ： <u>Unfortunately</u>, this security policy failed to prevent the terrorist attack from happening.

（很不幸地，這個安全政策未能防止這起恐攻的發生。）

⇨ 副詞 unfortunately 修飾逗號後方的整個句子。

重點2

情狀副詞的形成

(1) 大部分的情狀副詞是在形容詞的字尾加上 -ly 形成。

例如：quick → quickly、bad → badly

(2) 並非所有 -ly 字尾的字都是副詞，副詞也不一定都有 -ly 字尾。

例如：lovely（adj. 可愛的）、lonely（adj. 寂寞的）、well（adv. 好地）

例 ： Andy is competent enough to be promoted, but he doesn't mesh well with the team.

(Andy 雖然夠有能力被提拔晉升，不過他和團隊一向不能好好合作。)

⇨ 副詞 well 修飾動詞 mesh。

重點3

易混淆的副詞

有些副詞字尾加不加 -ly 會造成意義上的差異，在使用上要特別小心。
(1) close (靠近地) ⇨ closely (密切地)
(2) high (高高地) ⇨ highly (非常地)
(3) late (遲；晚) ⇨ lately (最近)
(4) hard (努力地) ⇨ hardly (幾乎不)
(5) deep (深) ⇨ deeply (深深地；非常)
(6) just (僅僅；剛剛；正好) ⇨ justly (公正地)
(7) near (近) ⇨ nearly (幾乎)

例1 : Don't stand too <u>close</u> to me. I don't want to pass on my flu to you.
(別站得靠我太近。我可不想害你感冒。)

例2 : According to the prosecutors, these two incidents are <u>closely</u> related.
(根據檢察官的說法，這兩起事件有密切關聯。)

例3 : I have to work <u>late</u> tonight; have dinner without me.
(我今晚要工作到很晚；晚餐就別等我了。)

例4 : Have you watched any good movie <u>lately</u>?
(你最近有看什麼好看的電影嗎？)

例5 : You need to work really <u>hard</u> to achieve your goal.
(你必須很努力才能實現目標。)

例6 : Would you please turn up your voice? I can <u>hardly</u> hear you at the back of the conference room.
(你可以大聲點嗎？在會議室後面我幾乎聽不見你的聲音。)

重點4

頻率副詞的位置

(1) 常見頻率副詞的種類：always（總是）、 usually（通常）、 often（經常）、 sometimes（有時候）、 seldom（很少）、 never（從未）。
(2) 頻率副詞的位置：
  ① be 動詞後方
  ② 一般動詞前方
  ③ 助動詞和一般動詞中間

例1 ：Marcus Lee is <u>always</u> late for the meeting.
(Marcus Lee 開會總是遲到。)

例2 ：He <u>seldom</u> goes to the movies because he prefers to stay home watching DVDs.
(他很少去看電影因為他寧願待在家看 DVD。)

例3 ：I have <u>never</u> been to France.
(我從未去過法國。)

Give it a try! 實力挑戰題

1 I find your actions _____ reckless, and I am suspending your driver's license.

(A) shockingly

(B) shocking

(C) shocked

(D) shock

Ⓐ Ⓑ Ⓒ Ⓓ

2 Your _____ pursuit of your dream has resulted in your getting this awesome position.

(A) relented

(B) relent

(C) relentlessly

(D) relentless

Ⓐ Ⓑ Ⓒ Ⓓ

3 Tom _____ adores Regina, but he is still not sure whether she wants to marry him.

(A) deep

(B) deeply

(C) depth

(D) deepen

Ⓐ Ⓑ Ⓒ Ⓓ

4 He _____ late for conference calls since he is busy placing orders for customers.

(A) usually is

(B) is ever

(C) is usually

(D) never is

Ⓐ Ⓑ Ⓒ Ⓓ

5 The child nearly drowned after falling into the _____ end of the swimming pool.

(A) deep

(B) depth

(C) deeply

(D) deepen   Ⓐ Ⓑ Ⓒ Ⓓ

- ▶

6 He _____ missed out on his opportunity to travel abroad for business due to attending his child's graduation ceremony.

(A) near

(B) highly

(C) deeply

(D) nearly   Ⓐ Ⓑ Ⓒ Ⓓ

- ▶

7 Mark looked at his _____ résumé, which was completely void of experience.

(A) compatible

(B) impartial

(C) imperfect

(D) periodic   Ⓐ Ⓑ Ⓒ Ⓓ

- ▶

8 The children's car seats need to be fastened _____ to the seats or they will fly forward in case of an accident.

(A) securely

(B) secure

(C) security

(D) be secure   Ⓐ Ⓑ Ⓒ Ⓓ

- ▶

9 Eighty percent of the villagers object _____ to the construction of a sports arena.

(A) strong

(B) strength

(C) strengthen

(D) strongly   Ⓐ Ⓑ Ⓒ Ⓓ

10 During the outbreak of Ebola, many countries are prohibiting travel to the most _____ affected regions of Africa.

(A) heavy

(B) heavily

(C) repeated

(D) repeat　　　　　　　　　　　　　　Ⓐ Ⓑ Ⓒ Ⓓ

11 I have purchased a transponder to _____ pay the toll when I drive past this toll booth twice a day.

(A) automatically

(B) automatic

(C) automation

(D) automated　　　　　　　　　　　　Ⓐ Ⓑ Ⓒ Ⓓ

12 Jennifer has the problem of asthma, which makes it _____ for her to run for too long.

(A) hardly

(B) hard

(C) harden

(D) hardness　　　　　　　　　　　　Ⓐ Ⓑ Ⓒ Ⓓ

13 Since this disease is _____ infectious, patients infected with it should be isolated.

(A) high

(B) height

(C) highly

(D) higher　　　　　　　　　　　　　Ⓐ Ⓑ Ⓒ Ⓓ

14 Sandy is a _____ aggressive salesperson; she will do whatever she can do to achieve her goal.

(A) fair

(B) fairness

(C) fairly

(D) fairy　　　　　　　　　　　　　Ⓐ Ⓑ Ⓒ Ⓓ

15 No matter how nervous you are, you have to try your best to stay _____ in an interview.

(A) calm

(B) calmly

(C) calmness

(D) quietly   Ⓐ Ⓑ Ⓒ Ⓓ

16 The old man was forced to _____ sell his convertible when the bank demanded that he immediately repay his loan.

(A) quick

(B) quickly

(C) quicken

(D) quickness   Ⓐ Ⓑ Ⓒ Ⓓ

17 Each member of our department is asked to submit their _____ analysis of the quarterly sales figures.

(A) respectable

(B) respectively

(C) respectful

(D) respective   Ⓐ Ⓑ Ⓒ Ⓓ

18 The manager was _____ impressed with the newcomer's ability to handle such a complicated case.

(A) particular

(B) particularity

(C) particularly

(D) particularities   Ⓐ Ⓑ Ⓒ Ⓓ

19 Being a business analyst is _____ more relaxing than being a programmer!

(A) definitely

(B) definite

(C) definitive

(D) definition   Ⓐ Ⓑ Ⓒ Ⓓ

20 If you can't be _____, I can't trust you to be a team leader.
   (A) punctually
   (B) punctual
   (C) punctuality
   (D) punctuation   Ⓐ Ⓑ Ⓒ Ⓓ

Unit ⑨ 關係子句

 徐薇老師小叮嚀　🎧 MP3:Unit9

關係代名詞類的題目要注意：

(1) 先行詞為「人」時，關代用 who、whose、whom、that。

(2) 先行詞為「物」或「動物」時，關代用 which、that，所有格則用 of which 或 whose。

(3) 若關代為受格時可省略，但前有介系詞時則不可省略。

(4) that 做關代時，前方不可有介系詞，也不可有逗點。

> **例1**：Tricia is the executive ＿＿＿＿＿ donated thousands of dollars to the political campaign.
> (A) which
> (B) who
> (C) whose
> (D) whom

> **例2**：I often ask Anthony about subjects of ＿＿＿＿＿ he has no knowledge.
> (A) which
> (B) that
> (C) whom
> (D) whose

(5) 複合關代 what = the thing(s) + which。

> **例3**：It's better to buy ＿＿＿＿＿ you need in the suburbs since the city has a 9% sales tax.
> (A) what
> (B) that
> (C) which
> (D) when

🔍 關係子句重點整理

重點1

關係代名詞

(1) 關係代名詞具有代名詞和連接詞之功用。
(2) 先行詞：關係代名詞所代替之字或字群。
(3) 關係子句 (形容詞子句)：關係代名詞所引導的子句，當形容詞用，修飾先行詞，原則上須緊靠先行詞後方。
(4) 關係代名詞 that 可代替 who, whom, which，但是 that 不可在介系詞或逗號之後。that 不可以代替 whose。
(5) 關係代名詞當受格時，可省略。但前有介系詞或逗號時則不可。

先行詞	主格	受格	所有格
人	who	whom	whose
動物、事物	which	which	whose / of which

例1 : Kelly is one of the staff members <u>who</u> help organize this event.
(Kelly 是協助籌辦這活動的員工之一。)
⇨ who 為形容詞子句主詞，代替表人的先行詞 staff members，所以用主格關代 who。

例2 : This is David Wagner, <u>whom</u> I told you about.
(這位是 David Wagner, 我跟你說過他。)
⇨ whom 為形容詞子句受詞，代替表人的先行詞 David Wagner，所以用受格關代 whom。雖然 whom 為受格，但是因為前方有逗號，所以不可以將 whom 省略，也不可以用 that 代替。

例3 : This award will be given to the employee <u>whose</u> performance is the best.
(這個獎將頒給表現最好的員工。)
⇨ whose 為受格關代，後方要接名詞。

例 4 : The antique <u>which</u> is made of ivory will be put up for auction next week.

(由象牙製成的那件古董將於下星期交付拍賣。)

⇨ which 為形容詞子句主詞，代替表事物的先行詞 the antique，所以用主格關代 which。

例 5 : The computer <u>which</u> you bought on eBay is a real bargain.

(你在 eBay 上買的電腦真是很便宜啊！)

⇨ which 為形容詞子句中動詞 bought 的受詞，代替表事物的先行詞 the computer，所以用受格關代 which。which 為受格關代，可以省略。

重點2

關係代名詞 that

(1) 必定要用 that 的情況：

① 先行詞同時有人和物的時候。

② 先行詞前方有最高級的時候。

③ 先行詞前方有 the only, the very, 序數的時候。

(2) 絕不可用 that 的情況：

① 不可以在逗號後方。

② 不可在介系詞後方。

例 1 : *Before I Go To Sleep* is the best novel that I've ever read.

(*Before I Go To Sleep* 是我看過最棒的小說。)

⇨ 前方有最高級 the best，所以要用 that。

例 2 : This is the very book that I am looking for.

(這正是我在找的書。)

⇨ 前方有 the very，所以要用 that。

例 3 : She is the first woman that was nominated as candidate in the presidential election.

(她是第一位被提名角逐參選總統的女性候選人。)

⇨ 前方有序數 the first，所以要用 that。

例4 : This is Dr. Chen, who always comes up with innovative ideas.

(這位是陳博士,她總是能想出創新的點子。)

⇨ 因為有逗號,所以不可以用 that 代替 who。

例5 : The committee asked her many questions to which she had no answers.

(委員會問了她很多她答不出來的問題。)

⇨ 因為有介系詞 to,所以不可以用 that 代替 which。

重點3

關係代名詞的非限定用法

(1) 先行詞是某個特定的人事物或專有名詞時,關係代名詞務必使用非限定用法。

(2) 當關係代名詞前有加逗點時,其所引導的形容詞子句,是用來補充說明先行詞。

例1 : <u>Mr. Newman, who</u> has just been promoted to department head, announced that he would resign at the meeting this morning.

(才剛被升上去做部長的 Newman 先生在今天早上的會議中宣布他將要辭職。)

⇨ 先行詞是人,所以關係代名詞用 who。此處關係代名詞不可以用 that 代替。

例 2 : We are still thinking about whether or not to sign the contract with <u>Hughes Inc., which</u> is said to be a company of bad reputation.

(我們還在考慮是否要跟 Hughes 公司簽訂這份合約，據説他們信譽並不好。)

⇨ 先行詞是公司，所以關係代名詞用 which。此處關係代名詞不可以用 that 代替。

重點4

複合關係代名詞 what

(1) 複合關代本身兼具先行詞和關係代名詞的作用，所以複合關代前不需先行詞。複合關係代名詞所引出的子句，在句中當「名詞」使用。

(2) what = the thing(s) + which

例 1 : <u>What I really need</u> is your encouragement and support.
(我真正需要的是你的鼓勵和支持。)

例 2 : It is good to know that the board of directors approved of <u>what I had done</u>.
(得知董事會贊同我所做的真是令人開心。)

重點5

關係副詞

---

(1) 關係副詞 = 介系詞 ＋ 關代

(2) 關係副詞有四：

① where ⇨ 用於先行詞表「場所」的時候

② when ⇨ 用於先行詞表「時間」的時候

③ why ⇨ 用於先行詞表「理由」的時候

④ how ⇨ 用於先行詞表「方法」的時候

例1 : Venice, <u>where</u> many couples spend their honeymoon, is likely to disappear from our world map in the future.

（威尼斯，很多夫妻度蜜月的地方，有可能在未來從世界地圖上消失。）

⇨ where = in which。

例2 : I will never forget the day <u>when</u> I gave birth to my first baby.

（我絕不會忘記我第一個孩子出生的那天。）

⇨ when = on which。

例3 : Everyone is curious about the reason <u>why</u> Frank resigned.

（大家對於 Frank 辭職的理由感到很好奇。）

⇨ why = for which。

例4 : Would you please tell me the way how you close a deal? (X)

= Would you please tell me <u>how</u> you close a deal? (O)

= Would you please tell me <u>the way</u> you close a deal? (O)

= Would you please tell me <u>the way in which</u> you close a deal? (O)

（可以請你告訴我你成交一筆生意的方法嗎？）

⇨ how = in which，how 和 the way 不同時並用，兩者擇一使用。

Give it a try! 實力挑戰題

1 Tricia is the executive _____ donated thousands of dollars to the political campaign.
(A) which
(B) who
(C) whose
(D) whom　　　　　　　　　　　　　　Ⓐ Ⓑ Ⓒ Ⓓ

2 This author is the one _____ I spoke so highly of last week.
(A) where
(B) which
(C) whose
(D) whom　　　　　　　　　　　　　　Ⓐ Ⓑ Ⓒ Ⓓ

3 The decorative bottles _____ used to be displayed atop the bar are now gone.
(A) which
(B) who
(C) whom
(D) whose　　　　　　　　　　　　　　Ⓐ Ⓑ Ⓒ Ⓓ

4 This is the worst keynote speaker _____ I have ever heard.
(A) whom
(B) that
(C) whose
(D) which　　　　　　　　　　　　　　Ⓐ Ⓑ Ⓒ Ⓓ

5 I often ask Anthony about subjects of _____ he has no knowledge.
(A) which
(B) that
(C) whom
(D) whose　　　　　　　　　　　　　　Ⓐ Ⓑ Ⓒ Ⓓ

6 Mary went to the press conference immediately with _____ she had discovered.

(A) that

(B) which

(C) what

(D) whom

Ⓐ Ⓑ Ⓒ Ⓓ

7 Henry's Bar is one of the places _____ I frequently meet co-workers for happy hour after work.

(A) when

(B) where

(C) which

(D) that

Ⓐ Ⓑ Ⓒ Ⓓ

8 When the boss gets furious, it is one of those times _____ you should just keep silent.

(A) why

(B) that

(C) where

(D) when

Ⓐ Ⓑ Ⓒ Ⓓ

9 No one could comprehend the reason _____ the factory suddenly shut down after being the major employer of this small town for forty years.

(A) when

(B) why

(C) where

(D) which

Ⓐ Ⓑ Ⓒ Ⓓ

10 This engineering job is the only one _____ I have ever had.

(A) that

(B) which

(C) when

(D) whom

Ⓐ Ⓑ Ⓒ Ⓓ

11 _____ our company lacks is creativity.
(A) That
(B) When
(C) Which
(D) What   Ⓐ Ⓑ Ⓒ Ⓓ

12 Ivy, _____ is my assistant, will show you around later.
(A) that
(B) who
(C) which
(D) whom   Ⓐ Ⓑ Ⓒ Ⓓ

13 The advice _____ my supervisor has given me for the past five years did help me climb up the corporate ladder faster than other colleagues.
(A) when
(B) whom
(C) that
(D) whose   Ⓐ Ⓑ Ⓒ Ⓓ

14 Thanks to the ad _____ successfully appealed to most young consumers, our new product brought in a big profit last year.
(A) who
(B) where
(C) when
(D) which   Ⓐ Ⓑ Ⓒ Ⓓ

15 This marketing specialist published many articles, some of _____ are about the effective ways to make profits.
(A) them
(B) which
(C) that
(D) whom   Ⓐ Ⓑ Ⓒ Ⓓ

16 After hours of discussion, the committee finally put together a plan _____ helps to boost the sales.

(A) who

(B) whom

(C) that

(D) where

Ⓐ Ⓑ Ⓒ Ⓓ

17 It's better to buy _____ you need in the suburbs since the city has a 9% sales tax.

(A) what

(B) that

(C) which

(D) when

Ⓐ Ⓑ Ⓒ Ⓓ

18 I am grateful for the hospitality of your brother, Vincent _____ let us stay at his place for a week while our electricity was out.

(A) who

(B) that

(C) , who

(D) which

Ⓐ Ⓑ Ⓒ Ⓓ

19 Would you please stop cracking jokes _____ are politically incorrect?

(A) what

(B) that

(C) who

(D) whose

Ⓐ Ⓑ Ⓒ Ⓓ

20 Little did I expect that I would see the day _____ my face was plastered on a billboard.

(A) where

(B) which

(C) that

(D) when

Ⓐ Ⓑ Ⓒ Ⓓ

Unit ⑩ 比較句構

徐薇老師小叮嚀　🎧 MP3:Unit10

(1) 形容詞與副詞的比較可以分為原級比較、比較級與最高級，

肯定句型：...as + 原級 adj. / 原級 adv. + as...(... 像 ... 一樣 ...)

否定句型：...not as / so + 原級 adj. / 原級 adv. + as...(... 不像 ... 那樣 ...)

例 1：Cheryl's cake looks _____ mine.
(A) as savory like
(B) as savory as
(C) more savory as
(D) less savory as

(2) 兩者比較與三者以上的比較時，其句型為：

兩者比較：① A + be V. / V. + 比較級 + than + B
② the + 比較級 + of the two

三者或三者以上比較：the + 最高級 { of the three / four... 以上
of all / in 團體

例 2：Sharon is _____ of the two candidates for mayor.
(A) the younger
(B) younger
(C) youngest
(D) the youngest

例 3：Of all the exceptional athletes who have ever attended this school, Greg is _____.
(A) most outstanding
(B) the most outstanding
(C) more outstanding
(D) the more outstanding

比較句構重點整理

重點1

原級的比較句

(1) 基本句型
① A... as + 原級 + as + B (A 和 B 一樣 ...)
② A... not as/so + 原級 + as + B (A 沒有像 B 一樣 ...)
(2) 特殊句型
as ～ as one can = as ～ as possible （盡可能地 ...）

例1 : Although Vincent is a newcomer, his performance is <u>as good as</u> others.
（雖然 Vincent 只是個新手，但是他的表現和別人一樣好。）

例2 : Christian works <u>as hard as</u> Jennifer.
(Christian 和 Jennifer 工作一樣認真。)

例3 : The writer's latest novel is <u>not so exciting as</u> her previous ones.
（這位作家的最新小說沒有像她先前的作品一樣精采。）

例4 : Mary doesn't dance <u>as well as</u> Vicky.
(Mary 跳舞沒有跳得像 Vicky 一樣好。)

例5 : I'll try to finish the scientific research project <u>as soon as possible</u>.
= I'll try to finish the scientific research project <u>as soon as I can</u>.
（我會盡快完成這個科學研究專案。）

重點2

比較級的比較句

(1) 基本句型
　① A + V. + 比較級 + than + B (A 比 B 較 ...)
　② A + V. + less + 原級 + than + B (A 比 B 較不 ...)
(2) 特殊句型
　① the + 比較級～，the + 比較級～ (越 ...，就越 ...)
　② 比較級 + and + 比較級 (越來越 ...)
　③ A + be + the + 比較級 + of the two (A 是兩者中較 ... 的)

例1 : House prices are <u>higher than</u> they were last year.
(今年房價比去年高。)

例2 : Paul is <u>more ambitious than</u> other job-seekers.
(Paul 比其他求職者更有野心。)

例3 : Her latest album sells <u>better than</u> those of other singers.
(她的最新專輯賣的比其他歌手的要好。)

例4 : The new manager is <u>less strict than</u> his predecessor.
(比起前任經理，新上任的經理比較沒有那麼嚴格。)

例5 : <u>The more qualified</u> you are, <u>the more likely</u> you are to be hired.
(你條件越好，你就越有可能被雇用。)

例6 : Due to the constant rise of oil prices, the demand for bikes is <u>higher and higher</u>.
(由於油價持續上揚，人們對於腳踏車的需求越來越高了。)

例7 : <u>The larger of the two companies</u> won the contract to remodel the airport.
(這兩家公司中較大的那間贏得了機場改造工程的合約。)

重點3

不用 than 的比較級

> 下列以 -ior 結尾的形容詞比較級要用 to，不用 than：
> ① be superior to ~ 比 ... 優秀
> ② be inferior to ~ 比 ... 差勁
> ③ be senior to ~ 比 ... 年長 / 資深
> ④ be junior to ~ 比 ... 年幼 / 資淺
> ⑤ prior to ~ 在 ... 之前

例1：The new product of this company <u>is superior to</u> that of its rival.
（這家公司的新商品比對手的要好。）

例2：Your performance <u>is inferior to</u> hers, and that's why she was chosen for the job.
（你的表現比她的糟，那就是為何她被選中做這份工作的原因。）

例3：When it comes to teaching, she <u>is senior to</u> me.
（講到教書，她比我資深。）

例4：My boss <u>is junior to</u> me.
（我的老闆比我還年輕。）

例5：<u>Prior to</u> the meeting, she was seen to cry bitterly in the restroom.
（在會議前，有人看到她在廁所痛哭流涕。）

重點4

最高級的句型

$$S. + V. + \begin{cases} \text{the + 形容詞最高級 + N.} \\ \text{the least + 原級 + N.} \end{cases} + \begin{cases} \text{of / among + 複數 N.} \\ \text{in + 範圍} \\ \text{that + S. + have/ has/had +ever +p.p.} \end{cases}$$

例1 : <u>Of all</u> the job applicants, Mr. Ellis is <u>the most experienced</u>.
(在所有求職者中，Ellis 先生是最有經驗的。)

例2 : This is <u>the most thrilling</u> book <u>that I have ever read</u>.
(這本書是我看過的書當中最精采刺激的。)

重點5

倍數句型

$$A + V. + \text{倍數} + \begin{cases} \text{as + 原級 + as + B} \\ \text{比較級 + than + B} \\ \text{the + height/length/size/weight/width + of + B} \end{cases}$$

例1 : The new conference room is <u>twice as big as</u> the old one.
(新的會議室是舊的兩倍大。)

例2 : In this company, the number of men is <u>three times larger than</u> that of women.
(這間公司男性的數目是女性的三倍。)

例3 : The new storage room is <u>ten times the size of</u> the old one.
(新倉庫是舊倉庫的十倍大。)

Give it a try! 實力挑戰題

1 _____ position you are in, the more responsibilities you have to take.
(A) The higher
(B) Higher
(C) Highest
(D) The highest   Ⓐ Ⓑ Ⓒ Ⓓ

2 The subway service in this city is far _____ the bus service.
(A) superior than
(B) better to
(C) superior
(D) superior to   Ⓐ Ⓑ Ⓒ Ⓓ

3 Cheryl's cake looks _____ mine.
(A) as savory like
(B) as savory as
(C) more savory as
(D) less savory as   Ⓐ Ⓑ Ⓒ Ⓓ

4 Samantha has demonstrated that she has _____ as Frank.
(A) as much ability
(B) more ability
(C) as more ability
(D) as ability   Ⓐ Ⓑ Ⓒ Ⓓ

5 Once I discovered that my dentist was _____ the one across the street, I switched immediately.
(A) worse to
(B) inferior than
(C) inferior to
(D) superior to   Ⓐ Ⓑ Ⓒ Ⓓ

6 Of all the exceptional athletes who have ever attended this school, Greg is _____.
(A) most outstanding
(B) the most outstanding
(C) more outstanding
(D) the more outstanding   Ⓐ Ⓑ Ⓒ Ⓓ

7 Maggie is _____ person in this department at handling customer complaints.
(A) least capable
(B) more capable
(C) the less capable
(D) the least capable   Ⓐ Ⓑ Ⓒ Ⓓ

8 The technological capability of smart phones is getting _____.
(A) better and better
(B) best and best
(C) the better and the better
(D) the best and the best   Ⓐ Ⓑ Ⓒ Ⓓ

9 Doing something is _____ than watching TV.
(A) as constructive
(B) more constructive
(C) the most constructive
(D) less more constructive   Ⓐ Ⓑ Ⓒ Ⓓ

10 You had better drive _____ on icy roads.
(A) as careful as possible
(B) as carefulness as possible
(C) as carefully as possible
(D) more carefully as possible   Ⓐ Ⓑ Ⓒ Ⓓ

11 I have to acknowledge the fact that you are _____ at programming software than I.

(A) good

(B) better

(C) well

(D) more good ⒶⒷⒸⒹ

12 In order to support your methodology, you need to compile _____.

(A) as many evidence as possible

(B) more evidence as you can

(C) as much evidence as possible

(D) as much evidence as you are ⒶⒷⒸⒹ

13 The user interface of our new software is not _____ to navigate as our old versions.

(A) as easy

(B) as easily

(C) more easily

(D) easier ⒶⒷⒸⒹ

14 Emma Johnson, _____ of the two candidates, has a better chance of landing this secretarial job.

(A) younger

(B) youngest

(C) the younger

(D) the youngest ⒶⒷⒸⒹ

15 This smartphone is _____ as that robot.

(A) twice as expensive

(B) twice more expensive

(C) as expensive twice

(D) as twice expensive ⒶⒷⒸⒹ

Unit ⑪ 介系詞

徐薇老師小叮嚀 🎧 MP3:Unit11

(1) 介系詞 on、at、in 等，後方可接地點表「在某處」，接時間則表「在某時」：

表地點時：at +(地圖上 / 某處的) 定點、in + 較大範圍的地點或空間
表時間時：at + (幾) 點鐘、on + 星期 / 日期、in + 月 / 季節 / 年

例 1：Our CEO is scheduled to deliver a speech _____ Friday morning.
(A) at
(B) in
(C) on
(D) for

(2) 搭乘交通工具的用法是 by + 交通工具，這裡 by 是指「藉由～」，後方的交通工具視為一種抽象的概念，當不可數名詞使用，所以前面不可加冠詞，也不能用複數。

例 2：I usually go to work by _____.
(A) a car
(B) car
(C) cars
(D) one car

(3) 在多益的介系詞考題中有很多都是在測驗片語中所搭配的介系詞，例如：on behalf of ~ 表「代表 ...」，make a note of ~ 表「將 ... 記下來」，in an effort to ~ 表「為了要 ...」，所以只要熟背片語就能輕鬆解題。

例 3：The chief operating officer accepted the award _____ behalf of the company.
(A) on
(B) in
(C) to
(D) with

介系詞重點整理

重點1

表時間的介系詞

> (1) on：後接星期名稱、特定日子、幾月幾號、某一天的早上、下午或晚上。
> (2) in：後接月份、年份、早上、下午或晚上、季節。
> (3) at：後接幾點幾分、正中午 (noon)、夜晚 (night)、午夜 (midnight)。
> (4) during/over：在…期間
> (5) after：在…之後
> (6) before：在…之前
> (7) since：自從…
> (8) from：從…開始
> (9) through：從…開始到結束
> (10) from ~ to ~：從…到…
> (11) around：大約…
> (12) until/till：直到…
> (13) for：為期…

例1 : The annual trade fair will be held <u>on December 12</u>.
(一年一度的商展將於十二月十二日舉行。)

例2 : Our CEO is scheduled to deliver a speech <u>on Friday morning</u>.
(我們執行長預定於週五早上發表演說。)

例3 : Getting up early is more difficult in winter than <u>in summer</u>.
(冬天早起比夏天困難。)

例4 : This non-profit organization was founded <u>in 2008</u>.
(這個非營利組織於 2008 年成立。)

例5 : An earthquake measuring 7 on the Richter scale struck the small town <u>at 4:25 A.M.</u> this morning.
(今早四點二十五分時芮氏規模七級的地震襲擊了這小鎮。)

例 6 : Never answer any phone <u>during the movie or performance</u>.
（在看電影或看表演期間絕不要接任何電話。）

例 7 : Dark clouds will be moving in <u>after the sunset</u>, and then rain showers are expected.
（日落後會開始有烏雲，而且有可能會下雨。）

例 8 : I used to eat an apple <u>before lunch</u>.
（我以前習慣在午餐前吃顆蘋果。）

例 9 : She has been working in this restaurant <u>since 2005</u>.
（自從 2005 年，她就在這間餐廳工作了。）

例 10 : Dinner will be served starting <u>from 5:30</u>.
（晚餐從五點半開始供應。）

例 11 : He nodded off <u>through the speech</u>.
（整場演講從頭到尾他都在打瞌睡。）

例 12 : Our clearance sales begin <u>from Monday to Saturday</u>.
（我們的清倉大拍賣從週一開始到週六結束。）

例 13 : The sunrise occurred <u>around 6 A.M.</u> this morning.
（今天早上太陽大約是六點升起的。）

例 14 : The concert lasted <u>until 11 P.M.</u>
（演唱會一直持續到晚上十一點為止。）

例 15 : I have been running this restaurant <u>for 10 years</u>.
（我經營這間餐廳有十年了。）

重點2

表地點或方向的介系詞

> (1) in：後接較大的空間 (在…裡面)、國名、城市、洲名、鄉下、容器。
> (2) on：表在某物的上面，而且有接觸。on 也可以接交通工具 (car 和 taxi 要用 in)。
> (3) at：後接小地方或是一個明確的地點。
> (4) over：在…上方，而且沒有接觸。
> (5) under/below/beneath：在…下方，而且沒有接觸。
> (6) beside/next to/by：在…旁邊
> (7) behind：在…後面
> (8) around：在…周圍
> (9) through：穿越 …
> (10) from ~ to ~：從…到…
> (11) along：沿著…
> (12) near：靠近 …

例1 : The 2018 FIFA World Cup will take place <u>in Russia</u>.
(2018 年世界盃足球賽將於俄羅斯舉行。)

例2 : One of the reasons why I live in the country is that I cannot afford a house <u>in the city</u>.
(我住在鄉下的原因之一是我買不起都市的房子。)

例3 : The toys <u>in the box</u> will be donated to the orphanage.
(箱子裡的玩具是要捐給孤兒院的。)

例4 : The secretary put the minutes <u>on the desk</u>.
(秘書將會議記錄放在桌上。)

例5 : Employee parking is permitted <u>on the second floor</u> of the parking garage.
(職員停車在停車場二樓。)

例6 : Since I don't like to take the bus, I will go <u>in my car</u>.
(因為我不喜歡搭公車，所以我會自己開車去。)

例7 : I have to pick up my mother <u>at the airport</u> later.
(稍後我得去機場接我媽。)

例 8 : The lamp hanging <u>over the dining table</u> is a gift from my best friend.
(餐桌上方的燈是我最好朋友送的禮物。)

例 9 : My dog likes to sleep <u>under my bed</u>.
(我的狗喜歡睡在我的床下。)

例 10 : The house <u>by the lake</u> is said to be haunted.
(那間河邊小屋據説鬧鬼。)

例 11 : The little boy always stands <u>behind his mother</u> because he is shy and introverted.
(因為害羞又內向,那個小男孩總是站在他媽媽後面。)

例 12 : I like to jog <u>around the lake</u>.
(我喜歡繞著湖跑步。)

例 13 : You had better keep your headlights on when driving <u>through the tunnel</u>.
(當你開車穿越隧道時,車子頭燈最好要一直開著。)

例 14 : It takes me about thirty minutes to walk <u>from my house to the office</u>.
(從我家走到辦公室要大約三十分鐘。)

例15 : My father makes it a rule to walk <u>along the river</u> every morning.

（我爸爸習慣每天早上沿著河邊散步。）

例16 : My house is <u>near the bus stop and the MRT station</u>, so I can do without a car.

（我家離公車站和捷運站很近，所以我沒有車也可以。）

重點3

其他重要介系詞

(1) against：反對…；對抗…
(2) amid/amidst：在…之中
(3) besides：除了…之外，還有…
(4) despite：儘管…
(5) except：將 … 除外（要和 every, any, all, no 連用）
(6) for：為了…；因為…
(7) following：在…之後
(8) like：像…；例如…
(9) throughout：遍布…

例1 : Every board member is <u>against</u> his proposal except James.

（除了 James 之外，每位董事會成員都反對他的提議。）

例2 : That comedian finished his performance <u>amid</u> boos and jeers.

（那位喜劇演員在一片噓聲和嘲笑聲中結束他的表演。）

例3 : <u>Besides</u> a ten percent discount, those who make reservations online can enjoy free membership of our sports club.

（在線上預訂的人除了可以打九折外，還可以享有我們運動俱樂部的免費會員資格。）

例4 : <u>Despite</u> repeated efforts to apologize for his mistake, the minister has been forced to resign.

（儘管反覆為自己的錯誤道歉，部長還是被迫要辭職下台。）

例 5 : <u>For</u> your safety, you had better wear a hard hat when you enter the construction site.

(為了你的安全著想，進入工地時最好要戴安全帽。)

例 6 : This city is famous <u>for</u> its Victorian buildings.

(這都市以維多利亞時期的建築而聞名。)

例 7 : <u>Following</u> the torrential rain, many streets were flooded.

(在豪雨過後，很多街道都淹水了。)

例 8 : Stop acting <u>like</u> a fool.

(拜託你舉止別再像笨蛋一樣了 !)

例 9 : I like to watch disaster movies, <u>like</u> *The Day After Tomorrow*.

(我喜歡看災難片，例如 ≪ 明天過後 ≫。)

例 10 : This product sells well <u>throughout</u> the world.

(這個商品在全球各地都賣得很好。)

Give it a try! 實力挑戰題

1 The phone has been ringing nonstop _____ this morning.
(A) since
(B) from
(C) on
(D) at   Ⓐ Ⓑ Ⓒ Ⓓ

2 The unpopular policy of employees having only fifteen minutes for lunch has been continued by management, _____ the outcries from staff members.
(A) against
(B) except
(C) besides
(D) despite   Ⓐ Ⓑ Ⓒ Ⓓ

3 The bicycle path runs _____ the banks of the Meyers River.
(A) against
(B) in
(C) at
(D) along   Ⓐ Ⓑ Ⓒ Ⓓ

4 The veteran soldier succeeded _____ all odds by getting a law degree and becoming a famous lawyer.
(A) despite
(B) amid
(C) against
(D) except   Ⓐ Ⓑ Ⓒ Ⓓ

5 _____ (for) Greg, none of the nurses on staff have received training on how to use the new X-ray machine.

(A) Except

(B) Despite

(C) Besides

(D) Following ⒶⒷⒸⒹ

6 In order to keep fit, I make it a rule to jog from my house _____ the park in the suburbs every day.

(A) at

(B) to

(C) over

(D) under ⒶⒷⒸⒹ

7 _____ the violent earthquake, many houses were reduced to rubble.

(A) Throughout

(B) Following

(C) Behind

(D) Beside ⒶⒷⒸⒹ

8 The EU summit this year will be held _____ Greece.

(A) at

(B) along

(C) in

(D) below ⒶⒷⒸⒹ

9 The new property we are thinking about purchasing is _____ Franklin Avenue.

(A) on

(B) in

(C) beneath

(D) through ⒶⒷⒸⒹ

10 Cameron works _____ dawn every day, coming home only to sleep.
(A) in
(B) under
(C) till
(D) around   Ⓐ Ⓑ Ⓒ Ⓓ

Unit ⑫ 助動詞

 徐薇老師小叮嚀　🎧 MP3:Unit12

(1) 常用助動詞包括：do/does、can/could(可以)、may/might(可能)、should(應該)、must(必須)、will(將、會 …)、have/has to(必須、得要 …)、had better(最好) 等，使用時要注意句意與時態，且助動詞後方要接原形 V。

例1：High employee turnover _____ lead to a drop in productivity.
(A) can't
(B) needn't
(C) may
(D) should

(2) 情態助動詞後方接完成式時主要是表示對於過去事情的推測或責難，例如：must have p.p. 表「過去必定 …」，should have p.p. 表「過去應該做但未做 …」。

例2：You _____ such sensitive customer data on your desk last night.
(A) should leave
(B) shouldn't have left
(C) should have left
(D) shouldn't leave

💡 助動詞重點整理

重點1

情態助動詞 can 和 could

> (1) can 的使用時機：
> ① 表現在或未來有能力做某事
> ② 請求許可
> ③ 表現在或未來的可能性（多用於否定句或疑問句中）
> (2) could 的使用時機：
> ① 表過去有能力做某事
> ② 表禮貌的請求
> ③ 表可能性
> * can, could 表示能力時也可用片語 be able to 代替。

例 1 : If you can speak Japanese and English, you are likely to be hired.
（如果你會說日文和英文，你就可能會被雇用。）
⇨ can 表能力。

例 2 : Can I park my car here?
（我可以將車停在這兒嗎？）
⇨ can 表請求許可。

例 3 : The news can't be true.
（這消息不可能是真的。）
⇨ can 表可能性。

例 4 : I could swim across the lake when I was young.
（我年輕時可以游泳橫渡這個湖。）
⇨ could 表過去的能力。

例 5 : Could I use your computer?
（我可以用你的電腦嗎？）
⇨ could 表請求。

例 6 : Vincent is absent from the meeting. He could be sick.
(Vincent 沒來開會，他可能生病了。)
⇨ could 表可能性。

例7 : Teresa is the only one that can do computer graphics in the team.

　　　= Teresa is the only one that is able to do computer graphics in the team.

　　(Teresa 是團隊中唯一一位會電腦繪圖的。)

　　⇨ can 表能力。

重點2

情態助動詞 may 和 might

(1) may 的使用時機：
　　① 表現在或未來的可能性
　　② 表請求
　　③ 表許可
　　④ 表祝福
(2) might 的使用時機：
　　① 表可能性
　　② 表許可

例1 : Don't be fooled by the sunshine. It may rain later.
　　(別被陽光給騙了，待會有可能會下雨喔。)
　　⇨ 表未來可能。

例2 : May I sit next to you?
　　(我可以坐在你旁邊嗎？)
　　⇨ 表請求。

例3 : Employees who wear an identification badge may park here.
　　(有配戴識別證的員工可以在這兒停車。)
　　⇨ 表許可。

例4 : May you have a happy marriage.
　　(祝你們婚姻幸福美滿。)
　　⇨ 表祝福。

例5 : He might go abroad for further study next year.
　　(他明年有可能出國深造。)
　　⇨ 表可能。

例 6 : You might stay here if you want to.
（如果你要的話你可以待在這兒。）
⇨ 表許可。

重點3

情態助動詞 will 和 would

(1) will 的使用時機：
　　① 表無意志的未來
　　② 表意願、承諾、決心
　　③ 表請求
(2) would 的使用時機：
　　① 表 will 的過去式
　　② 表請求

例 1 : My grandfather will be 100 years old next month.
（我爺爺下個月就一百歲了。）
⇨ 表無意志的未來。

例 2 : If it rains tomorrow, I will give you a lift.
（如果明天下雨，我就送你一程。）
⇨ 表意願。

例 3 : Will you do me a favor?
（可以請你幫我忙嗎？）
⇨ 表請求。

例 4 : He said he would take a day off tomorrow.
（他說他明天會請假。）
⇨ 表過去的未來。

例 5 : Would you mind lending me some money?
（你介意借我點錢嗎？）
⇨ 表請求。

重點4

情態助動詞 must

must 的使用時機：
① 表必須
② 表肯定的推測
③ must 的否定 must not 表禁止

例1 : The secretary must keep the manager posted.
(秘書必須向經理隨時報告最新狀況。)
⇨ 表必須。

例2 : You must be tired now because you have been working on the paper all day.
(你一整天都在做報告，你現在必定很累吧！)
⇨ 「must + 動詞原形」表對現在事情的肯定推測。

例3 : You were late this morning; you must have overslept.
(你今早遲到了；你必定是睡過頭了吧！)
⇨ 「must + have p.p.」表對過去事情的肯定推測。

例4 : You must not park your car here because this area is for management only.
(你不可以將車停在這兒，因為這區是給管理階層的人停的。)
⇨ must not 表不可以，可以縮寫成 mustn't。

重點5

情態助動詞 should 和 ought to

(1) should 的使用時機：
　① 表應該
　② should have p.p. ⇨ 表過去該做但未做
　③ shouldn't have p.p. ⇨ 表過去不該做但做了
(2) ought to = should

例1 : You should be ashamed of your behavior.
(你應該為自己的行為感到可恥。)
⇨ 表應該。

例2 : We should have advertised in the local newspaper.
(我們應該在當地報紙登廣告的。)
⇨ should have p.p. 表過去應該做但未做。

例3 : You shouldn't have talked back to your mother.
(你不應該跟你母親頂嘴的。)
⇨ shouldn't have p.p. 表過去不應該做但是做了。

例4 : You ought to apologize to her for your rudeness.
(你應該要為你的魯莽向她道歉。)
⇨ ought to = should。

Give it a try! 實力挑戰題

1 We _____ lose this client if we can't provide what he needs.
(A) might
(B) should
(C) need
(D) dare
Ⓐ Ⓑ Ⓒ Ⓓ

2 High employee turnover _____ lead to a drop in productivity.
(A) dare
(B) needn't
(C) may
(D) should
Ⓐ Ⓑ Ⓒ Ⓓ

3 You _____ such sensitive customer data on your desk last night.
(A) should leave
(B) shouldn't have left
(C) should have left
(D) shouldn't leave
Ⓐ Ⓑ Ⓒ Ⓓ

4 The recent downturn in the economy _____ be the reason why our product sales have sharply decreased.
(A) need
(B) dare
(C) ought
(D) could
Ⓐ Ⓑ Ⓒ Ⓓ

5 The bug in our computer software _____ delay our ability to process orders.
(A) could
(B) should
(C) need
(D) ought
Ⓐ Ⓑ Ⓒ Ⓓ

6 Completing several simple tasks successfully _____ boost the students' confidence.

(A) should have

(B) might

(C) needn't

(D) ought   Ⓐ Ⓑ Ⓒ Ⓓ

7 _____ you please stay on a few weeks longer until we get someone trained to do your job?

(A) Should

(B) Must

(C) Would

(D) Need   Ⓐ Ⓑ Ⓒ Ⓓ

8 In order to make good time, you _____ take the tunnel and not local roads.

(A) must

(B) ought

(C) shouldn't have

(D) need   Ⓐ Ⓑ Ⓒ Ⓓ

9 Tom _____ the reports last night instead of attending the party.

(A) should type

(B) shouldn't type

(C) shouldn't have typed

(D) should have typed   Ⓐ Ⓑ Ⓒ Ⓓ

10 It is hard to say how much the uptick in the economy _____ impact us.

(A) ought

(B) will

(C) should have

(D) need   Ⓐ Ⓑ Ⓒ Ⓓ

Unit ⑬ 常考片語及慣用語

Part1 **依語意分類**

* 與數量或範圍相關的片語

(1) a couple of ~ 一些 ... ; 零星的 ...
(2) a handful of ~ 少數 ...
(3) a number of ~ 幾個 ... ; 若干 ...

例1 : A couple of interns were late, so the workshop was delayed by an hour.
有幾個實習生遲到了,所以研討會延誤了一小時。

例2 : Only a handful of board members agreed to this proposal.
只有少數董事會成員同意這項提議。

例3 : We plan to open a number of branches in the near future.
我們計畫在不久的將來開一些分店。

(1) a crop of ~ 一批 ...
(2) a good/great deal of ~ 很多 ...
　　同 a large/great amount of ~ = plenty of = a lot of = lots of
　　　 = quite a little
(3) a stack of ~ 一疊 ... ; 一大堆 ...
(4) plenty of ~ 很多 ...

例1 : Our company needs a new crop of salespeople because of the opening of some new branches.
因為一些新分店的開幕,我們公司需要一批新的銷售人員。

例2 : There has been a great deal of controversy regarding the legalization of same-sex marriage.
一直以來關於同志婚姻的合法化有很多爭議。

例3 : She is holding a stack of files in her hands.
她手裡抱著一疊文件夾。

例 4 ： We still have plenty of time; there is no need to hurry.
我們還有很多時間；沒必要趕時間。

---

(1) a variety of ~ 各式各樣的 …
(2) a wide range of ~ 廣泛的 …

例 1 ： This restaurant serves a variety of foods which cater to foodies.
這家餐廳提供能迎合饕客的各種食物。

例 2 ： We discussed a wide range of topics during the meeting.
會議中我們討論了各種不同的主題。

---

(1) in all 總計
(2) amount to N. 共計 …
(3) equate to N. 等於 …
(4) add up 合計

例 1 ： In all, there are over 300 employees attending the seminar.
總計有超過三百位員工參加這場座談會。

例 2 ： The cost of the retirement party for Mr. Wilson amounts to $NT30,000.
為 Wilson 先生所舉辦的退休派對花費總計新台幣三萬元。

例 3 ： A ten percent raise equates to $NT5,000.
加薪百分之十相當於新台幣五千元。

例 4 ： Would you please add up these figures for me?
可以請你幫我將這些數字加總嗎？

(1) on a large scale 大規模
　　反 on a small scale
(2) range from A to B 範圍從 A 到 B

例1 : This company plans to lay off employees on a large scale.
這家公司計畫大規模裁員。

例2 : All the goods sold in this shop range in price from $30 to $ 500.
這家店販賣的所有商品價格從三十元到五百元不等。

＊與時間相關的片語

(1) ahead of schedule 在預定時間之前；(進度) 提前
(2) behind schedule 進度落後
(3) as scheduled 依照原先所預定的
(4) be scheduled to Vr. 預定要 ...

例1 : The renovation of the airport was completed ahead of schedule.
機場的翻修工程提前完工了。

例2 : The construction of the website has fallen behind schedule.
網站的建置進度已經落後了。

例3 : The job fair will be held as scheduled no matter what happens.
不論發生甚麼事，就業博覽會將會如期舉行。

例4 : The renovation of the conference room is scheduled to begin on December 31.
會議室的翻修預定於十二月三十一日開始。

(1) in advance 事先
(2) prior to ~ 先於 …

例1 : You had better book your flight in advance in peak season.
旅遊旺季你最好事先訂好班機。

例2 : I suggest that you get to the airport at least 2 hours prior to departure.
我建議你要在起飛前至少兩小時抵達機場。

(1) all the time 總是；一直
(2) at all times 隨時；永遠
(3) as usual 一如往常

例1 : There seems to be heavy traffic on this road all the time.
這條路的交通流量似乎一直都很大。

例2 : Make sure you have your passport with you at all times.
確認你的護照要一直在你身邊。

例3 : As usual, Kelly was late for the meeting again.
一如往常，Kelly 開會又遲到了。

(1) around the clock 日以繼夜
(2) on a daily/weekly/monthly/yearly basis 每日 / 週 / 月 / 年
(3) (every) once in a while 有時候；偶爾
　　同 (every) now and then = on occasion = occasionally
　　　 = from time to time

例1 : The rescuers searched for the missing child around the clock.
搜救人員日以繼夜地搜尋這名失蹤兒童。

例2 : You should practice on a daily basis to improve your computer skills.
你應該要每天練習以達到改善電腦技能的目的。

例 3 : I need to work overtime every once in a while at my new job.
我的新工作偶爾要加班。

---

(1) at first 起初
(2) at present 目前
(3) at last 最後
(4) at the latest 最晚

例 1 : At first, I thought the product was doomed to failure, but it turned out to be a huge commercial success.
起初我認為這商品註定會失敗,但是它最後獲利相當豐厚。

例 2 : At present, the MRT system is shut down due to a mechanical malfunction.
目前,MRT 系統因為機械故障暫停營運。

例 3 : After a long delay, the plane took off at last.
在經過很長時間的延遲後,飛機終於起飛了。

例 4 : Anyone who is interested in the employee picnic should reply to my email by tomorrow morning at the latest.
對員工野餐活動感興趣的人應該最晚在明天早上前回覆我的電子郵件。

---

(1) at once 立刻
    同 immediately = without delay
(2) in no time 立刻

例 1 : You had better deal with the customer's complaint at once.
你最好立刻處理那位客人的投訴。

例 2 : A customer service representative should deal with a complaint in no time.
客服人員應該要立刻處理投訴。

(1) before long 不久
(2) be about to Vr. 即將 ...

例1 : The singer's latest album will be released before long.
這位歌手的最新專輯不久就會發行了。

例2 : The application is about to be due, so you had better hurry.
申請期限就快要到了，你最好趕快。

(1) as of ~ 自 ... 起
(2) no later than ~ 不遲於 ...

例1 : The price of crude oil will go down as of next Monday.
自下週起，原油價格將會調降。

例2 : Application forms should be sent by e-mail no later than four o'clock on Thursday.
申請表最遲應該在週四四點之前以電子郵件方式寄出。

(1) in a row 成排；連續
(2) little by little 逐漸地

例1 : Oil prices have fallen for four days in a row.
油價已經連續下跌四天了。

例2 : Having waited for a long time, I lost my patience little by little.
因為等了好久，我漸漸地失去耐心了。

(1) in the meantime 同時；在此期間
(2) coincide with ~ 與 ... 同時發生

例1 : The renovation of your office won't be completed until next Monday; in the meantime, you'll have to share an office with David.
您辦公室的整修工作要到下週一才會完工；在此期間，您得和 David 共用一間辦公室。

例2 : Valentine's Day coincides with my birthday.
情人節和我生日是同一天。

(1) in time 及時
(2) on time 準時

例1 : Thanks to your help, I arrived just in time for my flight.
多虧您的幫忙，我剛好及時趕上飛機。

例2 : If you fail to make a payment on time, you will be charged a late fee.
如果你未能準時付款，你會被收取滯納金。

(1) date back to ~ 回溯到 ... 時
同 be traced back to ~
(2) to date 至今
(3) be out of date 過時的

例1 : This festival dates back to Victorian times.
這個節慶可以追溯至維多利亞時期。

例2 : The black box hasn't been found to date.
黑盒子至今依舊尚未尋獲。

例3 : These statistics are out of date.
這些統計數據過期了。

* 表語意加強或轉折的片語

(1) above all 最重要的是
(2) in particular 特別是；尤其
(3) on the contrary 相反地

例1 : To get a promotion, you have to be efficient, professional, and above all diligent.
想要獲得升遷，你必須有效率、專業，最重要的是你要很認真。

例2 : Every dish this restaurant serves is superb, the sweet-and-sour chicken in particular.
這家餐廳的每道菜都超讚，尤其是糖醋雞。

例3 : Our sales and profits didn't increase last year; on the contrary, they fell by 10%.
我們公司去年業績及獲利沒有增加；相反地，減少了百分之十。

(1) by contrast 對比之下
(2) in contrast to N. 和 ... 對比之下

例1 : By contrast, the latest model is easier to use than the old one.
對比之下，最新型號比舊款的容易操作。

例2 : In contrast to their new product, ours is more appealing.
和他們的新產品相比之下，我們的比較有吸引力。

(1) by and large 總的來說；大體上來說
(2) on the whole 總的來說；整體上來說
(3) on average 一般而言

例1 : By and large, this marketing strategy is a success.
大體上來說，這個行銷策略是成功的。

例2 : On the whole, her performance is good if you take her experience into account.
如果你將她的經驗考慮在內的話，她的表現在整體上來說是好的。

例3 : On average, this factory turns out 5,000 garments per day.
平均來說，這個工廠每天生產五千件衣服。

(1) in brief 簡言之
　同 in short
(2) in sum 總之
(3) sum up 總結

例1 : In brief, his performance is impeccable.
簡言之，他的表現無可挑剔。

例2 : In sum, we want to assure our customers that we provide the best products at reasonable prices.
總之，我們想要向客人保證我們提供的是價格合理的最佳商品。

例3 : Would you please sum up what you've just said?
可以請你總結一下你剛剛說的嗎？

(1) by chance 偶然地
(2) all of a sudden 突然地
　同 all at once = suddenly

例1 : They met by chance at the night market.
他們在夜市巧遇。

例2 : That company filed for bankruptcy all of a sudden.
那家公司突然聲請破產。

(1) after all 畢竟
(2) now that 既然
(3) at least 至少
(4) as long as 只要

例1 : I thought Jimmy might be promoted to sales manager; after all, he is hard-working and productive.

我以為 Jimmy 可能會被升為業務經理；畢竟他工作認真業績又好。

例2 : Now that you are unemployed, you should take some courses to improve your skills.

既然你現在沒有工作，你應該去上些課程來精進自己的技能。

例3 : Due to the traffic congestion, I have been stuck at least two hours on the highway.

因為交通阻塞，我已經被困在公路上至少兩小時了。

例4 : As long as you are not happy with our product, you will be given a refund upon presenting the receipt.

只要您對我們的產品不滿意，在出示收據時便可以獲得退款。

(1) in case 以防萬一；假如
(2) in the event of ~ 假如 ...

例1 : In case I am out of town, you can hand over the documents to my secretary.

假如我出城去了，你可以將文件交給我的秘書。

例2 : In the event of rain, the parade will be rescheduled.

假如下雨，遊行將會改期。

(1) in spite of ~ 儘管 …
(2) regardless of ~ 不管 …

例 1 : The department head insisted on launching the research project in spite of the shortage of funds.

儘管資金短缺，部門主管還是堅持要進行這專案。

例 2 : All 1000 employees of this company went on strike regardless of the bad weather.

這家公司所有一千名員工不管惡劣的天氣還是參加了罷工。

(1) in any case 無論如何
(2) not ~ on any account 無論如何也不 …
　　同 on no account

例 1 : Costs may be high, but in any case we'll try to meet every customer's demand.

花費可能會很高，但是無論如何，我們會想盡辦法符合每位顧客的需求。

例 2 : Once you make a promise, you should not break it on any account.

一旦你許下承諾，無論如何你都不應該違背它。

(1) as for ~ 至於 … ; 關於 …
(2) nothing but ~ 只有 ; 僅僅

例 1 : Stinky tofu is my favorite snack; as for drinks, I love milk tea most.

臭豆腐是我最愛的小吃；至於飲料，我最愛奶茶。

例 2 : He was so busy with the project that he ate nothing but an apple all day.

他是如此忙於專案以致於他一整天下來只吃了一顆蘋果。

(1) at all costs 不惜一切代價
　　同 at any cost = at any price
(2) without hesitation 毫不猶豫
(3) without reservation 毫無保留

例1 : The police said that they would save the kidnapped girl at all costs.
　　警方說他們會不計一切代價拯救被綁架的女孩。

例2 : Kelly said yes without hesitation when her boyfriend proposed to her.
　　Kelly 的男友跟她求婚時,她毫不猶豫地答應了。

例3 : I am grateful for your imparting your knowledge to me without reservation.
　　我很感激您毫無保留地將知識傳授給我。

(1) when it comes to N./V-ing 一談到 …
(2) with regard to N. 關於 …
　　同 with/in reference to = in regard to
(3) in reference to ~ 關於 …

例1 : When it comes to industrial design, Germany is second to none.
　　一談到工業設計,德國是首屈一指的。

例2 : If you have any questions with regard to the operation of this machine, don't hesitate to let me know.
　　如果你有關於操作這機器的任何問題,請立刻讓我知道。

例3 : I am calling in reference to your inquiry about our package tour.
　　我來電回覆關於您詢問我們的套裝行程一事。

(1) as far as someone be concerned 就某人而言；在某人看來
(2) in terms of ~ 從 ... 角度來看
(3) to some extent 在某種程度上

例 1 : As far as I am concerned, Lilian is not qualified for this position.
在我看來，Lilian 不夠資格做這工作。

例 2 : In terms of profits, this marketing strategy didn't work out.
從利潤方面來看，這個行銷策略並沒有成功。

例 3 : To some extent, I don't agree with you on the issue.
在某種程度上，我在這個議題上不同意你的看法。

(1) as well 也
(2) as well as ~ 以及 ...
(3) along with ~ 連同 ... ；以及 ...
    同 together with = as well as

例 1 : You will get reimbursement for any expenses incurred on the business trip and have a day off as well.
因公出差的話可以得到所有開銷的補償金，也可以休一天假。

例 2 : Board members as well as shareholders will attend the third annual Technology Awards.
董事會成員以及股東都將會出席第三屆年度科技獎頒獎典禮。

例 3 : The first 100 customers tomorrow morning will get additional 10% off along with a gift.
明天早上前一百名的客人將可以享有原有折扣再打九折以及一份禮物。

(1) apart from ~ 除了 … 之外

   同 aside from …

(2) except for ~ 除了 … 之外

(3) in addition to (+ N./V-ing) 除了 … 之外

* apart from 和 except for 都表示「除了 …(沒有)之外，其它都 …」；in addition to 則表示「除了 … 之外，還有 …」

例1 : All the equipment is in good condition apart from the photocopier.

除了影印機之外，所有設備狀況都很良好。

例2 : The shipment of all orders, except for those placed before Christmas, will be delayed because of the strike.

所有訂單的運送，除了耶誕節之前就下的訂單之外，其它的都會因罷工而延遲。

例3 : In addition to my monthly salary, I get many other perks at my new job.

除了月薪之外，我的新工作還有很多其他津貼。

(1) instead of ~ 而不是 … ，代替 …

(2) rather than ~ 而不是 …

例1 : Due to heavy traffic, we decided to go by MRT instead of taking a bus.

因為交通擁塞，我們決定搭捷運去而不要搭公車。

例2 : I think I'll stay home rather than go out on such a freezing day.

這麼冷的天我想我要待在家不要出門。

(1) no longer　再也不
(2) far from ~　一點也不 …

例1 : This company no longer manufactures car parts.
這家公司再也不生產汽車零件了。

例2 : According to the expert, the threat of the Ebola virus is far from over.
根據這位專家的說法，伊波拉病毒的威脅尚未結束。

(1) out of the question　不可能的
(2) under no circumstances　絕不
　同 by no means

例1 : Since two sides couldn't reach a consensus, the merger was out of the question.
因為雙方無法達成共識，併購是不可能的了。

例2 : Under no circumstances can you reveal anything about the new product.
你絕不可以洩漏任何關於這新商品的消息。

(1) be sure to Vr.　務必 …
(2) bear in mind　牢記在心

例1 : Be sure to submit your report no later than next Friday.
務必最慢要在下週五前交出你的報告。

例2 : Bear your past mistakes in mind and never make the same one twice.
將過去所犯的錯記住，絕不要再犯相同的錯。

(1) be destined to Vr. 注定 …
(2) be supposed to Vr. 應該 …

> **例1** : This project is destined to fail.
> 這個專案注定會失敗。

> **例2** : Judges are supposed to be objective and righteous.
> 法官應該要客觀且公正。

＊表因果關係的片語

(1) as a result of ~ 因為 …
> **同** because of = due to = owing to = on account of
(2) as a result 因此
> **同** therefore = thus = hence = consequently = as a consequence

> **例1** : As a result of a power outage, all the machines were shut down for two hours.
> 因為停電的關係，所有的機器都停擺了兩小時。

> **例2** : I left my briefcase behind in the taxi; as a result, I called the police to ask for help.
> 我將公事包遺留在計程車上了；因此，我報警尋求協助。

(1) result from ~ 起因於 …
(2) result in ~ 導致 …

> **例1** : The long delay of the flight resulted from the heavy fog.
> 班機的延誤多時是因為濃霧的關係。

> **例2** : The violent typhoon resulted in the loss of hundreds of lives.
> 這個強烈颱風造成數百人喪生。

(1) bring about ~ 導致 …
(2) lead to ~ 導致 …

例 1 : A too-rapid expansion may bring about the bankruptcy of this company.

擴展速度過快可能會導致這家公司破產。

例 2 : Low pay is the main cause that has led to the strike.

低工資是造成這次罷工的主要原因。

(1) in light of ~ 有鑑於 …
(2) according to ~ 根據 …
(3) on the basis of ~ 依據 …
(4) at the request of ~ 依 … 的請求

例 1 : In light of the recent stampede, the authorities decided to cancel all the New Year celebrations.

有鑑於最近發生的踩踏事件，有關當局決定要取消所有新年慶祝活動。

例 2 : According to the agenda, there will be a reception after the meeting.

根據議程，在會議結束之後會有一個歡迎會。

例 3 : We will choose the best candidate on the basis of communication and negotiation skills.

我們將依據溝通及談判技能選出最棒的候選人。

例 4 : Everyone on the staff joined in the fund-raising event at the request of the CEO.

在執行長的要求之下，每位員工都參加了募款活動。

(1) attribute A to B 將 A 歸因於 B
(2) thanks to N. 多虧 …
(3) with a view to (+ N./Ving) 為了要 …
(4) in an effort to Vr. 為了 …

例1 : The manager attributed the increase in sales to the success of the new promotion.
經理將銷售的增加歸功於是新促銷活動的成功。

例2 : Thanks to your timely help, I got the work done before the deadline.
多虧你即時的幫助，我才能在截止日前將工作完成。

例3 : With a view to making ends meet, she took three part-time jobs in college.
為了要收支平衡，她在大學時兼了三份差。

例4 : In an effort to appeal to more consumers, this store offered discounts of up to 40% on all merchandise.
為了要吸引更多消費者，這家店提供了所有商品最高打到六折的折扣價。

＊表情緒、喜好、意願的片語

(1) be concerned about ~ 擔心 …
(2) be sensitive to N. 對 … 敏感

例1 : People all over the world are concerned about the outbreak of the Ebola epidemic.
全球的人都很擔心伊波拉病毒的擴散。

例2 : Since she is sensitive to criticism, you had better be careful of what you say to her.
因為她對批評很敏感，所以跟她說話要小心。

(1) be grateful for ~ 感謝 …
(2) be impressed by/with ~ 對 … 印象深刻
(3) be pleased with ~ 對 … 感到滿意

例1 : I am grateful for Mr. Whitman's long-term service; without him, our company wouldn't have risen to the top of the field.
我很感激 Whitman 先生的長期效力；沒有他的話，公司就不會成為業界翹楚了。

例2 : All the interviewers were impressed with the youngest candidate's eloquence.
所有面試官都對最年輕應徵者的口才印象深刻。

例3 : I am pleased with your performance.
我對你的表現感到滿意。

(1) be delighted to Vr. 樂意去 …
(2) be willing to Vr. 願意 …

例1 : I am delighted to be the convener of the meeting.
我很樂意擔任會議召集人。

例2 : The key to his success is that he is always willing to learn anything new.
他的致勝關鍵在於他總是願意學習新事物。

(1) be eager to Vr. 渴望 …
(2) be keen on ~ 喜歡 … ；對 … 熱中
(3) care for ~ 喜歡 … （常用於否定句或疑問句）
(4) prefer A to B 喜歡 A 甚於 B

例1 : He is so eager to make a name for himself that he works hard day and night.
他是如此渴望揚名立萬，所以他日以繼夜地努力工作。

例2 : My son is keen on computer programming.
我兒子對電腦程式設計很熱愛。

例3 : I don't care for going shopping; I'd rather stay home.
　　　 我不喜歡逛街；我寧願待在家。

例4 : I prefer coffee to tea.
　　　 我喜歡咖啡更甚茶。

---

(1) pride oneself on ~　對 ... 自豪
(2) take pride in ~　以 ... 為榮
(3) speak highly of ~　讚美 ... ；推崇 ...

例1 : He prides himself on his efficiency.
　　　 他對自己的工作效率感到很自豪。

例2 : All the team members take pride in your achievement.
　　　 所有的團員都以你的成就為榮。

例3 : The manager speaks highly of your expertise and efficiency.
　　　 經理大力讚賞你的專業和效率。

---

(1) at random　隨機地
(2) at will　隨心所欲地
(3) feel free to Vr.　隨意 ...

例1 : All the participants have to choose a card on the table at random.
　　　 所有參加者必須從桌上的卡片中隨機挑出一張。

例2 : No one is allowed to leave in the midst of the show at will.
　　　 沒有人可以隨意地在表演中離開。

例3 : If you have any questions regarding your order, feel free to contact me.
　　　 如果你有任何關於你訂單的問題，儘管聯絡我。

(1) approve of ~ 贊成 …

　　反 disapprove of ~ 不贊成 …

(2) in favor of ~ 贊成 …

(3) object to N./V-ing 反對 …

例1 : According to the survey, 80% of people approve of the removal of the bridge.
根據調查，百分之八十的人贊成拆除這座橋樑。

例2 : All the board members voted in favor of his proposal.
所有董事會成員都投票贊成他的提議。

例3 : It is surprising that most of the board members object to the merger.
大部分的董事會成員都反對這併購案真是令人意外。

(1) agree on something 就某事達成協議

(2) agree with someone 贊同某人的看法；適合某人

例1 : Both parties fail to agree on the terms of a settlement.
雙方無法對和解條件達成協議。

例2 : I find it hard to agree with you on this issue.
針對這議題我覺得我很難同意你的看法。

例3 : The air in the country agrees with you.
鄉下的空氣適合你。

(1) be aware of ~ 知道 … ；意識到 …

(2) be stressed out 感到有壓力

例1 : He wasn't aware of the risk involved with the investment.
他沒有意識到這投資所涉及的風險。

例2 : I am stressed out about the coming interview.
對於即將到來的面試我感到很有壓力。

*表組成關係的片語

(1) associate A with B 將 A 和 B 聯想在一起
(2) think of A as B 視 A 為 B

例1 : It is common for people to associate bullfighting with Spain.
人們常將鬥牛和西班牙聯想在一起。

例2 : Most readers think of the writer's latest novel as a page-turner.
多數讀者都認為這位作家的最新小説是令人愛不釋手的一本書。

(1) combine A with B 結合 A 與 B
(2) incorporate A into B 將 A 納入 B
(3) separate A from B 將 A 和 B 分開

例1 : As an inventor, I have been dreaming of inventing something which combines practicality and creativity.
身為一個發明家，我一直夢想能發明出兼具實用性與創造力的東西。

例2 : I am happy to know that the team leader incorporated my idea into the design.
我很高興得知組長將我的想法納入設計中。

例3 : It's impossible to separate economics from politics.
要將經濟和政治切割開來是不可能的。

(1) be coupled with ~ 加上 ...
(2) cut down on ~ 減少 ...

例1 : Wisdom coupled with diligence makes him the top sales representative.
智慧加上努力使他成為頂尖銷售員。

例 2 : You had better cut down on the intake of sugar if you want to keep yourself in shape.
如果你想保持健康的話，你最好減少糖的攝取。

(1) be composed of ~ 由 ... 組成
　　同 consist of ~ = be made up of ~
(2) be made of ~ 由 ... 製成
(3) make A out of B 用 B 製成 A

例 1 : This organization is composed of people from all walks of life.
這個組織是由各行各業的人組成的。

例 2 : It is amazing that this dress is made of chocolate.
這件洋裝是用巧克力製成的真是令人覺得不可思議。

例 3 : The containers made out of polystyrene will pose a threat not only to our environment but also to our health.
用保麗龍做成的容器不僅會危害環境也會對人體健康造成威脅。

(1) be packed with ~ 擠滿 ...
　　同 be crowded with ~ = be filled with ~
(2) be inundated with ~ 充斥著 ...
(3) be rich in ~ 富含 ...

例 1 : Disneyland is always packed with tourists in peak season.
旅遊旺季時，迪士尼樂園總是擠滿遊客。

例 2 : All the customer service representatives are inundated with calls complaining about the flaw in the new product.
投訴新產品瑕疵的電話多到讓所有客服人員應接不暇。

例 3 : This country is rich in petroleum.
這個國家石油儲量豐富。

(1) pertain to ~ 和 ... 有關；涉及 ...
(2) relate to ~ 與 ... 有關

例1 : We will discuss issues that pertain to environmental protection.

我們將會討論和環保有關的議題。

例2 : His speech relates to the effects that global warming has on human beings.

他的演說是關於全球暖化對於人類的影響的。

(1) be linked to N. 和 ... 有關
　　同 be related to N. 和 ... 有關
(2) be restricted to ~ 被侷限在 ... 範圍內
(3) be exposed to N. 暴露在 ... 之中

例1 : It is widely accepted that smoking is closely linked to lung cancer.

大家都普遍認為抽菸和肺癌有密切關係。

例2 : Seats in the front row of the concert hall are restricted to foreign ambassadors.

音樂廳前排座位只限於外交使節。

例3 : This bottled water might be poisonous because it has been exposed to heat for a long time.

這罐瓶裝水因為長時間暴露於高溫下可能有毒。

(1) choose from ~ 從 ... 中選擇
(2) single out ~ 挑出 ...
(3) opt for ~ 選擇 ...

例1 : We provide a variety of management courses for you to choose from.

我們提供各種的管理課程供您選擇。

例 2 : It is an honor to be singled out for this award.
獲頒這個獎真是莫大的榮幸。

例 3 : On second thought, I opted for early retirement.
重新考慮之後，我選擇提前退休。

(1) be equipped with ~　配備有 …
(2) be accompanied by ~　由 … 陪同
(3) keep someone company　陪伴某人

例 1 : All our offices are equipped with air purifiers.
我們所有的辦公室都配備了空氣清淨設備。

例 2 : Visitors must be accompanied by staff members to enter the office.
訪客必須由員工陪同才能進入辦公室。

例 3 : Thanks for keeping me company while I was waiting for my flight.
謝謝你在我等飛機時一直陪著我。

(1) in conjunction with ~　與 … 聯合
(2) merge with ~　與 … 合併
(3) partner with ~　和 … 合夥

例 1 : The employees of these two departments are working in conjunction with each other on the project.
這兩個部門的員工合作進行這專案。

例 2 : The insurance company plans to merge with another in the near future.
這家保險公司計畫在不久的將來和另一家合併。

例 3 : Make sure that the person you choose to partner with is reliable and honest.
要確認你合夥的對象是可靠誠實的。

✱表能力的片語

(1) be able to Vr. 能夠 ...
　　同 be capable of　反 be unable to Vr.
(2) fail to Vr. 未能 ...
(3) succeed in ~ 成功 ...

例1：We will be able to sell a large number of our new products because of the innovative advertisement.
　　　因為這個創新的廣告，我們將能夠賣出很多新商品。

例2：Despite the fact that Mr. Lamos works hard, he still fails to win the manager's approval.
　　　儘管 Lamos 先生工作努力，他還是未能贏得經理的讚賞。

例3：By exercising regularly, he finally succeeded in losing weight.
　　　藉由規律地運動，他終於減重成功。

(1) be eligible for ~ = be eligible to Vr. 有資格 ...
(2) be qualified for ~ 適任 ...

例1：All the employees who are eligible for the retirement program should submit an application by Friday.
　　　符合退休方案資格的所有員工應該於週五前提出申請。

例2：Do you think that Mr. Wilson is qualified for the managerial position?
　　　你覺得 Wilson 先生適任管理職嗎？

(1) be familiar with ~ 熟悉 ...
　　反 be unfamiliar with ~ 不熟悉 ...
(2) familiarize someone with something 使某人熟悉某事
(3) acquaint oneself with ~ 使自己熟悉 ...

例1：Although he is a newcomer, he is familiar with our procedures.
　　　雖然他是個新手，但是他卻很熟悉我們的規定。

例 2 : I spent all day familiarizing myself with standard operating procedure.
我花了一整天時間讓自己熟悉標準作業程序。

例 3 : As a newcomer, the first thing you have to do is to acquaint yourself with the office's rules.
身為一個新進人員，你必須做的第一件事就是熟悉辦公室的規定。

(1) be responsible for ~ 為 … 負責
(2) take responsibility for ~ 為 … 負責
(3) in charge of 負責 …
(4) serve as ~ 充當 … ；擔任 …

例 1 : Who is responsible for the discrepancy between the two reports?
誰該為這兩份報告的不一致負責呢？

例 2 : Who has to take responsibility for the error in the financial report?
誰必須為財務報告上的錯誤負責呢？

例 3 : Marvin is in charge of this project.
Marvin 負責這個案子。

例 4 : David Wagner has been serving as our senior accountant for over ten years.
David Wagner 擔任我們的資深會計已經十多年了。

(1) credit someone with ~ 相信某人具有 … 優點或能力
(2) entitle someone to N./Vr. 授權某人 … ；使某人有資格 …
(3) bestow ~ on/upon someone 將 … 獻給某人

例 1 : Everyone credits Kevin Becker with the ability to complete a project on his own.
每個人都相信 Kevin Becker 具有獨立完成案子的能力。

例 2 : Membership in this club will entitle you to use all the facilities here.
本俱樂部的會員將可以有資格使用這裡的所有設施。

例 3 : The company founder bestowed the title of vice president on me before he retired.
這間公司的創辦人在退休前將副總裁的頭銜授予給我。

＊表比較關係的片語

(1) be commensurate with ~　和 ... 相稱
(2) in accordance with ~　依照 ... ；與 ... 一致
(3) vary with　隨著 ... 而改變

例 1 : Your salary is commensurate with your performance.
你的薪水會和你的表現相稱。

例 2 : If you fail to act in accordance with the terms of the contract, you will be subject to a fine.
如果你未能按照合約條文行事，你會被罰款。

例 3 : Prices vary with the seasons.
價格隨著季節有所不同。

(1) have ~ in common　有 ... 共同點
(2) be different from ~　和 ... 不同
(3) be inferior to N.　劣於 ...
　　反 be superior to N.　優於 ...

例 1 : Kelly is my best friend, but we have nothing in common.
Kelly 是我最好的朋友，但是我們兩人毫無共同點。

例 2 : The age group of our target customers is different from that of yours.
我們的目標客戶年齡層和你們的不一樣。

例 3 : The writer's latest novel is considered to be inferior to her previous works.
這位作家的最新小說被認為比她先前的作品要差。

(1) compared to N. 和 ... 比起來
(2) in comparison with 和 ... 相比之下
(3) compete with ~ 和 ... 競爭

例 1 : My car is more fuel-efficient compared to yours.
和你的車子相比，我的比較省油。

例 2 : In comparison with our old system, the new one is more complicated.
和我們的舊系統比起來，新系統比較複雜。

例 3 : We need to develop new products so that we can compete with our largest rival.
我們必須開發新商品才能夠和最大的對手競爭。

(1) keep up with ~ 跟上 ...
　　同 keep pace with
(2) catch up with ~ 趕上 ...

例 1 : To keep up with the times, you will need to know what is happening in the world.
想要跟上時代潮流，你必須知道世界上在發生的事。

例 2 : Since she is a late bloomer, it takes her a lot of time to catch up with other classmates.
因為她發展遲緩，她要花很多時間才能趕上其他同學。

＊表事物轉換的片語

(1) apply A to B 將 A 應用於 B
(2) introduce A to B 將 A 介紹給 B
(3) refer A to B 將 A 轉介給 B

例 1 : He tries his best to apply what he has learned to his new job.
他盡力將自己所學的一切應用於新工作上。

例 2 : I'd like to introduce myself to all of you.
我想向大家自我介紹一下。

例 3 : My family doctor referred me to an excellent chiropractor, who corrected my back issues.

我的家庭醫生將我轉介給一位很棒的脊椎指壓治療師,他治好了我的背部問題。

---

(1) adapt A into B 將 A 改編成 B
(2) change A into B 將 A 變成 B
(3) exchange A for B 將 A 換成 B

例 1 : The producer is good at adapting novels into movies.
這位製作人很擅長將小說改編成電影。

例 2 : The Japanese Yen has been depreciating for days; it's time for you to change your US dollars into Yen.
日圓已經連貶幾天了;你該去把美金換成日圓了。

例 3 : I would like to exchange this red hat for a green one.
我想要將這頂紅帽子換成綠色的。

---

(1) change into ~ 轉變成 …
　　同 turn into ~
(2) develop into ~ 發展成 …

例 1 : Advances in technology make it possible for the feces of animals to be changed into energy for human consumption.
科技的進步使得動物糞便得以變成可供人類使用的能源。

例 2 : It is surprising that this deserted prison has developed into a popular scenic spot.
這座廢棄監獄發展成熱門觀光景點真是令人意外。

✱ 表人際溝通的片語

(1) account for ~ 解釋 … ；是 … 的原因；(在數量或比例上) 佔 …
(2) apologize for ~ 為 … 道歉

例 1 : The manager asked Vincent to account for his absence from the seminar this morning.
經理要求 Vincent 解釋今早缺席研討會的原因。

例 2 : I am writing this letter to apologize for any inconvenience caused by the mix-up.
因為搞錯所造成的任何不便，我寫這封信是為了向您致歉。

(1) ask for ~ 要求 …
(2) call for ~ 需要 … ；呼籲 … ；要求 …
(3) solicit something from someone 向某人徵求某物

例 1 : I called the front desk and asked for some clean towels.
我打電話到櫃檯去要些乾淨的毛巾。

例 2 : Conducting a job search calls for patience, so don't give up now.
找工作是需要耐心的，所以別現在就放棄了。

例 3 : The aim of this event is to solicit donations from some organizations to help those in need.
這個活動的目的是要向一些機構募集捐款以幫助有需要的人。

(1) be critical of ~ 批評 …
(2) complain about ~ 抱怨 …

例 1 : David is always critical of his boss and complains about her unfair treatment of employees.
David 總是批評他的老闆以及抱怨老闆對員工的不公平對待。

例 2 : This morning, many consumers called to complain about the malfunction of our new product due to battery leakage.
今早很多客人打電話來抱怨因電池漏液導致我們的產品故障。

(1) comment on ~ 評論 …
(2) elaborate on ~ 詳盡說明 …

例 1 : The CFO refused to comment on the financial scandal.
財務長拒絕針對這起財務醜聞發表評論。

例 2 : The manager refused to elaborate on the reason why he resigned from his position.
經理拒絕對辭職的理由作詳盡說明。

(1) accuse someone of N./V-ing 控告某人做了某事
　　同 charge someone with N./V-ing
(2) convince someone of something 勸服某人相信某事
(3) inform someone of something 通知某人某事
(4) remind someone of something 提醒某人某事

例 1 : The writer was accused of plagiarizing.
這位作家遭控剽竊。

例 2 : The manager tried his best to convince the president of the necessity of downsizing the workforce.
經理想盡辦法要說服總裁減少勞動力人數的必要性。

例 3 : I will inform you of my decision as soon as possible.
我會盡快通知你我的決定。

例 4 : Thanks for reminding me of his birthday. I am going to buy him a gift.
謝謝你提醒我他的生日要到了。我要買個禮物送他。

(1) communicate with ~ 和 … 溝通
(2) inquire about ~ 詢問 …

例 1 : He is so stubborn that I find it hard to communicate with him.
他固執到我覺得要和他溝通很困難。

例2 : Many people called to inquire about the price of our new product this morning.

今早有很多人打電話來詢問我們新產品的價錢。

(1) keep in touch 保持聯繫
(2) touch base with ~ 聯絡 ...

例1 : Although my father has retired, he still keeps in touch with his former colleagues.

雖然我父親已經退休了，但是他還是和前同事保持聯絡。

例2 : I am in the middle of something now; I'll touch base with you later.

我現在有事情在忙；等一下我再跟你聯絡。

(1) keep track of ~ 了解 ... ; 持續追蹤 ...
(2) lose track of ~ 與 ... 失去聯繫 ; 忘記 ...

例1 : You can visit our website to keep track of your order.

您可以瀏覽我們網站以追蹤訂單狀況。

例2 : He was so busy with his paper that he lost track of time.

他忙報告忙到忘記時間了。

＊表處理執行的動詞片語

(1) attempt to Vr. 試圖去 ...
(2) manage to Vr. 做成某事
(3) tend to Vr. 傾向於 ... ; 易於 ...

例1 : Things might get worse if you attempt to fix the machine yourself.

如果你嘗試自己去修這機器的話，情況有可能更糟。

例2 : Judy managed to finish her presentation although she was under a lot of strain.

儘管壓力很大，Judy 還是成功地完成了簡報。

例3 : According to research, girls tend to learn better than boys in the acquisition of a language.
根據研究，在語言習得方面，女孩比男孩優秀。

---

(1) draw up 籌備 (計畫)；草擬
(2) plan on ~ 打算 (做某事)；預料 (某事會發生)
(3) fix up 安排

例1 : Before you draw up a contract, it is imperative that you ask Aston Owens for some advice.
在你草擬合約前，你有必要去向 Aston Owens 徵求一些建議。

例2 : I am planning on taking a trip to Germany next year.
我打算明年去德國旅行。

例3 : I am calling to fix up a meeting with you.
我打電話來是要跟你敲碰面時間。

---

(1) deal with ~ 處理 …
(2) take care of ~ 照顧 … ；處理 …
(3) work on ~ 從事 … ；修理；改善 …
(4) carry out ~ 實現 … ；執行 …

例1 : I admire the way you dealt with this problem.
我很欣賞你處理這問題的方法。

例2 : Lindsay used to be a tour guide, so you can rely on her to take care of the travel arrangements.
Lindsay 曾經當過導遊，所以你可以仰賴她處理所有旅遊安排事宜。

例3 : You will have to work on the thesis for a long time before you can get your doctoral degree.
在你可以取得博士學位之前，你將必須花很多時間在論文上。

例4 : The new immigration policy will be carried out as of next Monday.
新的移民政策將自下週一起實行。

(1) avail oneself of ~ 利用 …
(2) make use of ~ 利用 …
(3) take advantage of ~ 利用 …

例 1 : Newcomers are encouraged to avail themselves of this training session to get fully equipped.
我們鼓勵新進人員好好利用這次訓練課程的機會來讓自己做好充分準備。

例 2 : I think you should make use of this opportunity to fully develop your potential.
我認為你應該利用這機會充分發揮你的潛力。

例 3 : You can take advantage of all the facilities in the hotel.
你可以使用飯店的所有設施。

(1) fight for ~ 為 … 奮鬥
(2) strive to Vr. 努力 …
(3) see something through （尤指艱難地）堅持做完某事

例 1 : He is still fighting for the custody of his only child.
他還在為唯一的小孩的監護權奮鬥中。

例 2 : Once she sets a new goal, she will strive to achieve it.
她一旦設定新目標，她就會很努力去達成它。

例 3 : Thanks to your assistance, we could see this project through.
多虧您的協助，我們才能夠將這專案完成。

(1) concentrate on ~ 專注於 …
(2) focus on ~ 將焦點放於 …
(3) specialize in ~ 專門做 … ；專精 …
(4) follow up (on something) 後續追蹤

例 1 : I think you should concentrate on reducing the costs first.
我認為你應該先專注在降低成本上。

例2：This report focuses on the reasons why oil prices keep rising.
這份報告著重於探討油價持續上漲的原因。

例3：We need a person who specializes in staff training to help improve employee efficiency.
我們需要一位擅長員工訓練的人員來協助改善員工效率。

例4：The manager asked me to follow up on the consumer's complaint.
經理要求我後續追蹤這位客人的投訴。

---

(1) comply with ~ 遵守 …
(2) in compliance with ~ 遵守 …

例1：Every member has to comply with the rules of the club, and you are no exception.
每個會員都必須遵守俱樂部的規則，你也不例外。

例2：The construction company claimed that the dormitory was constructed in compliance with the building regulations.
這家建商聲稱他們是遵照建築法規蓋這間宿舍的。

---

(1) dispose of ~ 把 … 處理掉
(2) wipe out ~ 消滅 …
(3) kick out 開除
(4) shut down 停工
(5) switch off 關掉 (開關)
(6) end up 最後結果

例1：Finding a good way to dispose of nuclear waste is of great importance.
找到處理核廢料的好方法是相當重要的。

例2：The government pledged to enact stricter laws to wipe out adulterated food.
政府誓言要制定更嚴格的法律以掃除黑心食品。

例 3 : The board of directors decided to kick out the purchasing manager for taking kickbacks.
董事會決定開除採購部經理因為他收受回扣。

例 4 : The factory was forced to shut down because many workers went on strike.
因為很多工人參加罷工，工廠被迫停工。

例 5 : The plane is about to take off. Please make sure that your mobile device is switched off.
飛機即將起飛；請確認您的行動裝置已經關閉。

例 6 : He ended up in prison because of his involvement in insider trading.
他因涉及內線交易最後被關進監牢了。

---

(1) stop ~ from... 阻止 ... 做 ...
(2) prevent ~ from... 防止 ... 免於 ...
(3) protect ~ from... 保護 ... 免於 ...

例 1 : The heavy rain didn't stop us from going to the exhibition.
這場大雨並沒有阻止我們去看展覽。

例 2 : Something needs to be done to prevent the global warming from causing the earth to deteriorate.
我們必須做點什麼以防止全球暖化致使地球情況惡化。

例 3 : This silicon case can protect your phone from scratches.
這個矽膠殼可以保護你的手機免於刮傷。

＊表給予或取得某物的片語

(1) provide someone with something 提供某物給某人
(2) compensate someone for something 補償某人的 ...

例 1 : This brochure provides you with all the information about our company.
這個小冊子提供了你所有關於我們公司的資訊。

例2 : The victims of the accidents must be compensated for their loss.
這起意外的受害者必須得到損失賠償。

(1) at one's disposal 可供某人使用
(2) at the discretion of someone 由某人作主決定
   同 at one's discretion

例1 : This job allows me to have a car at my disposal.
這個工作讓我有車可以使用。

例2 : In most restaurants here, tipping is at a customer's discretion.
這裡大多數的餐廳，給不給小費都是由客人自己決定的。

(1) benefit from ~ 獲益於 ...
(2) in receipt of ~ 收到了 ...

例1 : I am convinced that every employee will benefit from the new policy.
我相信每位員工都可以從新政策中獲益。

例2 : He was in receipt of his order yesterday.
他昨天就收到了他訂的東西了。

(1) in return 作為回報
(2) pay off 得到回報；清償 (債務)

例1 : The billionaire gave the homeless person two hundred thousand dollars in return for his help.
這位億萬富翁給了這個流浪漢二十萬元以回報他的幫助。

例2 : I plan to use my yearly bonus to pay off a portion of my loan.
我計畫用我的年終獎金去付我一部份的貸款。

(1) on the house　店家招待
(2) free of charge　免費

例1 : Since he is a regular at the pub, the manager often sends over a drink on the house.
因為他是這間夜店常客，經理常會免費招待他飲料。

例2 : This hotel provides many services free of charge.
這間飯店提供很多免費服務。

＊尋找、想出、找出

(1) find out ~　發現或查明 (事實真相)
(2) figure out ~　弄明白 ... ; 想出 ...
(3) speculate on/upon ~　思索 ... ; 推測 ...

例1 : At the press conference, the mayor vowed to find out how the pregnant woman was murdered.
在記者會上，市長誓言要查明那位孕婦是如何被謀殺的。

例2 : The quality control manager asked me to figure out the reason for the defect.
品管經理要求我弄清楚造成瑕疵的原因。

例3 : The CEO said that he would never speculate on the cause of the plane crash while the investigation was underway.
執行長說在調查尚在進行中時他不願意對於飛機失事原因做推測。

(1) in search of ~　尋找 ...
(2) search for ~　搜尋 ...

例1 : The divers made their way down to the bottom of the sea in search of survivors.
潛水人員潛到海底為了尋找生還者。

例2 : He has been searching for a job for four months, but he has not gotten any interview offer so far.

他已經找工作找了四個月了，但是至今尚未得到任何面試機會。

---

(1) attend to N. 注意 ... ; 照顧 ...
(2) pay attention to N. 注意 ...
(3) take notice of ~ 注意 ... ; 留心 ...
(4) keep an eye on ~ 留意… ; 照看…

例1 : I have many things to attend to when my assistant is on sick leave.

當我助理請病假時，我就會有很多事情要處理。

例2 : Before you take the medicine, be sure to pay attention to the recommended dosage.

在你服用藥物之前，務必要注意建議劑量。

例3 : Remember to take notice of what the manager says. You can learn a lot from him.

記得要注意經理說的話，你可以從他身上學到很多的。

例4 : Will you keep an eye on my dog while I am out of town?

你願意在我出城時幫我看一下我的狗嗎？

＊表狀態的片語

(1) at work 在工作中
(2) in use 使用中
(3) in transit 運送中
(4) on the move 在移動中 ; 繁忙的
(5) on display 展示中

例1 : Our boss asks that every employee should not surf the Internet at work.

我們老闆要求每位員工在上班時不可以上網。

例 2 : The photocopier is in use right now. You have to wait a while.
影印機現在有人在使用，你得等一下。

例 3 : I am writing to apologize for the goods damaged in transit; we'll compensate you for the loss.
我寫這封信的目的是為了運送過程中有商品受損來向您致歉；我們會彌補您的損失。

例 4 : The doctors and nurses in the emergency room are always on the move.
急診室的醫生護士總是一直很忙碌。

例 5 : None of the paintings on display is for sale.
所有展示中的畫作都是非賣品。

---

(1) in working/running order 正常運轉；運作良好
(2) out of order 故障的；(行為) 不適當的
(3) out of service 停止服務
(4) break down 失敗；故障

例 1 : Since these computers are still in working order, there is no need to purchase new ones.
既然這些電腦都還可以正常運作，實在沒必要買新的。

例 2 : The heater is out of order again; it's freezing here in the office.
暖氣又故障了；辦公室好冷啊！

例 3 : The Maokong Gondola is out of service today due to routine maintenance.
因為例行保養，貓空纜車今日暫停服務。

例 4 : My car broke down and that's why I was late this morning.
我的車子拋錨了，那就是我今天早上遲到的原因。

(1) on call 待命；隨叫隨到
(2) on board 在 (交通工具) 上；到職
(3) on duty 值勤
　　反 off duty 不值班；下班
(4) on leave 在休假中

例 1 : As a doctor, he has to be constantly on call.
身為一位醫生，他必須隨時準備待命。

例 2 : It is reported that all the passengers on board survived.
根據報導所有乘客都存活了下來。

例 3 : We will have a marketing specialist on board tomorrow to help us boost profits.
我們公司明天即將有位行銷專家到職來協助我們提升獲利。

例 4 : Since we don't have enough customer service representatives on duty today, you will have to wait longer.
因為我們今天值班的客服人員不夠多，所以您的等候時間會久一點。

例 5 : When Sean is on leave, I will have to fill in for him.
Sean 休假時，我必須暫代他的職位。

(1) in stock 有存貨
　　反 out of stock 缺貨
(2) on the market 在出售；上市
(3) on back order 目前缺貨 (會再進貨)
(4) be sold out 銷售一空

例 1 : I regret to tell you that this hat is not in stock.
很抱歉這頂帽子已經沒有庫存了。

例 2 : Our panel is one of the best on the market.
我們的面板是市面上最好的之一。

例 3 : The item you are inquiring about is on back order now.
您所詢問的商品現在缺貨，之後會再進貨。

例 4 : Tickets to the show of *Cirque du Soleil* are sold out.
太陽劇團表演的票已全數售罄。

(1) in the dark 在暗處；對 ... 一無所知
(2) in vain 徒勞無功

例1 : Most of the employees are in the dark about the merger.
大多數員工並不知道合併的消息。

例2 : I tried in vain to make him sign the contract.
我想盡辦法要讓他簽合約，但沒有成功。

(1) in the extreme 極度地
(2) on impulse 一時衝動之下

例1 : Sometimes his behavior is violent in the extreme.
有時候他的行為極度暴力。

例2 : I bought this bike on impulse. Actually, I didn't need it at all.
我是一時衝動買這輛腳踏車的。事實上我根本不需要。

(1) in turn 輪流；依次
(2) take turns 輪流

例1 : The heads of all the departments made a presentation to the general manager in turn.
所有部門主管輪流向總經理做簡報。

例2 : All department directors took turns making their presentation.
所有部門主管輪流做簡報。

(1) in person 親自
(2) on one's own 靠自己

例1 : It is said that many celebrities will attend the ceremony to receive their awards in person.
聽說很多名人都會出席典禮親自領獎。

例2 : It is amazing that a child could draw such a painting on his own.
一個小孩能自己畫出這樣的畫作真是不可思議。

(1) on the spot 當場
(2) on loan 借來的

例1 : The police were on the spot right after the fire broke out.
火災一發生後警方立刻就趕到現場。

例2 : This book is on loan from the library; I have to return it in five days.
這本書是從圖書館借來的；五天後我就得將它歸還。

(1) at length 詳細地
(2) in detail 詳細地

例1 : He talked to us about what had happened to him at length.
他詳細地跟我們說發生在他身上的事情。

例2 : The police asked the security guard to describe the person who had burglarized the jewelry store last night in detail.
警方要求警衛詳細描述昨晚行搶珠寶店的人。

(1) on the edge of ~ 在 ... 邊緣
(2) on/to the verge of ~ 接近於 ... ; 幾乎要 ...
(3) on the side 另外；作為配菜

例1 : This restaurant is on the edge of bankruptcy due to bad service and food.
這家餐廳因為糟糕的服務與食物瀕臨破產邊緣。

例2 : She was on the verge of collapse when her pet dog died.
她的狗死去時她幾近崩潰。

例 3 ：I'd like a salad and fries on the side.
我的配菜要沙拉和薯條。

＊表開始、著手進行的片語

(1) begin with ~ 由 ... 開始
(2) start with ~ 由 ... 開始

例 1 ：The luncheon will begin with the CEO's speech.
午餐會將從執行長的演說揭開序幕。

例 2 ：The applicant started with a short story in his self-introduction.
這位應徵者在他的自我介紹中説了一則短故事作為開始。

(1) open up 開設
(2) kick off 開始；(足球比賽) 開球
(3) start off 開始；啟程
(4) take action 採取行動

例 1 ：There will be a new cinema opening up in town next month.
下個月鎮上會有一間新戲院開業。

例 2 ：The promotional campaign is about to kick off in five minutes.
宣傳活動即將於五分鐘後開始。

例 3 ：The luncheon started off with the president's address.
午餐會以總裁的演説作為開始。

例 4 ：The authorities must take action to stop the problem from getting worse.
當局必須採取行動以防止問題惡化。

(1) engage in ~ 從事 … ; 參加 …
(2) participate in ~ 參加 …
(3) take part in ~ 參加 …
(4) be involved in ~ 涉及 … ; 參與 …

例 1 : The minister has been engaging in economic reform for years.
部長已經從事經濟改革多年了。

例 2 : The fundraising event is star-studded; many A-list celebrities participated in it in the hope of making some contribution.
這個募款活動眾星雲集；許多一線明星都出席活動希望能有所貢獻。

例 3 : Every employee is encouraged to take part in the blood drive.
我們鼓勵每位同仁參加捐血活動。

例 4 : It is said that four employees are involved in embezzlement of company funds.
據說有四名員工涉及了挪用公司資金一案。

(1) apply for ~ 申請 … ; 應徵 (職缺)
(2) register for ~ 註冊 … ; 登記 …
(3) enroll in ~ 加入 … 會員 ; 登錄 … ; 註冊 …
(4) log onto ~ 登入 …
(5) fill out ~ 填寫 …

例 1 : It is expected that hundreds of people will apply for this coveted position.
預計會有數百人來應徵這個人人想要的職位。

例 2 : To register for the workshop, please call my assistant at 2708-8888.
要登記參加研討會的話，請撥打 2708-8888 找我的助理。

例 3 : In order to get promoted, Johnson enrolled in some night classes to improve his English.
為了升官，Johnson 修了一些夜間課程來改善自己的英文。

例 4 : For further information, log onto our website.
想了解更多資訊，請上我們的網站。

例 5 : If you don't know how to fill out the application form, don't hesitate to ask me.
如果你不知道如何填寫申請表，立刻問我。

(1) sign in 登記；登錄
(2) sign up 登記；報名

例 1 : All visitors are required to sign in at the security office before they can enter the building.
訪客在進入大樓前要先在警衛室登記。

例 2 : Those who sign up for the computer training session should bring their company ID badge.
報名參加電腦訓練課程的人應該要攜帶員工識別證。

(1) leave for ~ 出發前往 …
(2) head for ~ 前往 …
(3) move on to ~ 往 … 前進
(4) proceed to ~ 前往 …

例 1 : The train is about to leave for Kaohsiung in five minutes.
火車在五分鐘後即將開往高雄。

例 2 : The police decided to head for the woods to search for the missing child.
警方決定前往樹林裡去尋找失蹤的小孩。

例 3 : Let's move on to the next item on the agenda.
我們繼續進行議程中的下一個議題吧！

例4 : Passengers for Sydney should proceed to gate 12 for boarding.

前往雪梨的乘客請到十二號登機門準備登機。

---

(1) place an order　下訂單
(2) shop for ~　採購 ...

例1 : You can call our agent or visit our website to place an order.

您可以打給我們的專員或直接上網站來下訂。

例2 : Since the super typhoon is coming, many people are flooding into the supermarket to shop for food.

因為超級颱風要來了，很多人蜂擁到超市去採買食物。

---

(1) mail out ~　寄出 ...
(2) send out ~　寄出 ...

例1 : The brochure you asked for will be mailed out within three business days.

您要的小冊子將會在三個工作天之內寄出。

例2 : The brochure you asked for has been sent out yesterday.

您索取的小冊子昨天已經寄出。

Part2　其它常考片語及慣用語

1. at the expense of ~ 犧牲 …

　　例：Never meet deadlines at the expense of quality.
　　　　絕不要為了趕上截止期限卻犧牲了品質。

2. at the risk of ~ 冒 … 危險

　　例：The negotiators tried their best to save the hostages at the risk of losing their own lives.
　　　　談判人員冒著犧牲自己生命的危險盡力去搶救人質。

1. be absent from ~ 缺席 …

　　例：My colleague, Elsa, has been absent from work for days.
　　　　我同事 Elsa 已經好幾天沒來上班了。

2. be good at ~ 擅長 …

　　例：My mother is good at cooking Italian food.
　　　　我母親擅長做義大利菜。

3. be designated for ~ 被指定作為 …

　　例：This area of the conference room is designated for storage.
　　　　會議室的這區被指定為儲藏用。

4. be known for ~ 以 … 而聞名

　　同 be famous for ~ = be well-known for ~

　　例：Neilson Electronics is known for its quality products.
　　　　Neilson Electronics 以其高品質產品著稱。

5. be open to someone 對某人開放

　　例：The new museum is open to the general public.
　　　　新博物館開放給一般民眾參觀。

6. behind the wheel 開車

　　例：Don't be a phubber when you are behind the wheel.
　　　　開車時絕不要當低頭族。

7. bounce back 反彈；恢復

例 : Most financial analysts predict that the stock market will bounce back.
大多數的金融分析師都預測股市將會回彈。

1. call ~ into question 質疑 …

例 : The manager's ability was called into question because of his mishandling of the financial crisis.
因為財務危機處理不當，經理的能力遭到質疑。

2. culminate in ~ 以 … 作壓軸

例 : The year-end party will culminate in A-mei's performance.
尾牙將以阿妹的表演作為壓軸。

1. dress up 盛裝打扮

例 : The head of the department asked everyone to dress up for the farewell party.
部門主管要求每個人盛裝出席歡送會。

2. do/run an errand 去辦事

例 : I have to run some errands for my boss now, so I'll meet you later.
我現在得去幫我老闆辦些事情，所以我們晚點碰面。

1. escape from ~ 從 … 逃出

例 : It is reported that only four passengers escaped from the capsized ferry.
根據報導只有四名乘客從翻覆的渡輪中逃出。

1. fit someone in　安排時間見某人

　例　: I am in the middle of drawing a design; I'll try to fit you in when I am done.

　　　我正忙著畫設計圖；等我結束時我會想辦法安排時間和你碰面。

1. graduate from ~　從 … 畢業

　例　: It is said that the intern graduated from Harvard.
　　　據說那位實習生是從哈佛畢業的。

1. hang out　消磨時間

　例　: My parents don't allow me to hang out at night clubs.
　　　爸媽不允許我去夜店。

2. hear about ~　聽說 …

　例　: Did you hear about news of the merger?
　　　你有聽說關於合併的事情嗎？

1. in honor of ~　向 … 致敬

　例　: A banquet will be held in honor of Paul Johnson, who devotes all his life to the care of stray dogs.

　　　Paul Johnson 奉獻一生照顧流浪狗，為了向他致敬，將會舉辦一場宴會。

2. in the process of ~　在 … 的過程中

　例　: The soy sauce is contaminated in the process of production.
　　　這醬油在製作過程中受到汙染。

3. indulge in ~　沉迷於 … ；縱情於 …

　例　: After the completion of the project, I now have every good reason to indulge in a drink.

　　　專案完成之後，我現在有充分的理由可以好好喝一杯。

1. jump on the bandwagon 順應潮流；跟進

　　例 : The Central Bank has announced that it's going to lower the interest rate next month, which led many others to jump on the bandwagon.

　　中央銀行宣布下個月要調降利率，這消息讓很多其他銀行決定跟進。

1. keep someone posted 隨時讓某人了解情況

　　例 : My boss asks me to keep him posted when he is out of town.
　　我老闆要求我在他出城時要隨時告知他最新狀況。

1. let go of ~ 放開 …

　　例 : If you don't let go of my hand now, I am going to scream.
　　如果你現在不放開我的手，我就要大叫囉！

2. line up 排成一列

　　例 : Hundreds of people lined up to buy tickets to the show of Cavalia.
　　數百人排隊購買 Cavalia 表演的門票。

3. live on ~ 以 … 維生

　　例 : My grandfather has retired, so he has to live on his pension.
　　我祖父已經退休了，所以他必須靠退休金過日子。

1. make a fortune 賺大錢

   例 : This travel agency made a fortune during the peak tourist season.

   這家旅行社在旅遊旺季時賺了一大筆錢。

2. make a note of ~ 把…記下來

   例 : Be sure to make a note of the date for the next meeting.

   務必將下次開會日期記下來。

3. make ends meet 收支平衡

   例 : In order to make ends meet, I took two part-time jobs when I was in college.

   為了收支平衡，我在大學時兼了兩份差。

4. make room for ~ 為…騰出空間

   例 : My father removed the treadmill to make room for the piano.

   我爸爸將跑步機移走好騰出空間放鋼琴。

5. make sure 確認

   例 : Make sure you lock all the windows and turn off the heater when you leave the office.

   離開辦公室時，確認鎖好所有窗戶還有要關掉暖氣。

1. on behalf of ~ 代表 …

   同 on one's behalf

   例 : The chief operating officer accepted the award on behalf of the company.

   營運長代表公司領獎。

2. on/at short notice 倉促通知

   例 : I am sorry for rescheduling our appointment on such short notice.

   在這麼短時間內將我們的約會改期真是抱歉。

1. play a role in ~ 在 ... 上扮演重要角色

例 : Teamwork plays a leading role in the success of the project.
團隊合作在這次專案的成功上扮演了主要的角色。

1. recover from ~ 從 ... 恢復

例 : With the help of these financial advisors, the country's economy is likely to recover from recession.
有了這些財務顧問的協助,這個國家的經濟可望從不景氣中復甦。

2. roll up 捲起來

例 : Everyone rolled up their sleeves and began to clean up the mess.
大家都捲起衣袖開始清理髒亂。

1. sit in 旁聽;列席

例 : Mr. Spacey, our new CEO, will sit in on today's board meeting.
我們的新執行長 Spacey 先生將會列席今天的董事會議。

2. speak out 堅定而公開地表明

例 : Every employee in this company is encouraged to speak out.
這家公司鼓勵每位員工勇於發表意見。

3. stay up 熬夜

例 : In this company, many employees often stay up late working at the office to move up the corporate ladder.
這家公司有很多員工常熬夜到很晚是為了能在公司一路往上爬。

4. step down as ~ 辭退 ... 的職位

例 : Mr. Davis decided to step down as vice president of public relations.
Davis 先生決定要辭去公關部副總的職位。

5. strip someone of … 剝奪某人的 …

　　例 : The CFO was found guilty and stripped of his position.
　　財務長被發現有罪後遭到免職。

6. suffer from ~ 遭受 … 之苦

　　例 : My father has been suffering from long-term backache.
　　我父親一直為背痛所苦。

1. take a rain check （用於婉拒邀請）下次吧

　　例 : May I take a rain check on the dinner? I've made an appointment with the dentist.
　　你改天再請我吃晚餐好嗎？我已經預約要去看牙了。

2. trick someone into V-ing 騙某人去做 …

　　例 : The financial adviser tricked the old lady into investing all her pension in stocks.
　　這位財務顧問騙這位老婦人將所有退休金投資在股票上。

3. try on ~ 試穿 …

　　例 : I would like to try on this shirt. Where is the fitting room?
　　我想試穿這件襯衫。請問試衣間在那兒呢？

4. tune in to ~ 收聽 / 收看節目

　　例 : Tune in to our program for the news updates.
　　收聽我們的節目以獲得最新新聞消息。

1. use up ~ 用光 … ; 耗盡 …

　　例 : I used up all my pocket money during my trip in Italy.
　　我在義大利之旅中花光所有零用錢了。

2. used to Vr. 過去習慣 …

　　例 : I used to go to work by bus, but now I go on foot.
　　我以前搭公車上班，但是我現在走路上班。

1. wait for ~ 等待 …

　　例 : I had waited for the train for two hours before it arrived.
　　　　在火車進站前我等了兩小時。

Give it a try! 實力挑戰題

1 _____ the merger, everyone in our department was laid off.

(A) As a result of

(B) Along with

(C) Except for

(D) Instead of ⒶⒷⒸⒹ

. . . . ▶

2 _____ you follow the office guidelines, you will have no problem getting a raise at your performance review.

(A) Regardless of

(B) Now that

(C) As a result

(D) As long as ⒶⒷⒸⒹ

. . . . ▶

3 My supervisor discussed the new business opportunity _____, detailing the role I might play in it.

(A) at will

(B) at length

(C) at random

(D) at once ⒶⒷⒸⒹ

. . . . ▶

4 Our entire team _____ Anna's story that she had not been manipulating our financials.

(A) backed up

(B) applied for

(C) appealed to

(D) accounted for ⒶⒷⒸⒹ

5 This company _____ providing great customer service along with competitive prices.

(A) is keen on

(B) is known for

(C) is involved in

(D) is equipped with　　　　　　　　　Ⓐ Ⓑ Ⓒ Ⓓ

6 Mike _____ his own firing when he sent out an inflammatory email about the boss.

(A) called for

(B) approved of

(C) carried out

(D) brought about　　　　　　　　　Ⓐ Ⓑ Ⓒ Ⓓ

7 The company president insisted that all departments _____ one another better to increase efficiency and decrease mistakes.

(A) comment on

(B) come across

(C) comply with

(D) communicate with　　　　　　　　　Ⓐ Ⓑ Ⓒ Ⓓ

8 Our supervisor always knows that he can _____ Kevin to work overtime whenever a deadline is approaching.

(A) count on

(B) contribute to

(C) conform to

(D) compete with　　　　　　　　　Ⓐ Ⓑ Ⓒ Ⓓ

9 Tom has _____ one of the foremost experts in software development.

(A) drew up

(B) developed into

(C) come with

(D) coincided with　　　　　　　　　Ⓐ Ⓑ Ⓒ Ⓓ

10 The reporter let the politician know _____ about the tough questions he would be asking.

(A) in comparison

(B) in all

(C) in advance

(D) in person   Ⓐ Ⓑ Ⓒ Ⓓ

11 _____ the university, we have devised an internship program to recruit future employees.

(A) In conjunction with

(B) In contrast to

(C) In favor of

(D) In reference to   Ⓐ Ⓑ Ⓒ Ⓓ

12 _____ the scandal your company is associated with, we will take our business elsewhere.

(A) In the event of

(B) In light of

(C) In case of

(D) In place of   Ⓐ Ⓑ Ⓒ Ⓓ

13 This email is to inform you that I am _____ your refund check for the malfunctioning camera you sent me.

(A) in honor of

(B) in response to

(C) in receipt of

(D) in order of   Ⓐ Ⓑ Ⓒ Ⓓ

14 The bug in our software is _____ being fixed.

(A) in the face of

(B) in terms of

(C) in search of

(D) in the process of   Ⓐ Ⓑ Ⓒ Ⓓ

15 I expect you to _____ our contractor to make sure they are staying on schedule with the project.

(A) kick out

(B) inquire about

(C) keep in touch with

(D) kick off　　　　　　　　　　　　　Ⓐ Ⓑ Ⓒ Ⓓ

....▶

16 Steve _____ finish all the coding after two straight days of sitting in front of his computer.

(A) objected to

(B) felt free to

(C) managed to

(D) contributed to　　　　　　　　　　Ⓐ Ⓑ Ⓒ Ⓓ

....▶

17 I called the restaurant _____ to order enough food for 50 people and was told it could not be ready so quickly.

(A) on impulse

(B) on short notice

(C) on loan

(D) on leave　　　　　　　　　　　　Ⓐ Ⓑ Ⓒ Ⓓ

....▶

18 We are _____ signing a deal that would lead to the opening of our first chain store in the suburbs.

(A) on the basis of

(B) on behalf of

(C) in accordance with

(D) on the edge of　　　　　　　　　　Ⓐ Ⓑ Ⓒ Ⓓ

....▶

19 _____ the reason, you have been late to work five times this month, and you will lose one vacation day for it.

(A) Regardless of

(B) Rather than

(C) On the verge of

(D) On behalf of　　　　　　　　　　　Ⓐ Ⓑ Ⓒ Ⓓ

20 Bob has _____ our beloved mayor for eight years, and now he thinks it's time for him to step down.

(A) set about

(B) served as

(C) registered for

(D) referred to

Ⓐ Ⓑ Ⓒ Ⓓ

21 Anyone who did not _____ early for the seminar will need to pay the full price of $US 70.

(A) sit in

(B) single out

(C) sign up

(D) set up

Ⓐ Ⓑ Ⓒ Ⓓ

22 Ken always _____ all the details, which is what separates him from average employees.

(A) takes notice of

(B) takes over

(C) stands for

(D) shops for

Ⓐ Ⓑ Ⓒ Ⓓ

23 _____ the new models, the old models received much wider acceptance.

(A) On the contrary

(B) In accordance with

(C) By contrast

(D) In contrast to

Ⓐ Ⓑ Ⓒ Ⓓ

24 I'll call him back in a minute. There are _____ things I have to do first.

(A) a handful of

(B) a variety of

(C) a couple of

(D) a great deal of

Ⓐ Ⓑ Ⓒ Ⓓ

25 The committee was entirely _____ specialists.
(A) consist of
(B) composed of
(C) made of
(D) inundated with

Ⓐ Ⓑ Ⓒ Ⓓ

Unit ⑭ 常見動詞片語與易混淆片語

✳ check 的動詞片語

(1) check in 登記入住；辦理報到
(2) check out 結帳離開；檢查
(3) check with ~ 和 ... 確認

> **例1** : The hotel just called to remind us to check in before 2 o'clock.
> 飯店剛打來提醒我們在兩點前登記入住。

> **例2** : We will check out of the hotel right after breakfast.
> 早餐後我們會立刻辦理退房手續。

> **例3** : You can check with my assistant about the deadline.
> 你可以跟我助理確認截止日期是何時。

✳ come 的動詞片語

(1) come about 發生
(2) come across ~ 偶然遇見或發現 ...
(3) come down with ~ 染上 ... 病
(4) come up with ~ 想出 ...
(5) come with ~ 具備 ...

> **例1** : The police are still investigating how the crash came about.
> 警方還在調查這起墜機發生的原因。

> **例2** : I came across my high school classmate at the airport yesterday.
> 我昨天在機場偶然遇見我中學時的同學。

> **例3** : David has come down with the flu, so he is taking a sick leave today.
> David 感冒了，所以他今天請病假。

> **例4** : After a lengthy discussion, we finally came up with an innovative way to promote our new product.
> 經過漫長的討論後，我們終於想出一個推銷新商品的創新方法。

例 5 : Every room of this hotel comes with a Jacuzzi.
這間飯店每間房間都配備了按摩浴缸。

∗ fall 的動詞片語

(1) fall apart 散開
(2) fall in love (+ with ~) 愛上 …
(3) fall off (數量或價值) 減少；降低
(4) fall over 倒下
(5) fall short of ~ 達不到 …

例 1 : It seems that this machine is going to fall apart.
這機器似乎快解體了。

例 2 : The first time I saw her, I fell in love with her.
我初次見到她就愛上她了。

例 3 : Sales of the singer's album fell off last year.
去年這位歌手的專輯銷量下滑。

例 4 : He lost his balance and fell over.
他失去平衡然後就摔倒了。

例 5 : To my disappointment, his performance fell short of my
expectations.
令我失望的是，他的表現未能達到我的期望。

∗ get 的動詞片語

(1) get away from ~ 擺脫 (舊思想或老舊觀念)；離開 …
(2) get back to ~ 回覆 …
(3) get on 繼續 (做某事) (+ with N.)；進展 (+ with N.)；與某人處得
來 (+ with sb.)
(4) get over ~ 克服 …；恢復
(5) get rid of ~ 擺脫 …；清除 …；丟棄 …；處理掉 …；賣掉 …

例 1 : If you want to get away from the hustle and bustle of the city, book our package tour.
如果您想逃離城市的喧囂，參加我們的套裝行程吧！

例 2 : I will be out of town tomorrow, so get back to me as soon as possible.
我明天會出城去，所以請盡快回覆我。

例 3 : Can we stop arguing and get on with the discussion?
我們可以停止爭執繼續討論嗎？

例 4 : It took him a while to get over the death of his pet dog.
他的寵物狗死後，他花了一段時間才恢復過來。

例 5 : This store is going to have a clearance sale to get rid of all the merchandise.
這家店將要舉辦清倉大拍賣把所有商品都出清賣掉。

✻ give 的動詞片語

(1) give away ~ 贈送 … ；洩露 (秘密)；流露 (情感)
(2) give birth to ~ 生 (小孩)
(3) give in 屈服
(4) give off ~ 散發出 …
(5) give out ~ 發放 … ；公布 …
(6) give up 放棄
(7) give way to ~ 屈服於 …

例 1 : This shop gave away a gift to every customer yesterday.
這家店昨天贈送每位顧客一份禮物。

例 2 : Our general manager gave birth to twins last night.
我們總經理昨晚生了一對雙胞胎。

例 3 : The president stressed that the government would never give in to terrorism.
總統強調政府絕不會向恐怖主義低頭的。

例 4 : His room always gives off a disgusting smell.
他的房間總是會有噁心的味道。

例5 : That restaurant decided to give out discount vouchers to ease public anger.
那家餐廳決定發折價券平息眾怒。

例6 : The rescuers didn't give up searching for survivors despite the bad weather.
儘管天候不佳，搜救人員不放棄尋找生還者。

例7 : The CEO vowed that he would never give way to hackers.
執行長誓言他絕不會向駭客低頭。

* go 的動詞片語

(1) go after ~ 爭取 ...
(2) go by ~ 根據 ... 判斷
(3) go off (警報) 響起來；爆炸；(燈) 熄滅
(4) go on 繼續
(5) go over ~ 從頭到尾看過 ...；審查 ...
(6) go through ~ 瀏覽 ...；徹底檢查；(法律) 被通過；熬過 (困境)；從頭到尾練習
(7) go up 上漲；提高

例1 : This is such a good opportunity that you should try your best to go after it.
這是個你應該要盡力去爭取的好機會。

例2 : It is not always correct to go by past experiences.
根據過去經驗判斷並非總是正確的。

例3 : The reason why I was late yesterday was that my alarm clock didn't go off.
昨天我遲到的原因是我的鬧鐘沒有響。

例4 : If they go on like this, they won't be able to reach a consensus.
如果他們繼續這樣下去，他們將無法達成共識。

例5 : Be sure to go over your report before you turn it in.
在交出報告前務必要再從頭到尾看過一遍。

例6 : I suggest that you go through your lines again to make sure that you won't forget them on the stage.

我建議你將台詞從頭到尾再練習一遍以確保你不會在台上忘詞。

例7 : Because the labor costs are going up, company profits are down.

因為人事成本提高了，公司獲利就減少了。

✳ look 的動詞片語

(1) look after ~ 照顧 …
(2) look down on/upon ~ 輕視 …
(3) look for ~ 尋找 …
(4) look forward to N./V-ing 期待 …
(5) look into ~ 調查 …
(6) look over ~ 仔細檢查 …
(7) look up 好轉或改善；抬起頭來；查閱

例1 : He asked me to look after the flowers on his desk while he was away.

他請我當他不在時幫他照顧桌上的花。

例2 : You shouldn't look down on him just because he is junior to you.

你不應該因為他比你資淺就輕視他。

例3 : The largest law firm in town is looking for an energetic assistant.

鎮上最大的律師事務所正在尋找一位充滿活力的助理。

例4 : We look forward to doing business with your company.

我們期待和貴公司有生意往來。

例5 : The prosecutors are still looking into the secretary's embezzlement of company funds.

檢察官還在調查秘書挪用公司資金的事情。

例 6 : You had better look over these figures before you submit the report.

在你將報告交出前你最好檢查一下這些數字。

例 7 : This company's financial situation is starting to look up under new management.

在新的領導下，這家公司的財務狀況開始改善了。

✳ make 的動詞片語

(1) make up 編造；和好；組成；化妝；補足或湊齊
(2) make up for ~ 補償 …
(3) make up with ~ 和 … 和好

例 1 : Neilson didn't show up for the meeting, so he made up an excuse about being sick.

Neilson 沒有來開會，所以他編了個藉口說自己生病了。

例 2 : Nothing can make up for the loss of health.

沒有任何東西可以彌補健康的失去。

例 3 : Jacob made such a big mistake that his girlfriend refused to make up with him.

Jacob 犯了如此嚴重的錯誤，所以他女朋友拒絕跟他和好。

✳ pass 的動詞片語

(1) pass someone by 未被某人注意
(2) pass on ~ 傳遞 (某物)；把疾病傳染給 …
(3) pass out 昏倒

例 1 : You shouldn't let such a good opportunity pass you by.

你不應該錯過這麼好的機會。

例 2 : The speech has been cancelled. Please pass the message on to the students.

演講已取消。請將這個訊息傳達給學生們。

例3 : Many people who joined in the rally passed out because they had been exposed to the sun for a long time.
很多參加集會的人因為長時間曝曬在陽光下而昏倒了。

✻ pick 的動詞片語

(1) pick on someone 找某人碴
(2) pick out ~ 選出 ...
(3) pick up 撿起 ... ；學會 ... ；搭載某人

例1 : Vincent wanted to quit because he thought his boss was always picking on him.
Vincent 想辭職是因為他覺得老闆一直在找他碴。

例2 : Michelle Chen was picked out as the coordinator for this promotional event.
Michelle Chen 被選為是這次宣傳活動的策劃人。

例3 : Generally speaking, children pick up a language faster than adults.
一般來說，小孩學會語言的速度比成人快。

✻ put 的動詞片語

(1) put about/around ~ 散佈 (謠言)
(2) put away ~ 將 ... 放回原處；存錢
(3) put in ~ 花費 (時間)
(4) put together ~ 完成 ... ；匯整 ... ；組合 ...
(5) put up with ~ 忍受 ...

例1 : Who put the rumor about that the company is filing for bankruptcy?
是誰散布謠言說公司正在申請破產的？

例2 : You had better put some money away every month for your retirement.
你最好每個月存點錢以備將來退休用。

例3 : Kate put in at least 55 hours a week at her previous job.
Kate 之前的工作一週至少工作五十五小時。

例4 : It took me about ten days to put together this proposal.
我花了約十天才完成這專案。

例5 : Allen finds it hard to put up with his supervisor's short temper.
Allen 覺得要忍受他主管的暴躁脾氣是很難的。

✽ run 的動詞片語

(1) run down　撞倒；(不公正地) 批評或詆毀
(2) run low on ~　短缺 …
(3) run out of ~　用光 …
(4) run over ~　輾過 …；練習或排演 …；反覆考慮 …

例1 : He is always running his boss down.
他總是在批評自己的老闆。

例2 : We're running low on rice. Buy some on your way home.
我們的米快沒了；回家順路買些回來。

例3 : We're running out of time; hurry up.
我們快沒時間了；快一點啦！

例4 : Take a moment to run over your lines before you go on stage.
在上台前，撥個空把台詞演練一下。

✽ set 的動詞片語

(1) set about ~　開始做 …
(2) set off　出發；使爆炸
(3) set forth ~　提出 …；闡明 …
(4) set out　(書面) 詳述或闡明
(5) set up ~　設立 …；安排 …

例1 : After mopping the floor, my mother set about doing the dishes.

拖完地之後，我媽媽開始洗碗。

例2 : It's better that you set off for the airport now; there might be traffic congestion.

你最好現在就出發前往機場；可能會塞車。

例3 : All the employees are welcome to set forth their ideas.

我們歡迎所有員工提出自己的想法。

例4 : Once you sign the contract, you have to observe all the terms set out in it.

你一旦簽下這份合約，你就必須遵守所有合約上的條款。

例5 : Let's set up a time for the meeting.

我們來安排個時間開會吧！

* take 的動詞片語

(1) take apart ~ 拆開 …
(2) take in 理解；欺騙；攝取
(3) take off 脫掉 (衣物)；起飛
(4) take over ~ 接手 … ；接管 …
(5) take on ~ 承擔 (責任)

例1 : He took apart his iPhone to see what was wrong with it.

他拆開他的 iPhone 看看出了什麼問題。

例2 : I have difficulty taking in what he said. Would you please explain it to me?

我不懂他說的是什麼意思。你可以解釋給我聽嗎？

例3 : The plane is scheduled to take off at ten o'clock.

飛機預計十點起飛。

例4 : Susan Chang will take over as director of human resources when Philips Wong retires next week.

下個月 Philips Wong 退休後將由 Susan Chang 接任人資部主任。

例 5 : I have to take on more responsibilities at my new job.
我的新工作必須承擔更多的責任。

* turn 的動詞片語

(1) turn around （使）好轉，（使）扭轉，（使）有起色
(2) turn down 拒絕；調低 (音量)
(3) turn in 交還；將某人送交警方；獲得 (利潤)
(4) turn into ~ 變成 …
(5) turn out 結果為 … ；生產 … ；出席
(6) turn to N. 求助於 …

例 1 : Many investors hope that the ailing company will turn around under new management.
許多投資者希望這家營運不善的公司會在新的管理下有所好轉。

例 2 : She turned down the job offer in spite of the good benefits package.
儘管員工福利很優渥，她還是拒絕了這工作。

例 3 : It is reported that this company turned in post-tax profits of thirty million dollars last year.
根據報導這家公司在去年賺了三千萬的稅後利潤。

例 4 : This small town turned into a popular tourist attraction after a UFO was rumored to have been seen.
在有人謠傳說看到了幽浮之後，這個小鎮變成了很夯的觀光景點。

例 5 : Most of the solar panels on the market are turned out by our company.
市面上大部分的太陽能板都是我們公司所生產的。

例 6 : It is estimated that five thousand people turned out for the rally last night.
根據估計昨晚有五千人到場參加這場集會。

例 7 : Not knowing what to do, he turned to me for help.
因為不知如何是好，他向我求助。

＊介系詞 to 後接名詞或動名詞的片語

(1) adapt to N.~ 適應 ...

　　同 adjust to ~

(2) apply to N. 適用於 ...

> **例 1** : I have difficulty adapting to the new job.
> 我很難以適應新工作。

> **例 2** : The new regulation applies only to motorcyclists.
> 這個新規定只適用於摩托車騎士。

(1) be committed to N./V-ing 致力於 ...

(2) be dedicated to N./V-ing 奉獻於 ... ; 致力於 ...

　　同 be devoted to N./V-ing

> **例 1** : The CEO is committed to the expansion of the business.
> 執行長致力於業務的拓展。

> **例 2** : The writer is dedicated to writing a novel which he expects to be a page-turner.
> 這位作家致力於寫出人人愛不釋手的小說。

(1) conform to N. 順從 ... ; 遵照 ...

(2) live up to ~ 符合 (期望) ; 遵循 ...

(3) cling to N. 堅持 ... ; 忠實於 ...

(4) testify to ~ 證明 ...

> **例 1** : The company recalled thousands of strollers because of failure to conform to safety standards.
> 因為未能符合安全標準，這家公司回收了數千輛嬰兒車。

> **例 2** : His performance lived up to his supervisor's expectations.
> 他的表現一點都不辜負他主管的期望。

例 3：He clung to the hope that his wife would survive the plane crash.
他一直抱持著希望覺得他的妻子會在這次的墜機意外中存活下來。

例 4：The long lines testified to the popularity of organic food.
長長的人龍證明了有機食品受歡迎的程度。

(1) appeal to someone　吸引某人
(2) refer to ~　提及 … ；參考 …
(3) cause damage to N.　對 … 造成損害

例 1：This product appeals to people of all ages.
這產品吸引各個年齡層的人。

例 2：In his autobiography, he often refers to his parents.
在他的自傳中，他常提到自己的父母親。

例 3：This incident will cause damage to the relations between these two countries.
這起事件將會對兩國關係造成傷害。

(1) respond to ~　回應 …
(2) in response to ~　回應 …

例 1：The legislator will hold a press conference to respond to his scandal.
這位立委將要舉行記者會回應他的醜聞。

例 2：The president of the company promised to recall all its flawed products in response to public outrage.
面對大眾的憤怒，這家公司的總裁允諾會將所有有問題的商品下架回收。

✱ 易混淆的片語

(1) depend on ~ 取決於 … ；依靠… ；信任…
(2) lie in ~ 在於 …
(3) be subject to N. 取決於 … ；遭受 …
(4) count on ~ 依靠…
(5) rely on ~ 依賴… ；依靠…

例1 : Whether the employee picnic will be held depends on the cost.
要不要辦員工野餐取決於費用問題。

例2 : You can depend on Kathie to take care of your baby while you're away.
Kathie 會在你們不在時照顧你們的孩子，你們可以信任她。

例3 : The key to his success lies in his ability to motivate employees to work harder.
他成功的關鍵在於他具有激勵員工更加努力的能力。

例4 : The show is subject to weather.
表演會因天候狀況做調整。

例5 : You are subject to a fine if you fail to follow the new traffic regulations.
如果你未能遵守新的交通法規，你會被罰款。

例6 : You can always count on Kevin because he is the most honest man that I have ever seen.
你絕對可以仰賴 Kevin，因為他是我看過最正直的人。

例7 : You can rely on Westin Catering Service to hold a wonderful banquet.
要舉辦一場很棒的宴會，您可以仰賴 Westin 外燴服務公司。

(1) in place 處於適當或正確的位置；準備就緒的
(2) in place of ~ 取代 …
(3) out of place 突兀的；格格不入的

例1 : All the arrangements for the CFO's retirement party are all in place.
為財務長辦的退休派對的所有安排都準備就緒了。

例2 : When cooking this dish, you can use chicken in place of pork.
煮這道菜時，你可以用雞肉代替豬肉。

例3 : Shy and introverted, he often feels out of place at any social event.
因為生性害羞內向，在任何社交活動中他常覺得格格不入。

(1) take place 發生；舉行
(2) take the place of ~ 取代 …

例1 : The annual board meeting will take place next Friday.
年度董事會議將於下週五舉行。

例2 : In many offices, notebooks have taken the place of desktops.
在很多辦公室，筆記型電腦已經取代了桌上型電腦。

(1) be based on ~ 以 … 為依據
(2) be based in ~ 以 … 為總部

例1 : You will get either a raise or a promotion based on your performance.
依據你的表現，你將得到加薪或是升職。

例2 : This company is based in Vancouver.
這家公司總部在溫哥華。

(1) on and off 斷斷續續地
(2) to and fro 來來回回地
(3) ups and downs 盛衰；起伏

例 1 : It has been raining on and off for four days.
這雨已經斷斷續續下了四天了。

例 2 : Would you please stop walking to and fro? It makes me really nervous.
你可以不要走來走去嗎？搞得我很緊張。

例 3 : This book is about the ups and downs of the pitcher's baseball career.
這本書是關於這位投手棒球生涯的起起伏伏。

(1) back up ~ 支持 ...
(2) back out of ~ 退出 ...

例 1 : I am grateful to my parents for backing me up all the time.
我很感謝我的家人一直支持我。

例 2 : He backed out of his promise to lend me money.
他本來答應要借我錢的，但是又打退堂鼓了。

(1) stand for ~ 代表 ...
(2) stand by 支持；待命

例 1 : Do you know what those letters on the box stand for?
你知道箱子上的字母代表甚麼嗎？

例 2 : I am grateful to my husband for standing by me all the time.
我很感激我先生一直支持著我。

(1) hand in ~ 提交 …
(2) hand out ~ 分發 …

例 1 : It is surprising that the head of our department decided to hand in his resignation.
我們部門主管決定要提交辭呈真是令人驚訝。

例 2 : In order to pay her way through college, she takes a part-time job of handing out leaflets.
為了自己支付大學學費，她兼差發傳單。

(1) hold on 等一下
(2) hold on to N. 緊握 … ; 堅持 …

例 1 : Please hold on; I'll put you through to the manager.
請稍等，我幫您轉接給經理。

例 2 : The road is bumpy; you had better hold on to the straps.
這條路很顛簸；你最好拉緊吊環。

(1) be faced with ~ 面對 …
(2) in the face of ~ 不顧 (困難等)

例 1 : The president is now faced with a dilemma about how to rise above financial difficulties.
總裁正面臨要如何解決財務困難的困境。

例 2 : The governor insisted on legalizing euthanasia in the face of strong opposition.
州長不顧強烈反對還是堅持將安樂死合法化。

(1) out of pity 出於同情
(2) out of practice 疏於練習
(3) out of shape 體力不佳；健康狀況不好

例1 : Wilson gave the beggar one hundred dollars and some food out of pity.
Wilson 出於憐憫給了這個乞丐一百元和一些食物。

例2 : I haven't played the piano for a while, so I am a bit out of practice.
我有一段時間沒有彈鋼琴了，所以有點生疏了。

例3 : If you don't make it a rule to exercise, you will get out of shape.
如果你沒有養成運動的習慣，你的健康狀況就會變得不好。

(1) sell off ~ 賣出 …
(2) shell out (for ~) (不情願地) 支付 … 或拿出錢

例1 : The shop decided to sell off all the merchandise at half price.
這家店決定以半價賣出所有商品。

例2 : Since he lost the bet, he shelled out three thousand dollars for the dinner.
因為他打賭輸了，他不情願地拿出三千元來付這頓晚餐的錢。

(1) wear off 慢慢消失 (效果)
(2) wear out ~ 使 … 筋疲力盡

例1 : The effects of this drug will wear off after ten hours.
這藥的效果會在十小時後慢慢消失。

例2 : Sitting at the desk and typing all day really wore me out.
坐在書桌前打字一整天真的累死我了。

(1) drop off ~ 放下 (行李等東西)
(2) stop by 經過；順道來訪
   同 drop by/in

例 1 : I'll need to drop off my luggage first before I can go shopping.
我得先將行李放下才能去逛街。

例 2 : You can stop by my house on your way to Kaohsiung.
你可以在去高雄途中順道來我家一趟。

(1) in order of ~ 按照 ... 順序
(2) in order to~ 以便 ... ; 為了要 ...

例 1 : These issues will be taken care of in order of priority.
這些議題會按照重要順序處理。

例 2 : She arrived at the auditorium early in order to get a good seat.
她早早抵達禮堂以便有個好位子。

Give it a try! 實力挑戰題

1 Our company _____ the real estate deal when we discovered the unscrupulous nature of the seller.

(A) benefited from

(B) brought about

(C) backed out of

(D) backed up   Ⓐ Ⓑ Ⓒ Ⓓ

2 The smartphone _____ the idea that all our personal information could be stored on a mobile device.

(A) gave out

(B) gave in

(C) gave birth to

(D) got rid of   Ⓐ Ⓑ Ⓒ Ⓓ

3 My boss and I _____ the key points of the presentation before finalizing it.

(A) went by

(B) went after

(C) got over

(D) went over   Ⓐ Ⓑ Ⓒ Ⓓ

4 Tom's assistant _____ a copy of the meeting agenda to every person who was crammed into the small conference room.

(A) handed out

(B) handed in

(C) went through

(D) focused on   Ⓐ Ⓑ Ⓒ Ⓓ

5 To quickly master the new programming language, I _____ some great tutorial web sites.
(A) turned down
(B) testified to
(C) took in
(D) turned to   Ⓐ Ⓑ Ⓒ Ⓓ

6 To keep our factory workers from getting _____, it is mandatory that they take two 30-minute breaks per day.
(A) worn off
(B) worn out
(C) wiped out
(D) worked on   Ⓐ Ⓑ Ⓒ Ⓓ

7 The company sold off a number of their assets to _____ their considerable debt.
(A) give way to
(B) pay off
(C) hear about
(D) hold on to   Ⓐ Ⓑ Ⓒ Ⓓ

8 If you don't _____ your side of the bargain, our contract will be void.
(A) log onto
(B) live up to
(C) look down on
(D) look into   Ⓐ Ⓑ Ⓒ Ⓓ

9 Employers are seeking employees with the ability to _____ changes.
(A) apply to
(B) adapt to
(C) cling to
(D) refer to   Ⓐ Ⓑ Ⓒ Ⓓ

10 We'll _____ a proposal, including detailed costings, free of charge.
(A) put together
(B) put up with
(C) put away
(D) put in   Ⓐ Ⓑ Ⓒ Ⓓ

11 I'll _____ for her until she gets back from her spring break.
(A) get over
(B) get on
(C) take over
(D) take on   Ⓐ Ⓑ Ⓒ Ⓓ

12 Whether we will have to cut down on the budget _____ the sales performance this quarter.
(A) lies in
(B) counts on
(C) depends on
(D) comes with   Ⓐ Ⓑ Ⓒ Ⓓ

13 Please _____ the handrail so that you won't fall.
(A) hold on to
(B) hold on
(C) stop by
(D) stand by   Ⓐ Ⓑ Ⓒ Ⓓ

14 The company offered some special discounts _____ the customer complaints.
(A) in place of
(B) in order to
(C) in the face of
(D) in response to   Ⓐ Ⓑ Ⓒ Ⓓ

15 Mr. Cliff has _____ a conference call for Wednesday afternoon.
(A) set up
(B) picked up
(C) made up
(D) looked up

Ⓐ Ⓑ Ⓒ Ⓓ

文法實力挑戰詳解

♛ Unit 1

1. When all the board members _____, the meeting will commence.
   (A) arrived
   (B) will arrive
   (C) has arrived
   (D) arrive

1. 當所有董事會成員抵達時,會議將會開始。
   正確答案:(D)

> : 本題考副詞子句和主要子句的時態關係。從主要子句 the meeting will commence 用未來式可以得知本句是在描述未來的事情,但是表時間或條件的副詞子句不可以用未來式,必須用現在簡單式代替未來式,所以答案選 (D)。

2. She _____ one thousand dollars each week for five years.
   (A) has been saving
   (B) had saved
   (C) will save
   (D) saves

2. 她每週存一千元已經長達五年了。
   正確答案:(A)

> : 從 for five years 可以得知動詞是表從過去持續至今的動作或狀態,時態要搭配現在完成進行式,所以答案選 (A)。

3. The politician _____ before the agents tackled the gunman.
   (A) has been shot
   (B) will have shot
   (C) had been shot
   (D) had shot

3. 在探員制伏這名槍手前,那位政治人物已經遭到槍殺。
   正確答案:(C)

：從 before 引導的副詞子句用過去簡單式動詞 tackled，可以得知主要子句是表更早發生的動作，動詞應用過去完成式，另外，主詞 the politician 是遭到槍殺的人所以要搭配被動，因此答案選 (C)。

4. Before the night comes to an end, we _____ the lifetime achievement award.
   (A) have presented
   (B) will present
   (C) had presented
   (D) present

4. 在今夜進入尾聲前，我們將要頒發終身成就獎。
   正確答案：(B)

 ：從副詞子句 Before the night comes to an end 動詞時態用現在簡單式 comes，可以得知副詞子句是用現在代替未來，此時主要子句應使用未來式，所以答案選 (B)。

5. Ellen had hosted the last ten dinner parties before Regina _____ to host this one.
   (A) agreed
   (B) agrees
   (C) will agree
   (D) had agreed

5. 在 Regina 同意主辦這次的晚宴之前，過去的十場晚宴都是 Ellen 主辦的。
   正確答案：(A)

 ：從主要子句 Ellen had hosted the last ten dinner parties 動詞時態用過去完成式 (had hosted)，可以得知副詞子句要用過去簡單式表較晚發生的動作，所以答案選 (A)。

6. Your son _____ from senior high school by the time you receive your Ph.D.
   (A) will graduate
   (B) has graduated
   (C) will have graduated
   (D) graduates

6. 當你取得博士學位時，你兒子將已經從高中畢業了。
   正確答案：(C)

> : by the time (當…時) 等同連接詞，引導的副詞子句用現在簡單式 (receive) 時，代表主要子句是在描述未來某時為止已經完成或仍在進行的動作，此時要用未來完成式，所以答案選 (C)。

7. As long as the temperature _____ mild, our family reunion will take place at the park.
   (A) was
   (B) is
   (C) has been
   (D) will be

7. 只要天氣暖和，我們就會在公園舉行家庭聚會。
   正確答案：(B)

> : 從主要子句 our family reunion will take place at the park 動詞時態用未來簡單式 will take，可以得知副詞子句要用現在式代替未來式，要填入現在簡單式動詞，所以答案選 (B)。

8. Mark has been employed by this firm since he _____ from law school.
   (A) graduates
   (B) has graduated
   (C) graduated
   (D) will graduate

8. 自從 Mark 從法學院畢業後，他就已經被這家律師事務所聘僱了。
正確答案：(C)

 ：從主要子句 Mark has been employed by this firm 動詞時態用
現在完成式 (has been employed)，可以得知 since 引導的副
詞子句要用過去簡單式，所以答案選 (C)。

---

9. The study _____ by the time you return from your trip abroad.
(A) will finish
(B) will have finished
(C) finishes
(D) finished

9. 當你從國外旅遊回來時，這份研究將已經完成了。
正確答案：(B)

 ：by the time(當…時) 等同連接詞，引導的副詞子句用現在簡
單式 (return) 時，代表主要子句是在描述未來某時為止已經
完成或仍在進行的動作，此時要用未來完成式，所以答案選
(B)。

---

10. The financial error has gone unnoticed _____.
(A) for the last three quarters
(B) since you are on board
(C) since three quarters
(D) since he takes over as manager

10. 過去三季以來，這個財務錯誤一直沒有被注意到。
正確答案：(A)

 ：句子動詞用現在完成式 has gone，因此可以搭配「for + 一
段時間」、「since + 過去時間」、「since + 一段時間 +
ago」、「since + 過去簡單式子句」，所以答案選 (A)。(B)
中的 are 要改成 were。(C) 要再加上 ago。(D) 中的 takes 要
改成 took。

11. Brian _____ an elaborate backyard garden over the past five years.
   (A) had been constructing
   (B) will have constructed
   (C) has been constructing
   (D) is constructing

11. 過去的五年來，Brian 一直在建造一座精心設計的後院花園。
   正確答案：(C)

：從時間副詞片語 over the past five years (過去五年來) 可以得知句子動詞要用現在完成式或現在完成進行式表從過去持續至今的動作或狀態，所以答案選 (C)。

12. Dallas, Texas has just recently become one of the most popular places to host international events _____.
   (A) in the past three years
   (B) for three years ago
   (C) among the last three years
   (D) since three years

12. 德州的達拉斯在過去的三年來成為主辦國際活動的最受喜愛地點之一。
   正確答案：(A)

：句中動詞用現在完成式 (has become)，因此可以搭配「for + 一段時間」、「since + 過去時間」、「since + 一段時間 + ago」、「since + 過去簡單式子句」、「in/for/over/during + the + last/past + 一段時間」，所以答案選 (A)。(B) 可以改成 for three years 或是 since three years ago。(C) 中的 among 要改成 in/for/over/during。(D) 可以改成 for three years 或是 since three years ago。

13. The financial report had already been released before the CFO
_____ the numbers had been inflated.
(A) realizes
(B) will realize
(C) has realized
(D) realized

13. 在財務長發現數字被誇大之前，這份財務報告早已經被公布了。
正確答案：(D)

: 從主要子句 The financial report had already been released
動詞時態用過去完成式 (had been released)，可以得知副詞
子句要用過去簡單式表較晚發生的動作，所以答案選 (D)。

14. You _____ over two million dollars by the time you retire if you
keep up this pace.
(A) have saved
(B) had saved
(C) will have saved
(D) saved

14. 如果你以這樣的速度繼續下去的話，到了你退休時，你將已經存到兩百
多萬元了。
正確答案：(C)

: by the time (當⋯時) 等同連接詞，引導的副詞子句用現在
簡單式 (retire) 時，代表主要子句是在描述未來某時為止已經
完成或仍在進行的動作，此時要用未來完成式，所以答案選
(C)。

15. The tech giant _____ to release their new tablet before the market tanked.
    (A) plans
    (B) had planned
    (C) has planned
    (D) will plan

15. 在市場衰退前，這家科技大廠早已經計劃要推出他們的新平板電腦。
    正確答案：(B)

 ：從 before 引導的副詞子句用過去簡單式動詞 tanked，可以得知主要子句是表更早發生的動作，動詞應用過去完成式，所以答案選 (B)。

16. It _____ that the regional manager has been embezzling money since 1998.
    (A) has been unearthed
    (B) have been unearthed
    (C) has unearthed
    (D) will have been unearthed

16. 自從 1998 年這位區經理一直在挪用公款的事情早已經被發現。
    正確答案：(A)

 ：從時間副詞 since 1998 可以得知動詞是表從過去持續至今的動作或狀態，時態要搭配現在完成式或是現在完成進行式；另外因為主詞 it 是指一件事，所以動詞 unearth (v. 發現) 要用被動態，所以答案選 (A)。(B) 中的 have 要改成 has，因為主詞 it 是單數。

17. As long as everyone _____ in, we will be able to open the shop in under one week.
    (A) will pitch
    (B) pitches
    (C) will have pitched
    (D) pitched

17. 只要每個人都投入參與，我們就能夠在一週之內開店。
    正確答案：(B)

 ：從主要子句動詞時態用未來簡單式 will be，可以得知副詞子句要用現在式代替未來式，要填入現在簡單式動詞，所以答案選 (B)。

18. The stream _____ for five years by the corrupt chemical company.
    (A) have polluted
    (B) has been polluted
    (C) was polluted
    (D) had polluted

18. 這條溪流已經被這間貪贓舞弊的化學公司汙染長達五年了。
    正確答案：(B)

 ：從 for five years 可以得知動詞是表從過去持續至今的動作或狀態，時態要搭配現在完成式或是現在完成進行式；另外因為主詞溪流是被汙染的，所以動詞 pollute 要搭配被動態，所以答案選 (B)。

19. All of Rick's dreams had been realized before he _____ thirty years old.

   (A) had been

   (B) is

   (C) was

   (D) will be

19. Rick 的所有夢想都在他三十歲前已經實現了。

   正確答案：(C)

 ：從主要子句 The financial report had already been released 動詞時態用過去完成式 (had been realized)，可以得知副詞子句要用過去簡單式表較晚發生的動作，所以答案選 (C)。

---

20. Our stock has shot up in value _____ the past two weeks.

   (A) since

   (B) at

   (C) within

   (D) over

20. 我們的股價在過去的兩週以來一直在上漲。

   正確答案：(D)

 ：由動詞 has shot 可知本句是現在完成式，要搭配由過去到現在的一段時間。本題考時間副詞「in/for/over/during + the + last/past + 一段時間」表過去的一段時間以來，所以答案選 (D)。選項 (C)「within + 一段時間」表「在某期限之內」。

♛ Unit 2

1. If I _____ you, I would continue to argue with your insurance company until they compromise.
   (A) am
   (B) were
   (C) had
   (D) will be

1. 如果我是你，我會一直跟保險公司據理力爭直到他們妥協為止。
   正確答案：(B)

 ：本題考和現在事實相反的假設句。從主要子句的動詞 would continue 可以得知條件子句要用 were 或是過去簡單式，所以答案選 (B)。

2. If you _____ the presentation, you would have gotten a better grasp of how the new software works.
   (A) attended
   (B) attends
   (C) had attended
   (D) will attend

2. 如果你有出席簡報會議的話，你就會更加了解新軟體是如何運作的了。
   正確答案：(C)

 ：本題考和過去事實相反的假設句。從主要子句的動詞 would have gotten 可以得知條件子句要用 had p.p.，所以答案選 (C)。

3. If you should run into a problem with logging in, you _____ the help desk.
   (A) called
   (B) had called
   (C) should call
   (D) have called

3. 萬一你有登入的問題,你應該打電話給客服中心。
   正確答案:(C)

 :本題考表萬一的假設句。從條件子句的動詞 should run 可以得知主要子句可以搭配祈使句、would/should/could/might + V.、will/can/may/should + V.,所以答案選 (C)。

----

4. If you hadn't given me that stock tip last year, I _____ so well off financially now.
   (A) wouldn't be
   (B) will not be
   (C) wouldn't have been
   (D) would be

4. 如果你去年沒有指點我買那檔股票的話,我現在也不會這麼有錢。
   正確答案:(A)

 :本題考混和型的假設句。從主要子句出現的時間副詞 now 可以得知主要子句是和現在相反,不是和過去相反,所以要搭配 would/should/could/might + V.,再另外從語意可以選出答案是 (A)。

5. If I _____ that this truck was going to break down so often, I would not have bought it.
  (A) have known
  (B) had known
  (C) knew
  (D) know

5. 如果我早知道這輛卡車會這麼常拋錨的話，我是不會買它的。
  正確答案：(B)

> : 本題考和過去事實相反的假設句。從主要子句的動詞 would have bought 可以得知條件子句要用 had p.p.，所以答案選 (B)。

6. Sally wishes she _____ the time and money to play golf once a week now.
  (A) had
  (B) has
  (C) had had
  (D) have

6. Sally 希望自己現在有時間和金錢可以一週打一次高爾夫球。
  正確答案：(A)

> : 本題考 wish 的假設句。從時間副詞 now 可以得知本句是和現在事實相反的假設句，wish 之後要搭配過去簡單式動詞，所以答案選 (A)。

7. _____ you created your profile, the company would never have recruited you.
  (A) If
  (B) Hadn't
  (C) Should
  (D) Were

7. 如果你沒有建立自己的簡介，這家公司是絕不會錄用你的。

正確答案：(B)

 ：本題考和過去事實相反的假設句。從主要子句的動詞 would have recruited 可以得知條件子句要用 had p.p.，即 if you hadn't created your profile。而 if 省略後就寫成 Hadn't you created your profile，所以答案選 (B)。

---

8. It is natural that you _____ so many questions as you are a new employee.

(A) asked

(B) had asked

(C) should ask

(D) to ask

8. 因為你是新進員工，你會問這麼多問題是很正常的。

正確答案：(C)

 ：本題考固定句型 It is natural that + S. + (should) + 動詞原形~，所以答案選 (C)。

---

9. My boss demanded that I _____ working on such a pointless project.

(A) ceased

(B) to cease

(C) ceasing

(D) cease

9. 我的老闆要求我停止做這個無意義的案子。

正確答案：(D)

 ：本題考「要命堅建」的假設句型。S. + 要命堅建動詞 + that + S. + (should) + (not) + 原形動詞，所以答案選 (D)。

10. Becky advised that her husband _____ his job until he finds a new one.
(A) not quit
(B) not to quit
(C) quit not
(D) should quit

10. Becky 建議她先生在找到新工作前不要辭職。

正確答案：(A)

> ：本題考「要命堅建」的假設句型。S. + 要命堅建動詞 + that + S. + (should) + (not) + 原形動詞。而選項 (D) 不符合語意，所以答案選 (A)。

11. It is about time that you _____ your back examined by a chiropractor.
(A) have
(B) to have
(C) had
(D) had had

11. 你該去請脊椎指壓治療師檢查你的背部了。

正確答案：(C)

> ：本題考固定句型 It is about time + that + S. + 過去式動詞，所以答案選 (C)。

12. If I _____ business instead of literature, I might have obtained employment more quickly.
(A) studied
(B) should study
(C) had studied
(D) study

12. 如果我是學商而不是文學的話，我就有可能更快找到工作了。

正確答案：(C)

: 本題考和過去事實相反的假設句。從主要子句的動詞 might have obtained 可以得知條件子句要用 had p.p.，所以答案選 (C)。

---

13. If I _____ a reliable car, I would not have to take public transportation every day.
    (A) were
    (B) had
    (C) have
    (D) had had

13. 如果我有一輛能開的車，我就不用每天搭大眾運輸工具了。

   正確答案：(B)

 : 本題考和現在事實相反的假設句。從主要子句的動詞 would not have to 可以得知條件子句要用過去簡單式動詞，所以答案選 (B)。

---

14. _____ Ken's generosity, the museum wouldn't have had the funding to stay open.
    (A) But for
    (B) But that
    (C) Were it for
    (D) With

14. 要不是 Ken 的樂善好施，博物館就不會有資金繼續營運了。

   正確答案：(A)

 : 本題考「若非；要不是」的假設句。從主要子句的動詞 would not have had 可以得知本句描述的是和過去事實相反的情況，所以可用 But for + N. 或是 If it had not been for + N. 或是 Had it not been for + N.，因此答案選 (A)。(B) But that 後方要接句子，不可接名詞。(C) 要改成 Were it not for。(D) 要改成 Without。

15. But that you _____ me, I might not have pursued engineering as my major in the first place.
    (A) encouraged
    (B) encouragement
    (C) had encouraged
    (D) have encouraged

15. 要不是你鼓勵我，當初我也不會選擇工程學當作主修。
    正確答案：(A)

> ：本題考「若非；要不是」的假設句。從主要子句的動詞 might not have pursued 可以得知本句描述的是和過去事實相反的情況，but that 後方的句子要用過去簡單式，所以答案選 (A)。

16. It is vital that Angela _____ the server tonight while we do some web site maintenance.
    (A) monitors
    (B) monitored
    (C) had monitored
    (D) monitor

16. 今晚當我們在維修網站時，Angela 有必要監測伺服器。
    正確答案：(D)

> ：本題考 It is vital that + S. + (should) + 動詞原形～，所以答案選 (D)。

17. If you _____ sick, you might want to try this newly approved medicine that I brought back from Europe.
    (A) had felt
    (B) feel
    (C) should feel
    (D) are feeling

17. 萬一你覺得不舒服，你或許可以試試看我從歐洲帶回來的新批准的藥。
    正確答案：(C)

：本題考表「萬一」的假設句。從主要子句的動詞 might want 可以得知條件子句有幾種可能：表萬一時要搭配 should + 動詞原形；表和現在事實相反時要搭配過去簡單式，所以答案選 (C)。

18. If you were as talented as Bobby, you _____ an athletic scholarship to any university you wanted.
    (A) can get
    (B) could get
    (C) could have gotten
    (D) should have gotten

18. 如果你像 Bobby 一樣有才華，你就能夠得到任何一所你想要進入的大學的體育獎學金了。

正確答案：(B)

 ：本題考和現在事實相反的假設句。從條件子句的動詞 were 可以得知主要子句要用 would/should/could/might + 動詞原形，所以答案選 (B)。

19. I wish I _____ a better understanding of computer operating systems.
    (A) have
    (B) will have
    (C) had
    (D) have had

19. 但願我對於電腦操作系統有更深入的了解。

正確答案：(C)

 ：本題考 wish 的假設句。和現在相反時要用過去簡單式，和過去相反時要用過去完成式，所以答案選 (C)。

20. If our company had relocated our factories to Vietnam, we _____ so many issues with government regulations now.
    (A) wouldn't have
    (B) wouldn't have had
    (C) had
    (D) won't have

20. 如果我們公司將工廠遷到越南，我們現在就不會有這麼多牽扯到政府法規的問題了。

    正確答案：(A)

     ：本題考混和型的假設句。從主要子句出現的時間副詞 now 可以得知主要子句是和現在相反，不是和過去相反，所以要搭配 would/should/could/might + V.，因此可以選出答案是 (A)。

♛ Unit 3

1. It is the duty of this department _____ our finances accurately.
   (A) audit
   (B) to audit
   (C) to auditing
   (D) will audit
1. 正確稽核我們公司的財務是這個部門的職責。
   正確答案：(B)

> :本題中的 It 為虛主詞，語意上真正的主詞是不定詞，所以答案選 (B)。

2. Tom aims _____ the conflict with his neighbors by erecting a fence around his yard.
   (A) to resolve
   (B) to resolving
   (C) resolving
   (D) resolved
2. Tom 打算在自家院子周圍築一道籬笆來解決和鄰居的衝突。
   正確答案：(A)

> :本題考固定用語 aim + to Vr. 表示「打算做某事」，所以答案選 (A)。

3. You always urge me _____ close attention to all the details before signing a contract.
   (A) pay
   (B) to paying
   (C) paid
   (D) to pay
3. 你總是會敦促我在簽合約之前要注意所有細節。
   正確答案：(D)

:本題考固定用語 urge + O. + to Vr. 表示「敦促受詞去做某事」，所以答案選 (D)。

4. She joined an athletic club with an eye to _____ ten kilograms.
   (A) losing
   (B) lose
   (C) lost
   (D) loss

4. 她為了要減重十公斤參加了運動俱樂部。

正確答案：(A)

 : with an eye to + V-ing 表示「為了要 ...」，所以答案選 (A)。

5. If you attempt _____ your cell phone service before the two-year agreement expires, you will incur a significant fine.
   (A) to cancel
   (B) canceling
   (C) to canceling
   (D) canceled

5. 如果你想要在你的兩年合約終止前先取消行動電話服務，你會被收取一筆可觀的費用。

正確答案：(A)

 :本題考固定用語 attempt + to Vr. 表示「企圖去做某事」，所以答案選 (A)。

6. The salesman tempted me _____ the highest quality smart phone in the shop.
   (A) purchasing
   (B) to purchase
   (C) to purchasing
   (D) purchase

6. 這個銷售員慫恿我買店裡最高品質的智慧型手機。

正確答案：(B)

：本題考固定用語 tempt + O. + to Vr. 表示「引誘受詞去做某事」，所以答案選 (B)。

7. My sister bought a sleek luxury car _____ off her wealth to everyone.
   (A) showing
   (B) to showing
   (C) to show
   (D) for showing

7. 我姊姊買了一輛流線型的豪華車是為了向大家炫耀她的財富。

正確答案：(C)

：本題考 to 引導的不定詞片語表示「為了要 ...」，所以答案選 (C)。

8. The sign warns park patrons _____.
   (A) not to litter
   (B) to not litter
   (C) not litter
   (D) not littering

8. 這個標誌警告常來公園的人不要亂丟垃圾。

正確答案：(A)

：本題考固定用語 warn + O. + (not) + to Vr. 表示「警告受詞 (不要) 去做某事」，所以答案選 (A)。

9. _____ child obesity, the mayor lobbied for the construction of a new community recreation center.
   (A) So as to combat
   (B) To combatting
   (C) With a view to combat
   (D) To combat

9. 為了要對抗兒童肥胖問題，市長極力遊說支持建設新的社區娛樂中心。

   正確答案：(D)

   > : 本題考 to 引導的不定詞片語表示「為了要 ...」，所以答案選 (D)。(A) so as to 不可以放在句首。(C) with a view to 後方要接動名詞，不可接原形動詞，所以改成 With a view to combating 就可以。

10. You finally persuaded me _____ my house on the market.
    (A) to putting
    (B) to put
    (C) putting
    (D) put

10. 你終於說服了我出售我的房子。

    正確答案：(B)

    > : 本題考固定用語 persuade + O. + to Vr. 表示「說服受詞去做某事」，所以答案選 (B)。

11. _____ peace with our neighboring countries is the political aim of my administration.
    (A) To making
    (B) Make
    (C) Made
    (D) To make

11. 和鄰近國家和諧相處是我在執政時的政治目標。

正確答案：(D)

 ：由動詞 is 可知題目缺少主詞，故空格要填入不定詞或動名詞，只有選項 (D) 是正確的，所以答案選 (D)。

---

12. The city government refuses _____ recycling pickup more frequently than once a week.

(A) to offer

(B) to offering

(C) offer

(D) offering

12. 市政府拒絕一週收資源回收物超過一次。

正確答案：(A)

 ：本題考固定用語 refuse + to Vr. 表示「拒絕去做某事」，所以答案選 (A)。

---

13. The secretary recorded a new voice mail greeting _____ a list of the office's holiday hours.

(A) providing

(B) to provide

(C) to providing

(D) provided

13. 秘書錄製了一段新的語音問候語是為了要提供公司的休假時間表的訊息。

正確答案：(B)

 ：本題考 to 引導的不定詞片語表示「為了要 ...」，所以答案選 (B)。

14. Kevin took the family out to a high-end restaurant _____ the special occasion of his big job promotion.
    (A) to mark
    (B) marking
    (C) as to mark
    (D) in order to marking

14. 為了慶祝升官，Kevin 帶全家到一家高檔餐廳用餐。
    正確答案：(A)

> ：本題考 to 引導的不定詞片語表示「為了要 ...」，所以答案選 (A)。(C) 要改為 so as to mark。(D) 要改為 in order to mark。

15. It is the vision of our nonprofit organization _____ all children with access to great after-school programs.
    (A) providing
    (B) to provide
    (C) to providing
    (D) provided

15. 我們這個非營利組織的未來目標是提供所有兒童很棒的課後課程。
    正確答案：(B)

> ：本題中的 It 為虛主詞，語意上真正的主詞是不定詞，所以答案選 (B)。

16. I would like _____ my gratitude to you for covering for me when I was out sick with the flu.
    (A) expressing
    (B) to expressing
    (C) to express
    (D) express

16. 因為你在我感冒時幫我代班，我想對你表達我的感激之意。
    正確答案：(C)

：本題考固定用語 would like to Vr. 表示「想要去做某事」，
所以答案選 (C)。

17. _____ technology trends several months in advance is risky.
    (A) Predict
    (B) To predicting
    (C) Predicted
    (D) To predict

17. 提前好幾個月預測科技趨勢是有風險的。
    正確答案：(D)

：從句中動詞 is 可以得知本題考不定詞當主詞，所以答案選
(D)。

18. He took classes _____ upgrade his skill set and improve his job
    prospects.
    (A) so as to
    (B) as to
    (C) so that
    (D) with a view to

18. 為了提升自己的技能以及改善自己的工作前景，他上了很多課。
    正確答案：(A)

：本題考「為了要 ...」的表達法，可以用 so as to Vr./in order
to Vr./with a view to V-ing/so that + 句子，因為空格後方的
upgrade 為動詞原形，所以答案選 (A)。(B) as to 指「至於…」，
後方要加名詞。

19. The tension between these two countries caused oil prices _____
    sharply.
    (A) rise
    (B) to rise
    (C) rising
    (D) to rising

19. 這兩國間的緊張氣氛使得油價急遽上升。

正確答案：(B)

> :本題考固定用語 cause + O. + to Vr. 表示「致使受詞 ...」，所以答案選 (B)。

20. My mentor taught me _____ to know a customer before I try to
    recommend anything to him or her.
    (A) to getting
    (B) getting
    (C) to get
    (D) get

20. 我的指導者教導我在推薦任何東西給顧客前要先了解他 (她)。

正確答案：(C)

> :本題考固定用語 teach + O. + to Vr. 表示「教導受詞去做某事」，所以答案選 (C)。

21. _____ new software allows me _____ up with the newest
    trends in the field of graphic design.
    (A) Purchasing; to keep
    (B) Purchasing; keeping
    (C) To purchase; keeping
    (D) Purchase; keep

21. 購買新軟體使我得以跟上平面設計的最新流行趨勢。

正確答案：(A)

：本句的動詞是 allows，因此代表前方的是句子主詞，所以第一個空格是考動名詞或不定詞當主詞；第二個空格考的是固定用語 allow + O. + to Vr.，所以答案選 (A)。

22. The marketing department has delayed _____ out their new campaign.
    (A) to roll
    (B) to rolling
    (C) rolling
    (D) rolled

22. 行銷部門延遲了新宣傳活動的推出。
    正確答案：(C)

：本題考固定用語 delay + V-ing 表示「延遲做某事」，所以答案選 (C)。

23. It is no use _____ the truth in light of the new evidence.
    (A) to deny
    (B) to denying
    (C) of denying
    (D) denying

23. 有鑑於新證據的出現，否認事實真相是沒有用的。
    正確答案：(D)

：本題考固定句型 It is no use + V-ing 表示「做⋯是沒有用的」，所以答案選 (D)。

24. We couldn't help _____ why the policy remains unchanged.
    (A) wondering
    (B) wonder
    (C) but wondering
    (D) but to wonder

24. 我們忍不住納悶為何這個政策還是沒有改變。
正確答案：(A)

 ：本題考固定句型 can't help + V-ing 表示「忍不住…」，而 can't help but 後方要加原形動詞，所以答案選 (A)。

---

25. I have a hard time _____ that Gary got the manager position and not me.
(A) to accept
(B) accepting
(C) to accepting
(D) accepted

25. 對於 Gary 得到經理職位而不是我這件事，我很難以釋懷。
正確答案：(B)

 ：本題考固定句型 have a hard time + V-ing 表示「做…很困難」，所以答案選 (B)。

---

26. When it comes to _____ the best products, this Japanese company has no equal.
(A) innovate
(B) innovating
(C) innovation
(D) innovated

26. 說到創造最佳商品這件事，這間日本公司是無人能比的。
正確答案：(B)

 ：本題考固定用語 when it comes to + V-ing 表示「一談到…」，所以答案選 (B)。

27. The new private school is devoted to _____ students the best education money can buy.
    (A) giving
    (B) give
    (C) gave
    (D) given

27. 這所新的私立學校致力於提供學生金錢所能買到的最優質教育。

正確答案：(A)

> 🧑 ：本題考固定用語 be devoted to + V-ing 表示「致力於做…」，所以答案選 (A)。

---

28. _____ the report was time-consuming, but it was vital for every employee _____ the current status of the company.
    (A) Preparing; understanding
    (B) To prepare; understanding
    (C) Prepare; to understand
    (D) Preparing; to understand

28. 準備這份報告是費時的，但是對於每位員工而言，了解公司現狀是重要的。

正確答案：(D)

> 🧑 ：第一個空格考動名詞當主詞；第二句的主詞 it 是虛主詞，真正的主詞是不定詞，所以答案選 (D)。

---

29. The news editor opposed _____ the scandalous story to the public.
    (A) to release
    (B) to releasing
    (C) releasing
    (D) being released

29. 這位新聞編輯反對將這個醜聞公諸於世。

正確答案：(C)

：本題考「反對」的表達法。oppose + V-ing = be opposed to + V-ing = object to + V-ing，所以答案選 (C)。

---

30. I have become accustomed to _____ in this college town.
    (A) living
    (B) live
    (C) lived
    (D) being lived

30. 我已經習慣居住在這個大學城了。
    正確答案：(A)

 ：本題考固定用語 be/become accustomed to + V-ing 表示「習慣 ...」，所以答案選 (A)。

---

31. I have become a vegetarian in addition to _____ my daily calorie intake.
    (A) lower
    (B) lowering
    (C) lowered
    (D) being lowered

31. 除了減少我每日的卡路里攝取量之外，我還成為了一名素食者。
    正確答案：(B)

 ：本題考固定用語 in addition to + V-ing 表示「除了 ... 之外，還有」，所以答案選 (B)。

---

32. _____ when Mr. Andrews will make a decision.
    (A) There is not second-guessing
    (B) It is impossible second-guessing
    (C) It is no second-guessing
    (D) There is no second-guessing

32. 我們不可能去揣測 Andrews 先生何時會做決定。

正確答案：(D)

 ：本題考固定句型 There is no + V-ing 表示「不可能 ...」，所以答案選 (D)。(B) 要改成 It is impossible to second-guess。

---

33. I am busy _____ my car's engine and can't come to the party.
   (A) repairing
   (B) to repair
   (C) with repairing
   (D) to repairing

33. 我正忙著修理我汽車的引擎，所以無法前去參加派對。

正確答案：(A)

 ：本題考固定用語 be busy + V-ing 表示「忙於 ...」，所以答案選 (A)。(C)「be busy with + 名詞」表忙於某事。

---

34. It is common for overworked, stressed out employees to get addicted to _____ drinks which contain caffeine.
   (A) have
   (B) having
   (C) had
   (D) have had

34. 對於勞累過度、壓力過大的職員而言，喝含有咖啡因的飲料成癮是很常有的情況。

正確答案：(B)

 ：本題考固定用語 get addicted to + V-ing 表示「對 ... 上了癮」，所以答案選 (B)。

35. I am looking forward _____ our 25-year class reunion.
   (A) to attend
   (B) of attending
   (C) in attending
   (D) to attending

35. 我很期待參加我們畢業二十五年的同學會。
   正確答案：(D)

> :本題考固定用語 look forward to + V-ing 表示「期待 ...」，所以答案選 (D)。

36. _____ the most efficient way to produce microchips is essential to our business.
   (A) Research
   (B) To researching
   (C) Researching
   (D) Researched

36. 研究生產微晶片最有效率的方法對我們企業是很重要的。
   正確答案：(C)

> :從句中動詞 is 可以得知從空格到 microchips 為句子主詞，因此動詞要用動名詞或不定詞才能當主詞，所以答案選 (C)。

37. I have a problem _____ Charles as a creative genius.
   (A) imagining
   (B) to imagine
   (C) to imagining
   (D) with imagining

37. 我真是無法想像 Charles 是個有創意的天才。
   正確答案：(A)

> :本題考固定用語 have a problem + V-ing 表示「做 ... 有困難」，所以答案選 (A)。

38. Granting employees an hour-long lunch break _____ them re-energize for the afternoon rush.
    (A) lets
    (B) make
    (C) have
    (D) get

38. 給員工一小時的午餐休息時間使他們可以有充沛的精力應付繁忙的下午。

正確答案：(A)

: Granting employees an hour-long lunch break 為動名詞當本句主詞，因此動詞要取單數，所以答案選 (A)。

39. I couldn't help _____ depressed when I learned that we might need to make job cuts to avoid bankruptcy.
    (A) but to feel
    (B) but feeling
    (C) feeling
    (D) felt

39. 當我得知我們公司為了避免破產而可能必須裁員時，我忍不住覺得很沮喪。

正確答案：(C)

: 本題考固定句型 can't help + V-ing 表示「忍不住⋯」，所以答案選 (C)。

40. _____ that our main competitor's product is superior to ours.
    (A) It is not denying
    (B) There is no denying
    (C) It is not impossible denying
    (D) It is no denying

40. 無可否認的我們的主要對手的產品比我們的好。

正確答案：(B)

：本題考固定句型 There is no + V-ing 表示「不可能…」，所以
答案選 (B)。

👑 Unit 4

1. The _____ food commercial successfully appeals to many housewives.
   (A) freeze
   (B) frozen
   (C) freezing
   (D) froze

1. 這個冷凍食品廣告成功地吸引了很多家庭主婦。

   正確答案：(B)

    ：因為空格後方有名詞，所以空格要放形容詞用以修飾名詞。本題考分詞當形容詞用，現在分詞表主動或進行，過去分詞表被動或完成，冷凍食品是指已經結凍的食品，所以用過去分詞表已經完成結凍的動作，因此答案選 (B)。

2. The _____ cars were all mashed into a pile on the icy road.
   (A) wrecking
   (B) wreck
   (C) wrecked
   (D) wreckage

2. 那些車子在結冰的道路上撞爛成一堆。

   正確答案：(C)

    ：因為空格後方有名詞，所以空格要放形容詞用以修飾名詞。本題考分詞當形容詞用，現在分詞表主動或進行，過去分詞表被動或完成。wrecked 表「被毀的；遭到嚴重破壞的」，修飾 cars，所以答案選 (C)。

3. The movie _____ 500 million US dollars will be released on DVD this week.
   (A) made
   (B) which making
   (C) which make
   (D) making
3. 賺了五億美金的這部電影將在這週發行 DVD。
   正確答案：(D)

   :本題考分詞片語。making 500 million US dollars 為分詞片語，來自形容詞子句 which made 500 million US dollars，所以答案選 (D)。

4. He focused intently on the money as it was being counted, _____ by greed.
   (A) consumed
   (B) consuming
   (C) to consume
   (D) having consumed
4. 當對方在數錢時，他目不轉睛的盯著看，內心充滿了貪念。
   正確答案：(A)

   :本題考對等子句簡化的分詞構句。consumed by greed 來自 and he was consumed by greed，所以答案選 (A)。

5. _____ the lifetime achievement award, he couldn't help but weep.
   (A) Receiving
   (B) To receive
   (C) Received
   (D) Receipt
5. 因為獲得終身成就獎，他忍不住哭了。
   正確答案：(A)

：本題考副詞子句簡化的分詞構句。Receiving the lifetime achievement award 來自 Because he received the lifetime achievement award，所以答案選 (A)。

---

6. Watching the football team's _____ comeback victory left me galvanized, and I decided to play sports again.
   (A) inspired
   (B) inspire
   (C) inspiring
   (D) inspiration

6. 看這支足球隊激勵人心勝利復出的故事使我為之一振，我決定要繼續運動了。
   正確答案：(C)

：inspiring 為動詞 inspire 的現在分詞，表「鼓舞人心的」，修飾名詞 comeback victory。

---

7. _____ by the customer, Harold hung up the phone in disgust.
   (A) To scold
   (B) Scolding
   (C) Scold
   (D) Scolded

7. 因為遭到客人的責罵，Harold 厭惡地掛斷電話。
   正確答案：(D)

：本題考副詞子句簡化的分詞構句。Scolded by the customer 來自 Because he was scolded by the customer，所以答案選 (D)。

8. _____ at having sent out so many résumés with no response, I got an uplifting call for a job interview.
   (A) Frustrating
   (B) Frustrated
   (C) To frustrate
   (D) Frustration

8. 就在我對於寄出那麼多履歷都音訊全無感到很挫折的時候，我接到了一通令人振奮的面試通知電話。

正確答案：(B)

： 本題考副詞子句簡化的分詞構句。Frustrated at having sent out so many résumés with no response 來自 When I was frustrated at having sent out so many résumés with no response，frustrated 在此修飾主詞 I，表「感到受挫的」，所以答案選 (B)。

9. The shopkeeper glared at the noisy student, her eyes _____.
   (A) burning
   (B) burned
   (C) burn
   (D) be burned

9. 店老闆瞪向那名很吵的學生，眼中燃著怒火。

正確答案：(A)

： 本題考對等子句簡化的分詞構句。her eyes burning 來自 and her eyes were burning，所以答案選 (A)。(B) burned 表示被燒傷。

10. Any dollar bills _____ a special blue watermark on the back can be considered counterfeit.
    (A) which not have
    (B) not had
    (C) which not having
    (D) not having

10. 任何背面沒有特殊藍色浮水印的一元紙鈔都會被認為是假鈔。
    正確答案：(D)

 ：本題考分詞片語。not having a special blue watermark on the back 來自形容詞子句 which do not have a special blue watermark on the back，所以答案選 (D)。

---

11. The conflicting reports made our executives _____ about the direction of the company.
    (A) confusing
    (B) confuse
    (C) confused
    (D) confusion

11. 這些有衝突的報告使我們的主管對於公司未來走向感到困惑。
    正確答案：(C)

 ：本句動詞 make 的用法為「make + 受詞 + 受詞補語」。本句受詞 our executives 為人，所以用情緒動詞的過去分詞修飾人，因此答案選 (C)。

---

12. All customers _____ before 8 AM will be sent directly to a voice mailbox.
    (A) calling
    (B) called
    (C) who calling
    (D) which call

12. 任何在早上八點前來電的客戶電話都會直接轉進語音信箱。
    正確答案：(A)

 ：本題考分詞片語。calling before 8 AM 來自形容詞子句 who call before 8 AM，去掉主格關代 who 後再將主動動詞 call 改為現在分詞 calling，因此答案選 (A)。

13. _____ that the company would need to take drastic measures to avoid a collapse, the president took a deep breath and sighed.
    (A) Concluded
    (B) Concluding
    (C) To conclude
    (D) Conclusion

13. 總裁在下了結論說公司為了避免倒閉而必須採取嚴厲措施後,他深呼吸了一下並嘆了一口氣。
    正確答案:(B)

：本題考分詞構句。Concluding that the company would need to take drastic measures to avoid a collapse 來自 After he concluded that the company would need to take drastic measures to avoid a collapse,兩邊主詞相同所以去掉 he,再將主動動詞 concluded 改為現在分詞 concluding,連接詞 after 可保留也可以去掉,因此答案選 (B)。

14. Witnessing such a traumatizing event as the fatal car crash made Carol feel _____.
    (A) satisfying
    (B) depressing
    (C) delighted
    (D) shocked

14. 親眼目睹像這場致命車禍那樣使人精神受創的事情使 Carol 很震驚。
    正確答案:(D)

：本題考情緒動詞的分詞。本句受詞 Carol 為人,所以用情緒動詞的過去分詞修飾人,因此答案選 (D)。(C) delighted 是愉快的。

15. Bradley was hired as an executive for the firm right after _____ his Ph.D.
    (A) getting
    (B) he getting
    (C) he gets
    (D) gotten

15. Bradley 在取得博士學位之後立即受雇為這家公司的主管。
    正確答案：(A)

> : 本題考分詞構句。after getting his Ph.D. 來自副詞子句 after he got his Ph.D.，因此答案選 (A)。

16. Most employees are unhappy about the new policy _____ each employee to give three weeks' notice for vacation requests.
    (A) to require
    (B) which requiring
    (C) requiring
    (D) that require

16. 大部分的員工對於要求每位員工放假要提前三週提出申請的新政策感到不滿。
    正確答案：(C)

> : 本題考分詞片語。requiring each employee to give three weeks' notice for vacation requests 來自形容詞子句 which requires each employee to give three weeks' notice for vacation requests，去掉主格關代 which 後再將主動動詞 requires 改為現在分詞 requiring，因此答案選 (C)。

17. If you fail to abide by the policies _____ in our agreement, we might switch to other contractors.
    (A) which outlined
    (B) outlined
    (C) outlining
    (D) which outlining

17. 如果你未能遵守我們合約中所提到的規定，我們有可能要換其他承包商。

正確答案：(B)

 ：本題考分詞片語。outlined in our agreement 來自形容詞子句 which were outlined in our agreement，去掉主格關代 which 後再將 be 動詞去掉，保留過去分詞，因此答案選 (B)。

18. The accusations _____ by the whistleblower did damage the reputation of our company.
   (A) brought forth
   (B) which brought forth
   (C) bringing forth
   (D) which was brought forth

18. 告密者對我們公司的指控的確傷害了我們公司的聲譽。

正確答案：(A)

 ：本題考分詞片語。brought forth by the whistleblower 來自形容詞子句 which were brought forth by the whistleblower，去掉主格關代 which 後再將 be 動詞去掉，保留過去分詞，因此答案選 (A)。

19. You had better do a thorough assessment of the new fast food chain before _____ to sign a franchise agreement.
   (A) agreed
   (B) agreeing
   (C) you agreeing
   (D) agree

19. 在同意簽屬特許加盟協議之前，你最好先針對新的速食連鎖店做一個徹底的評估吧。

正確答案：(B)

：本題考分詞構句。before agreeing to sign a franchise agreement 來自副詞子句 before you agree to sign a franchise agreement，因此答案選 (B)。

20. The carbon dioxide _____ by this factory has exceeded the standard amount.
    (A) which emitted
    (B) emitting
    (C) which emits
    (D) emitted

20. 這間工廠所排放出的二氧化碳已經超出了標準量。
    正確答案：(D)

：本題考分詞片語。emitted by the factory 來自形容詞子句 which was emitted by the factory，去掉主格關代 which 後再將 be 動詞去掉，保留過去分詞，因此答案選 (D)。

♛ Unit 5

1. Being gifted _____ self-motivated, Melissa had no problem ascending the corporate ladder at an accelerating rate.
   (A) but
   (B) as well as
   (C) or
   (D) but also

1. 因為有才華又有上進心，Melissa 在公司內部晉升的很快。
   正確答案：(B)

   👩 : 本題考對等連接詞。as well as (以及) 連接兩個形容詞 gifted 和 self-motivated，所以答案選 (B)。

2. The family reunion will take place in _____ a public park or a restaurant.
   (A) as well as
   (B) neither
   (C) either
   (D) not only

2. 家庭聚會不是在公園就是在餐廳舉行。
   正確答案：(C)

   👩 : 本題考對等連接詞。either ~ or ~ 表「不是 ... 就是 ...」，所以答案選 (C)。

3. Tom's failure in college was not for lack of effort, _____ for lack of financial support.
   (A) but also
   (B) and
   (C) but
   (D) as well as

3. Tom 之所以大學未能順利畢業不是因為他不努力，而是因為缺乏經濟方面的援助。
正確答案：(C)

 ：本題考對等連接詞。not ~ but ~ 表「不是 ... 而是 ...」，所以答案選 (C)。

---

4. The athletic director as well as I _____ concerned about cuts in funding to the sports programs at our school.
    (A) is
    (B) are
    (C) am
    (D) has

4. 體育主任和我都對本校體育經費遭到刪減的事情感到擔心。
正確答案：(A)

 ：本題考對等連接詞 as well as。as well as 連接兩個名詞當主詞時動詞要由前方的名詞決定，因此本句要由 the athletic director 決定，另外 be concerned about 表「擔心 ...」，所以答案選 (A)。

---

5. Neither we nor Ken _____ found any evidence of wrongdoing at the government agency.
    (A) have
    (B) are
    (C) is
    (D) has

5. 我們和 Ken 都沒有發現政府做錯事的證據。
正確答案：(D)

：本題考對等連接詞 neither ~ nor ~。neither ~ nor ~ 連接兩個名詞當主詞時動詞要由靠近的主詞決定，因此本句要由 Ken 決定；另外因為本句主詞是人，所以發現證據要用主動態，故答案選 (D)。

---

6. _____ our database administrator is on vacation this week, no significant issues in the IT department can be dealt with.
   (A) Since
   (B) Although
   (C) No matter
   (D) For

6. 因為我們的資料庫管理者本週在度假中，所以 IT 部門沒有人可以處理重要的問題。

正確答案：(A)

：本題考從屬連接詞。因為空格後方有兩個完整的句子，可知空格要填入從屬連接詞連接兩句子。因副詞子句的語意表示原因，主要子句表示結果，所以空格內為引導原因的附屬連接詞，答案要選 (A)。since 在此句中表「因為」。

---

7. _____ the stressful office environment, we have had high turnover of staff these past few years.
   (A) Because
   (B) Despite
   (C) As a result
   (D) As a result of

7. 因為我們的辦公室環境充滿壓力，所以在過去的幾年來，人事流動率一直很大。

正確答案：(D)

：因為空格後方的 the stressful office environment 為名詞，所以空格要用介系詞或介系詞片語，此時 (B) 和 (D) 符合，再從語意呈現因果關係選出答案為 (D)。

8. _____ the city has built many centers to provide job training to the poor, very few residents have taken advantage of these resources.

(A) Because

(B) Although

(C) When

(D) As soon as

8. 雖然市政府已經建立了很多提供貧窮者職業訓練的中心，但是會利用這些資源的居民卻很少。

正確答案：(B)

 ：本題考從屬連接詞。因為空格後方有兩個完整的句子，因此要以從屬連接詞連接兩個句子，四個選項皆為從屬連接詞，所以再從語意選出答案為 (B)。

9. _____ the suspension of all trading on the stock market, we were able to mitigate some of our losses.

(A) Instead of

(B) In addition to

(C) Thanks to

(D) Compared with

9. 還好股市交易全面停擺，我們的損失才得以減輕。

正確答案：(C)

 ：因為空格後方的 the suspension of all trading on the stock market 為名詞，所以空格要用介系詞或介系詞片語，此時四個選項都符合，所以最後由語意選出答案為 (C) 多虧。(A) 表「而不是；取代」。(B) 表「除了 ... 之外」。(D) 表「和 ... 比起來」。

10. _____ the approaching winter storm, schools and businesses announced that they would not open the following day.
   (A) Since
   (B) On account of
   (C) In spite of
   (D) Thanks for

10. 因為冬季風暴即將來襲，學校以及公司行號宣布隔天停班停課。
   正確答案：(B)

 ：因空格後方的 the approaching winter storm 為名詞，所以空格要用介系詞或介系詞片語，且由語意可知前後有因果關係，所以選出答案為 (B) 因為。(A) since 當介系詞表「自從」，但表「因為」時為連接詞，要連接句子。(C)表「儘管」。(D)表「謝謝」。

- -

11. _____ this bar has perfect equipment and facilities, the location is not ideal.
   (A) When
   (B) With all
   (C) Because
   (D) Even though

11. 即使這間酒吧有很棒的設備設施，但是它的地點並不理想。
   正確答案：(D)

 ：本題考從屬連接詞。因為空格後方有兩個完整的句子，可知空格要填入從屬連接詞連接兩句子。依語意選出答案為 (D) 即使。(A) 表「當 ...」。(B) 介系詞片語，表「儘管」。(C) 表「因為」。

12. _____ the effort he has gone through to solicit funds, the non-profit company still went belly up in the end.
    (A) For all
    (B) As a result of
    (C) In comparison with
    (D) Owing to

12. 儘管他很努力去募集資金，但是這個非營利公司最後還是破產了。
    正確答案：(A)

> : 因為空格後方的 the effort he has gone through to solicit funds 為名詞，所以空格要用介系詞或介系詞片語，此時四個選項都符合，所以最後由語意選出答案為 (A) 儘管。(B) 表「因為」。(C) 表「和 ... 比起來」。(D) 表「因為」。

13. _____ how many sales calls I made, I still could not close the deal with enough customers.
    (A) Although
    (B) As
    (C) No matter
    (D) Despite

13. 不論我打了多少銷售電話，我還是無法成功地和足夠多的客戶達成交易。
    正確答案：(C)

> : no matter + wh- 表「無論」。

14. _____ repairs we attempted to make, the server would still no longer function exactly right.
    (A) However
    (B) Whatever
    (C) No matter
    (D) Although

14. 不論我們修了多少次，伺服器還是無法正常運作。
    正確答案：(B)

: whatever repairs we attempted to make = no matter what repairs we attempted to make。(A) 雖然也是連接詞,相當於 no matter how,但是此處不符合語意。(C) no matter 後方的第一個字必須是 wh- 開頭的疑問詞。

---

15. Your business plan is so ambitious that it's unrealistic; _____, you are projecting fifty million dollars in sales in just your first year!
    (A) in addition
    (B) therefore
    (C) for example
    (D) however

15. 你的商業計劃太有野心了所以不切實際;例如,你估計在第一年就會有五千萬的銷售額!
    正確答案:(C)

 : 本題四個選項都是轉承副詞,所以最後從語意呈現舉例關係選出答案為 (C) 例如。(A) 表「此外」。(B) 表「因此」。(D) 表「然而」。

---

16. There were so many disappointing aspects to this presentation; _____, it was depressing to watch.
    (A) to sum up
    (B) instead
    (C) otherwise
    (D) last but not least

16. 這個簡報有太多令人失望的地方了;總之,繼續看下去很令人沮喪。
    正確答案:(A)

 : 本題四個選項都是轉承副詞,所以最後從語意選出答案為 (A) 總之。(B) 表「取而代之地」。(C) 表「否則」。(D) 表「最後」。

17. _____ the professor was explaining the problem in another way, the students rudely began to get up and leave the classroom.
    (A) As long as
    (B) Until
    (C) While
    (D) Since

17. 當教授正用另一種方式解釋這個問題時，學生們無禮地起身開始離開教室。
    正確答案：(C)

 ：本題四個選項都是從屬連接詞，所以最後從語意選出答案為
    (C) 當。(A) 表「只要」。(B) 表「直到」。(D) 表「因為；自從」。

18. _____ Kingston met the client for lunch, he went to the dentist to have his teeth professionally whitened.
    (A) When
    (B) Before
    (C) Because of
    (D) In spite of

18. Kingston 去跟客戶碰面吃午餐之前，他先去了牙醫診所美白牙齒。
    正確答案：(B)

 ：本題考從屬連接詞。因為空格後方有兩個完整的句子，因此要
    以從屬連接詞連接兩個句子，此時 (A)(B) 符合，所以最後由
    語意選出答案為 (B) 在～之前。(A) 表「當」。(C) 表「因為」，
    後方接名詞。(D) 表「儘管」，後方接名詞。

19. The retirement package for this position is excellent; _____, it has flexible scheduling.
    (A) in addition to
    (B) as a result
    (C) to begin with
    (D) moreover

19. 這個職位的退休福利很好；此外，它的工時很彈性。

正確答案：(D)

：從空格前方的分號以及後方的逗號可以判斷出要用轉承副詞，**(B)(C)(D)** 皆為轉承副詞，最後從語意選出答案為 **(D)** 此外。**(A)** 表「除了 ... 之外」，後方要接名詞。**(B)** 表「因此」。**(C)** 表「首先」。

20. My responsibility is to double check every order _____ it ships out.
    (A) since
    (B) because
    (C) before
    (D) although

20. 我的責任是在出貨前要複查清楚每一張訂單。

正確答案：(C)

：因為空格前後方都是完整句子，所以要用連接詞將兩個句子連接，本題四個選項皆為連接詞，最後從語意選出答案為 **(C)**。

♔ Unit 6

1. That this operating system will soon be replaced _____ a relief to all my co-workers.
   (A) is
   (B) has
   (C) are
   (D) were

1. 這個操作系統即將被替換掉讓我所有的同事感到輕鬆無比。
   正確答案：(A)

   > : That this operating system will soon be replaced 為名詞子句當主詞，因此動詞要用單數，所以答案選 (A)。

2. I doubt _____ all these old files will be saved when we move to the new building.
   (A) this
   (B) what
   (C) whether
   (D) that

2. 我懷疑當我們搬到新大樓後，這些舊檔案是否會被保存下來。
   正確答案：(C)

   > : whether all these old files will be saved when we move to the new building 為名詞子句當作 doubt 的受詞，所以答案選 (C)。

3. The congressman debriefed us all on _____ was in the new bill proposed by the President.
   (A) that
   (B) how
   (C) whether
   (D) what

3. 國會議員詢問我們關於總統所提議的新法案內容。

正確答案：(D)

: what was in the new bill proposed by the President 為名詞子句當作 on 的受詞，又因為空格本身要是名詞子句的主詞，故選具有名詞性質的 what 來做為名詞子句的主詞，所以答案選 (D)。

---

4. I doubt _____ we will have enough funds to finish this project.
   (A) that
   (B) what
   (C) why
   (D) whether

4. 我懷疑我們是否有足夠的資金來完成這個專案。

正確答案：(D)

: whether we will have enough funds to finish this project 為名詞子句當作 doubt 的受詞，所以答案選 (D)。

---

5. When you get the chance, would you mind describing _____ the advertising campaign will look like?
   (A) what
   (B) that
   (C) if
   (D) when

5. 有機會的話，你介意描述一下廣告活動是什麼樣子嗎？

正確答案：(A)

: what the advertising campaign will look like 為名詞子句當作 describe 的受詞，所以答案選 (A)。

6. Ken is worried about _____ we have tested the new software enough before releasing it.

(A) that

(B) what

(C) whether

(D) it

6. Ken 很擔心我們的新軟體在發行之前是否做過足夠的測試。

正確答案：(C)

> : whether we have tested the new software enough before releasing it 為名詞子句當作 about 的受詞，所以答案選 (C)。

7. _____ the boss will grant Joe some time off or not depends on how busy he thinks we will be during the holidays.

(A) If

(B) That

(C) What

(D) Whether

7. 老闆是否會給 Joe 休息一些時間取決於他認為我們在放假時有多忙碌。

正確答案：(D)

> : whether the boss will grant Joe some time off or not 為名詞子句當作主詞，因為有 or not，所以要選 whether 搭配 or not，因此答案選 (D)。

8. _____ the fourth quarter report exceeded expectations encouraged all the company employees.

(A) What

(B) That

(C) If

(D) Whether

8. 第四季的財報超出預期鼓舞了所有員工。

正確答案：(B)

: that the fourth quarter report exceeded expectations 為名詞子句當作主詞，所以答案選 (B)。

---

9. We are debating _____ customers should be charged an extra fee for next-day shipping.
   (A) that
   (B) whether
   (C) what
   (D) this

9. 我們正在討論是否要對要求隔天出貨的客戶額外收費。
   正確答案：(B)

 : whether customers should be charged an extra fee for next-day shipping 為名詞子句當作 debate 的受詞，所以答案選 (B)。

---

10. The matter under discussion is _____ we can regain the trust of our customers.
   (A) that
   (B) what
   (C) why
   (D) how

10. 我們正在討論的事情是要如何重新取得客戶的信任。
   正確答案：(D)

 : how we can regain the trust of our customers 為名詞子句當作主詞補語，所以答案選 (D)。

11. I have to acknowledge the fact _____ his idea is more innovative than mine.
    (A) whether
    (B) if
    (C) that
    (D) why

11. 我必須承認他的想法比我的創新。
    正確答案：(C)

> : that his idea is more innovative than mine 為名詞子句當作 the fact 的同位語，所以答案選 (C)。

12. I want to underline the fact _____ safety is our major concern when it comes to making a new product.
    (A) that
    (B) when
    (C) whether
    (D) where

12. 我想要強調，說到製造新產品時，安全是我們主要關心的事情。
    正確答案：(A)

> : that safety is our major concern when it comes to making a new product 為名詞子句當作 the fact 的同位語，所以答案選 (A)。

13. The results of the survey show _____ consumers think the quality of a product is more important than its price.
    (A) whether
    (B) that
    (C) if
    (D) when

13. 這份調查的結果顯示消費者認為產品品質比價格更重要。
    正確答案：(B)

: that consumers think the quality of a product is more important than its price 為名詞子句當作 show 的受詞，所以答案選 (B)。

---

14. Since our boss is quite demanding, I don't know _____ your performance lived up to his expectations.
    (A) that
    (B) if
    (C) why
    (D) where

14. 因為我們老闆要求很高，所以我不知道你的表現是否有符合他的期望。

正確答案：(B)

 : if your performance lived up to his expectations 為名詞子句當作 know 的受詞，所以答案選 (B)。

---

15. It is predicted _____ 70 percent of manual jobs will be taken over by robots in the near future.
    (A) what
    (B) whether
    (C) if
    (D) that

15. 有人預測在不久的將來，百分之七十的勞力工作將由機器人代勞。

正確答案：(D)

 : it 為虛主詞，that 70 percent of manual jobs will be taken over by robots in the near future 為名詞子句當作語意上的真主詞，所以答案選 (D)。

16. Since most people now get their news from the Internet, it is no surprise _____ our print division will be closed.
    (A) that
    (B) whether
    (C) if
    (D) what

16. 因為現在大部分的人都從網路上取得資訊，所以我們印刷部門會關閉也不令人意外。
    正確答案：(A)

> : it 為虛主詞，that our print division will be closed 為名詞子句當作語意上的真主詞，所以答案選 (A)。

---

17. The problem with your proposal is _____ it is too impractical.
    (A) why
    (B) that
    (C) if
    (D) whether

17. 你的提案的問題就在於它太不實際了。
    正確答案：(B)

> : that it is too impractical 為名詞子句當作主詞補語補充說明主詞 the problem，所以答案選 (B)。

---

18. We take pride in the fact _____ our company has an extremely diverse work force.
    (A) when
    (B) if
    (C) what
    (D) that

18. 我們對於我們公司有多元的員工團隊引以為傲。
    正確答案：(D)

: that our company has an extremely diverse work force 為名詞子句當作 the fact 的同位語,所以答案選 (D)。

19. Alice only has two weeks of training, so I don't think _____ she is able to handle this on her own.
    (A) whether
    (B) when
    (C) that
    (D) where

19. Alice 只受過兩週的訓練,所以我認為她沒有能力獨自處理這件事。
    正確答案:(C)

 : that she is able to handle this on her own 為名詞子句當作 think 的受詞,所以答案選 (C)。

20. _____ Lawrence had been dismissed from his duties as supervisor was shocking to his wife.
    (A) That
    (B) Whether
    (C) If
    (D) When

20. Lawrence 被免除主管職位的事情讓他老婆很震驚。
    正確答案:(A)

 : that Lawrence had been dismissed from his duties as supervisor 為名詞子句當主詞,所以答案選 (A)。

♛ Unit 7

1. She always insists that her work schedule is worse than _____.
   (A) ours
   (B) our
   (C) us
   (D) we

1. 她總是堅稱說她的工作日程表比我們的還要糟。

   正確答案：(A)

    ：ours 在此代替了 our work schedule，所以答案選 (A)。

---

2. She didn't give _____ enough time to finish the project.
   (A) her own
   (B) I
   (C) herself
   (D) hers

2. 她沒有給自己足夠的時間來完成這個專案。

   正確答案：(C)

    ：因空格前是動詞，可知空格內為受詞；而句子主詞是 she，因此當受詞也是同一人時會用反身代名詞 herself，所以答案選 (C)。選項 (B) I 應改為 me。

---

3. The storage space in this warehouse is ten times bigger than _____ of what we had at our shop.
   (A) this
   (B) that
   (C) those
   (D) these

3. 這個倉庫的儲藏空間比之前我們店裡的要大十倍。

   正確答案：(B)

：依題意，空格表示前面提到的 the storage space，因此空格內要填入代名詞。因為 the storage space 是不可數名詞，所以要用 that 代替，答案選 (B)。

4. Little of what Kim says _____ any real importance.
   (A) have
   (B) is
   (C) were
   (D) has

4. Kim 所説的話沒有甚麼重要性。
   正確答案：(D)

 ：little 表「幾乎沒有」，是不可數的代名詞，因此動詞要搭配單數；而表示「重要的」是用「have... importance」或是「be 動詞 + important」，所以答案選 (D)。

5. Few of the warnings regarding our financial insolvency _____ heeded.
   (A) have
   (B) were
   (C) is
   (D) has

5. 關於我們公司破產的警告幾乎沒有被理會。
   正確答案：(B)

 ：few 表「幾乎沒有」，是複數的代名詞，因此動詞要搭配複數，另外 heed 表「注意」，因此要以被動態（be 動詞 + 過去分詞）表示警告被理會，所以答案選 (B)。

6. Several of my colleagues _____ registered for the upcoming seminar.
   (A) have
   (B) has
   (C) is
   (D) was

6. 我的幾個同事已經登記參加即將來臨的座談會了。

正確答案：(A)

：several 表「幾個」，是複數的代名詞，因此動詞要搭配複數，四個選項中只有 (A) 是複數，所以答案選 (A)。

6. None of the stolen money _____ in the apartment of the suspect.
   (A) were found
   (B) have found
   (C) has found
   (D) was found

7. 被偷走的錢都沒有在嫌犯的公寓中找到。

正確答案：(D)

：none 表「全無」，當後方名詞為複數時，動詞取複數；當後方名詞為不可數時動詞則搭配單數，the stolen money 為不可數名詞，所以動詞用單數，另外 money 和動詞 find 的關係應是被動關係，所以答案選 (D)。

8. Sharon makes _____ a point to keep up with all the latest technological developments.
   (A) that
   (B) this
   (C) it
   (D) which

8. Sharon 很重視自己是否有跟上科技發展的速度。

正確答案：(C)

: it 為虛受詞，真正的受詞是 to keep up with the latest technological developments，所以答案選 (C)。

---

9. I couldn't believe that _____ ideas were adopted instead of theirs.
   (A) myself
   (B) I
   (D) me
   (D) my

9. 我真是不敢相信是我的意見被採納而不是他們的。
   正確答案：(D)

    : 空格後方所接的 ideas 為名詞，因此前方要放所有格，所以答案選 (D)。

---

10. They _____ are to blame for this catastrophic failure.
    (A) themselves
    (B) them
    (C) their
    (D) theirs

10. 是他們自己造成了這次的重大失敗。
    正確答案：(A)

     : 句子的主詞是 they，因此要強調是主詞自己時要用主詞的反身代名詞，所以答案選 (A)。

---

11. I often lose _____ in a daydream during one of our boring conference calls.
    (A) me
    (B) myself
    (C) my
    (D) ourselves

11. 在進行我們其中一個無聊的電話會議時，我常會沉浸在自己的幻想中。
    正確答案：(B)

: lose oneself in ~ 表「全神貫注於某事中」，因為句子的主詞是 I，所以用 myself，因此答案選 (B)。

---

12. _____ file cabinets over there need all their contents to be transferred to digital files.

    (A) These

    (B) That

    (C) Those

    (D) This

12. 那兒的那些檔案櫃中的內容需要轉換成電子檔案。

    正確答案：(C)

 : 從 over there 可以得知東西距離較遠，所以用 that/those 表較遠的事物，又因為空格後方的名詞 file cabinets 是複數，所以用 those，因此答案選 (C)。

---

13. Each of these entrées _____ like a savory choice for dinner.

    (A) looks

    (B) look

    (C) were

    (D) has

13. 這些主菜中的每一道看起來都是很美味的晚餐選擇。

    正確答案：(A)

 : each 表「(眾多中的) 每一個」，視為單數，所以答案選 (A)。

---

14. A few of the customers' comments _____ valid concerns, but others were ridiculous.

    (A) is

    (B) were

    (C) has

    (D) was

14. 客人的評論中有些是合理的擔心，但是有些則是很荒謬的。

正確答案：(B)

 ：a few 表「一些」，為複數代名詞，動詞需搭配複數，所以答案選 (B)。

15. Some of the employees _____ eligible for the employee of the month award.

(A) is

(B) have

(C) has

(D) are

15. 這些員工中有些有資格可以領本月最佳員工獎。

正確答案：(D)

 ：some 可表複數名詞也可表不可數名詞，本句中後方的名詞 the employees 是複數，因此 some of the employees 還是表複數，此時動詞要搭配複數，(B)(D) 都是複數動詞，但是空格後方的 eligible 為形容詞，故前方要搭配 be 動詞，所以答案選 (D)。

16. _____ is my wish that you attain every goal that your heart desires.

(A) It

(B) That

(C) What

(D) This

16. 我希望你可以達成你心中所想的每一個目標。

正確答案：(A)

 ：it 為虛主詞，代替語意上的真主詞 that you attain every goal that your heart desires，所以答案選 (A)。

17. He finds _____ useful to have majored in Japanese in college.
    (A) that
    (B) it
    (C) this
    (D) himself

17. 他覺得在大學時主修日文是很有用處的。

正確答案：(B)

> 🧑 ：it 為虛受詞，代替語意上的真受詞 to have majored in Japanese in college，所以答案選 (B)。

18. _____ was my expectation that you would finish the financial report on your own.
    (A) That
    (B) This
    (C) It
    (D) What

18. 我期望你可以自己完成財務報告。

正確答案：(C)

> 🧑 ：it 為虛主詞，代替語意上的真主詞 that you would finish the financial report on your own，所以答案選 (C)。

19. We make _____ our mission to produce safe quality strollers for a fair price.
    (A) that
    (B) it
    (C) this
    (D) X

19. 生產安全品質好、價格又合理的嬰兒推車是我們的使命。

正確答案：(B)

：it 為虛受詞，代替語意上的真受詞 to produce safe quality strollers for a fair price，所以答案選 (B)。

---

20. One of the most important steps when you deal with any problem is the acceptance that _____ is real.
    (A) he
    (B) she
    (C) they
    (D) it

20. 當你在處理任何問題時，最重要的步驟之一就是要接受問題是真實存在的。

    正確答案：(D)

：it 在此代替前方提過的 any problem，所以答案選 (D)。

👑 Unit 8

1. I find your actions _____ reckless, and I am suspending your driver's license.
   (A) shockingly
   (B) shocking
   (C) shocked
   (D) shock

1. 我發現你的行為非常魯莽輕率，我要吊銷你的駕照。
   正確答案：(A)

   > 🙎‍♀️：空格後方已經有形容詞 reckless，因此要用副詞修飾形容詞，所以答案選 (A)。

2. Your _____ pursuit of your dream has resulted in your getting this awesome position.
   (A) relented
   (B) relent
   (C) relentlessly
   (D) relentless

2. 你持續不停追求你的夢想使你得以獲得這個很棒的職位。
   正確答案：(D)

   > 🙎‍♀️：空格後方的 pursuit 是名詞，因此用形容詞修飾名詞，所以答案選 (D)。relentless 表「持續強烈的」。

3. Tom _____ adores Regina, but he is still not sure whether she wants to marry him.
   (A) deep
   (B) deeply
   (C) depth
   (D) deepen

3. Tom 深愛著 Regina，但是他不確定她是否想嫁給他。

正確答案：(B)

 : 空格後方的 adore 是動詞，因此用副詞修飾一般動詞，所以答案選 (B)。

---

4. He _____ late for conference calls since he is busy placing orders for customers.
   (A) usually is
   (B) is ever
   (C) is usually
   (D) never is
4. 因為他忙著為客戶處理訂單，電話會議他經常晚到。
   正確答案：(C)

: 頻率副詞 usually 要放在 be 動詞後方，所以答案選 (C)。

---

5. The child nearly drowned after falling into the _____ end of the swimming pool.
   (A) deep
   (B) depth
   (C) deeply
   (D) deepen
5. 在跌進游泳池的最深處時，這個小孩差點溺死。
   正確答案：(A)

: 空格後方的 end 是名詞，因此用形容詞修飾名詞，所以答案選 (A)。

---

6. He _____ missed out on his opportunity to travel abroad for business due to attending his child's graduation ceremony.
   (A) near
   (B) highly
   (C) deeply
   (D) nearly

6. 因為參加小孩的畢業典禮,他差一點錯過了出國洽公的機會。
正確答案:(D)

：空格後方的 missed 是動詞,因此用副詞修飾動詞,本題四選項皆為副詞,因此最後從語意選出答案為 (D)。

7. Mark looked at his _____ résumé, which was completely void of experience.
(A) compatible
(B) impartial
(C) imperfect
(D) periodic

7. Mark 看著自己不完美的履歷,上面完全沒有經歷可言。
正確答案:(C)

：空格後方的 résumé 是名詞,因此用形容詞修飾名詞,本題四選項皆為形容詞,因此最後從語意選出答案為 (C) 不完美的。(A) 相容的。(B) 公正的。(D) 週期的。

8. The children's car seats need to be fastened _____ to the seats or they will fly forward in case of an accident.
(A) securely
(B) secure
(C) security
(D) be secure

8. 兒童安全座椅必須牢牢地固定在座位上,否則一旦發生意外,他們會往前飛出去。
正確答案:(A)

：空格前方的 be fastened 是被動語態,因此用副詞修飾過去分詞,所以答案選 (A) 牢固地。

9. Eighty percent of the villagers object _____ to the construction of a sports arena.
   (A) strong
   (B) strength
   (C) strengthen
   (D) strongly

9. 百分之八十的村民都強烈反對體育場館的興建。
   正確答案：(D)

: 空格前方的 object 是動詞，因此用副詞修飾一般動詞，所以答案選 (D) 強烈地。

---

10. During the outbreak of Ebola, many countries are prohibiting travel to the most _____ affected regions of Africa.
    (A) heavy
    (B) heavily
    (C) repeated
    (D) repeat

10. 在伊波拉爆發期間，很多國家都禁止前往疫情最嚴重的非洲疫區旅遊。
    正確答案：(B)

: 空格後方的 affected 是過去分詞，因此要用副詞修飾，所以答案選 (B) 嚴重地。

---

11. I have purchased a transponder to _____ pay the toll when I drive past this toll booth twice a day.
    (A) automatically
    (B) automatic
    (C) automation
    (D) automated

11. 我買了一個感應器可以在我一天兩次行經收費站時自動扣款。
    正確答案：(A)

：空格後方的 pay 是動詞，因此要用副詞修飾，所以答案選 (A) 自動地。

---

12. Jennifer has the problem of asthma, which makes it _____ for her to run for too long.
    (A) hardly
    (B) hard
    (C) harden
    (D) hardness

12. Jennifer 有氣喘的問題，這使得她無法長時間跑步。

正確答案：(B)

：句型 make it + O.C. + for somebody + to Vr. 中的 O.C. 要用形容詞或名詞，所以答案選 (B) 困難的。(A) hardly 是副詞，表「幾乎不」。(C) harden 是動詞，表「(使)變硬；(使)變嚴厲或堅強」。(D) hardness 是名詞，表「硬度」。

---

13. Since this disease is _____ infectious, patients infected with it should be isolated.
    (A) high
    (B) height
    (C) highly
    (D) higher

13. 因為這疾病具有高度傳染力，任何染上的人都應該被隔離。

正確答案：(C)

：空格後方的 infectious 是形容詞，所以要用副詞修飾，因此答案選 (C) 高度地。(A) high 雖然也可以當副詞，但是用於實際高度，而非抽象程度。(B) height 是名詞，表「高度」。(D) higher 是 high 的比較級。

14. Sandy is a _____ aggressive salesperson; she will do whatever she can do to achieve her goal.
    (A) fair
    (B) fairness
    (C) fairly
    (D) fairy

14. Sandy 是個相當有野心的人，她會盡一切能力達到自己的目標。
    正確答案：(C)

> : 空格後方的 aggressive 是形容詞，所以要用副詞修飾，因此
> 答案選 (C) 相當地。(A) fair 是形容詞，表「公平的；相當大的；
> 相當好的；(天氣)晴朗的」。(B) fairness 是名詞，表「公平」。
> (D) fairy 是名詞，表「小仙子；小精靈」。

15. No matter how nervous you are, you have to try your best to stay _____ in an interview.
    (A) calm
    (B) calmly
    (C) calmness
    (D) quietly

15. 面試時，不論你有多緊張，你都得盡力保持冷靜。
    正確答案：(A)

> : stay 表「保持」時，後方要接形容詞，因此答案選 (A) 冷靜的。
> (B) calmly 是副詞，表「鎮靜地」。(C) calmness 是名詞，表「冷
> 靜；鎮靜」。(D) quietly 是副詞，表「迅速地」。

16. The old man was forced to _____ sell his convertible when the bank demanded that he immediately repay his loan.
    (A) quick
    (B) quickly
    (C) quicken
    (D) quickness

徐薇教你懂新多益文法

16. 當銀行要求這個老人立即付貸款時，他被迫要很快賣掉自己的敞篷車。
正確答案：(B)

：空格後方的 sell 是動詞，因此要用副詞修飾，所以答案選 (B) 快速地。

17. Each member of our department is asked to submit their _____ analysis of the quarterly sales figures.
(A) respectable
(B) respectively
(C) respectful
(D) respective

17. 我們部門的每個人都被要求要交出各自的季銷售數字的分析報告。
正確答案：(D)

：空格後方的 analysis 是名詞，因此要用形容詞修飾，(A)(C)(D) 都是形容詞，所以再從語意去選擇答案，(A) respectable 表「可敬的」。(C) respectful 表「表示尊敬的」。(D) respective 表「各自的」。(B) respectively 是 respective 的副詞。

18. The manager was _____ impressed with the newcomer's ability to handle such a complicated case.
(A) particular
(B) particularity
(C) particularly
(D) particularities

18. 經理對於這位新進員工處理如此複雜案子的能力特別感到印象深刻。
正確答案：(C)

：在 be 動詞與過去分詞的中間只能放副詞，所以答案選 (C) 尤其；特別地。(A) particular 是形容詞，表「特定的；苛求的；挑剔的」。(B) particularity 是名詞，表「精確；詳細」。(D) particularities 是名詞，表「詳細情況」。

19. Being a business analyst is _____ more relaxing than being a programmer!
    (A) definitely
    (B) definite
    (C) definitive
    (D) definition

19. 當一名商業分析師必定比當一名程式設計師來得輕鬆。

正確答案：(A)

: 空格後方的 relaxing 為形容詞，因此要用副詞修飾，所以答案選 (A) 必定。(B) definite 是形容詞，表「確定的」。(C) definitive 是形容詞，表「最終的；確鑿的」。(D) definition 是名詞，表「定義」。

20. If you can't be _____, I can't trust you to be a team leader.
    (A) punctually
    (B) punctual
    (C) punctuality
    (D) punctuation

20. 如果你無法準時，我實在無法信任你當領導者。

正確答案：(B)

: be 動詞後方要接形容詞，所以答案選 (B) 準時的。(A) punctually 是副詞，表「準時地」。(C) punctuality 是名詞，表「準時」。(D) punctuation 是名詞，表「標點符號」。

👑 Unit 9

1. Tricia is the executive _____ donated thousands of dollars to the political campaign.
   (A) which
   (B) who
   (C) whose
   (D) whom

1. Tricia 就是捐了數千元給那場政治活動的主管。
   正確答案：(B)

> 👩 ：空格前方的先行詞 executive (n. 主管) 為人，後方又緊接動詞 (donated)，因此要主格關代，所以答案選 (B)。

2. This author is the one _____ I spoke so highly of last week.
   (A) where
   (B) which
   (C) whose
   (D) whom

2. 這位作者就是我上週給予高度評價的人。
   正確答案：(D)

> 👩 ：空格前方的先行詞 the one 在此指 the author (作者)，後方的結構為主詞加上動詞的結構，因此要用受格關代，所以答案選 (D)。

3. The decorative bottles _____ used to be displayed atop the bar are now gone.
   (A) which
   (B) who
   (C) whom
   (D) whose

3. 以前放在吧台上方的那些裝飾用的瓶子現在都不見了。

正確答案：(A)

：空格前方的先行詞 the decorative bottles 為事物，後方又緊接動詞 (used)，因此要用主格關代，所以答案選 (A)。

4. This is the worst keynote speaker _____ I have ever heard.
   (A) whom
   (B) that
   (C) whose
   (D) which

4. 這是我聽過最糟的主要演說者。

正確答案：(B)

：先行詞前方有最高級 (the worst)，關代只能用 that，所以答案選 (B)。

5. I often ask Anthony about subjects of _____ he has no knowledge.
   (A) which
   (B) that
   (C) whom
   (D) whose

5. 我常會問 Anthony 一些他不懂的事情。

正確答案：(A)

：本句先行詞 subjects 是表事物的名詞，而空格前方有介系詞 of，關代不能用 that，所以答案選 (A) which。

6. Mary went to the press conference immediately with _____ she had discovered.
   (A) that
   (B) which
   (C) what
   (D) whom

6. Mary 帶著她所發現的東西立即去參加記者會。

正確答案：(C)

：複合關代 what 在此代替了 the things + which，the things 作為 with 的受詞，which 則引導形容詞子句修飾先行詞 the things，所以答案選 (C)。

---

7. Henry's Bar is one of the places _____ I frequently meet co-workers for happy hour after work.

   (A) when

   (B) where

   (C) which

   (D) that

7. Henry's Bar 是我在下班後常和同事小聚度過歡樂時光的地方之一。

正確答案：(B)

：先行詞 the places 表地方，關係副詞 where 在此代替了 at which，所以答案選 (B)。

---

8. When the boss gets furious, it is one of those times _____ you should just keep silent.

   (A) why

   (B) that

   (C) where

   (D) when

8. 當老闆很生氣時，那就是你該保持沉默的時候。

正確答案：(D)

：先行詞 the times 表時間，關係副詞 when 在此代替了 in which，所以答案選 (D)。

9. No one could comprehend the reason _____ the factory suddenly shut down after being the major employer of this small town for forty years.
   (A) when
   (B) why
   (C) where
   (D) which

9. 沒有人了解這個在過去四十年來一直是這個小鎮主要雇主的工廠為何會突然關閉的原因。

   正確答案：(B)

   :先行詞 the reason 表原因，關係副詞 why 在此代替了 for which，所以答案選 (B)。

10. This engineering job is the only one _____ I have ever had.
    (A) that
    (B) which
    (C) when
    (D) whom

10. 這個工程設計工作是我從以前到現在唯一的一個工作。

    正確答案：(A)

    :先行詞前方有 the only，關代只能用 that，所以答案選 (A)。

11. _____ our company lacks is creativity.
    (A) That
    (B) When
    (C) Which
    (D) What

11. 我們公司缺乏的是創意。

    正確答案：(D)

：本句動詞為 is，可知 is 之前是句子主詞；而空格後是主詞加動詞的結構，表示缺少代替受詞的關係代名詞；因此空格要填入兼具先行詞和關代功能的複合關代 what。what our company lacks = the thing which our company lacks 表示「我們公司所缺乏的東西」，因此答案選 (D)。

---

12. Ivy, _____ is my assistant, will show you around later.
    (A) that
    (B) who
    (C) which
    (D) whom

12. 我的助理 Ivy 稍後會帶您參觀參觀。
    正確答案：(B)

：空格前方有逗號時，關代不能用 that，另外空格後方緊接動詞 is，因此要用關代主格，所以答案選 (B)。

---

13. The advice _____ my supervisor has given me for the past five years did help me climb up the corporate ladder faster than other colleagues.
    (A) when
    (B) whom
    (C) that
    (D) whose

13. 我的主管在過去五年所給我的建議確實幫助了我在公司內部晉升比別的同事快。
    正確答案：(C)

：先行詞 the advice 為表事物的名詞，另外空格後方的結構為主詞加上動詞，因此要用關代受格 which 或 that，所以答案選 (C)。

14. Thanks to the ad _____ successfully appealed to most young consumers, our new product brought in a big profit last year.
    (A) who
    (B) where
    (C) when
    (D) which

14. 多虧成功吸引多數年輕人的那個廣告，我們的新產品在去年賺進大筆利潤。
    正確答案：(D)

> : 先行詞 the ad 為表事物的名詞，另外空格後方緊接了動詞 (appealed)，因此要用關代主格 which 或 that，所以答案選 (D)。

15. This marketing specialist published many articles, some of _____ are about the effective ways to make profits.
    (A) them
    (B) which
    (C) that
    (D) whom

15. 這位行銷專家發表了很多文章，其中有一些是關於獲利的有效方法的。
    正確答案：(B)

> : 關代本身兼具代名詞以及連接詞的雙重作用，some of which 在此代替了 and some of them，所以答案選 (B)。

16. After hours of discussion, the committee finally put together a plan _____ helps to boost the sales.
    (A) who
    (B) whom
    (C) that
    (D) where

16. 經過幾小時的討論後，委員會終於制定了一個能有助於刺激業績的計畫。
    正確答案：(C)

：先行詞 a plan 為事物，又空格後方緊接動詞 helps，因此要用關代主格 which 或 that，所以答案選 (C)。

---

17. It's better to buy _____ you need in the suburbs since the city has a 9% sales tax.
    (A) what
    (B) that
    (C) which
    (D) when

17. 你最好在郊區買你需要的東西，因為都市有百分之九的銷售稅。
    正確答案：(A)

：複合關代 what 在此代替了 the things + which，the things 作為 buy 的受詞，which 則引導形容詞子句修飾先行詞 the things，所以答案選 (A)。

---

18. I am grateful for the hospitality of your brother, Vincent _____ let us stay at his place for a week while our electricity was out.
    (A) who
    (B) that
    (C) , who
    (D) which

18. 我很感激你哥哥 Vincent 的好客，他在我們停電時讓我們住在他家一星期。
    正確答案：(C)

：先行詞 Vincent 為專有名詞，因此要用非限定用法的形容詞子句，也就是關代前方要加上逗點，所以答案選 (C)。

19. Would you please stop cracking jokes _____ are politically incorrect?
   (A) what
   (B) that
   (C) who
   (D) whose

19. 可以請你不要再開這種政治不正確的玩笑嗎？

正確答案：(B)

 ：先行詞 jokes 為事物，因此要用 which 或 that 當關代，所以答案選 (B)。

. . . .

20. Little did I expect that I would see the day _____ my face was plastered on a billboard.
   (A) where
   (B) which
   (C) that
   (D) when

20. 我一點都沒有想過我的臉會出現在大型廣告看板上。

正確答案：(D)

 ：先行詞 the day 表時間，關係副詞 when 在此代替了 on which，所以答案選 (D)。

♛ Unit 10

1. _____ position you are in, the more responsibilities you have to take.
   (A) The higher
   (B) Higher
   (C) Highest
   (D) The highest

1. 你的職位越高,你要承擔的責任就越多。
   正確答案:(A)

> :本題考固定用語「the + 比較級~,the + 比較級~」表示「越 ...,就越 ...」,所以答案選 (A)。

---

2. The subway service in this city is far _____ the bus service.
   (A) superior than
   (B) better to
   (C) superior
   (D) superior to

2. 這個城市的地鐵服務遠比公車服務好。
   正確答案:(D)

> :本題考固定用語 be superior to~ 表「優於 ...」,所以答案選 (D)。

---

3. Cheryl's cake looks _____ mine.
   (A) as savory like
   (B) as savory as
   (C) more savory as
   (D) less savory as

3. Cheryl 的蛋糕看起來和我的 一樣美味。
   正確答案:(B)

: 本題考原級和比較級的基本句型，如果是原級要用 as savory as，比較級要用 more savory than，所以答案選 (B)。

---

4. Samantha has demonstrated that she has _____ as Frank.
   (A) as much ability
   (B) more ability
   (C) as more ability
   (D) as ability

4. Samantha 已經展現出她和 Frank 能力一樣好。
   正確答案：(A)

 : 從空格後方出現的 as 可以得知本題考原級的比較，表「一樣多的 ...」時要用「as many 複數名詞 as」或是「as much 不可數名詞 as」，所以答案選 (A)。

---

5. Once I discovered that my dentist was _____ the one across the street, I switched immediately.
   (A) worse to
   (B) inferior than
   (C) inferior to
   (D) superior to

5. 我一發現我的牙醫比對街的那位糟的時候，我便立刻換到那邊去了。
   正確答案：(C)

 : 本題考固定用語 be inferior to ~ 表「劣於 ...」，從本題語意判斷答案應選 (C)。

---

6. Of all the exceptional athletes who have ever attended this school, Greg is _____.
   (A) most outstanding
   (B) the most outstanding
   (C) more outstanding
   (D) the more outstanding

6. Greg 是所有就讀過這所學校的優異運動員中最傑出的。
   正確答案：(B)

 ：從句中的 of all~ 可以判斷出要搭配最高級，所以答案應選 (B)。

---

7. Maggie is _____ person in this department at handling customer complaints.
   (A) least capable
   (B) more capable
   (C) the less capable
   (D) the least capable

7. Maggie 是這個部門中最沒有能力處理客人投訴的。
   正確答案：(D)

 ：從句中的 in this department 可以判斷出要搭配最高級，另外形容詞的最高級前方一定要有 the，所以答案選 (D)。

---

8. The technological capability of smart phones is getting _____.
   (A) better and better
   (B) best and best
   (C) the better and the better
   (D) the best and the best

8. 智慧型手機的技術功能力越來越好了。
   正確答案：(A)

 ：本題考句型「比較級 and 比較級」表「越來越 ...」，所以答案選 (A)。

9. Doing something is _____ than watching TV.

(A) as constructive

(B) more constructive

(C) the most constructive

(D) less more constructive

9. 做點什麼事都比看電視來的有建設性。

正確答案：(B)

> ：從空格後方出現的 than 可以得知本題考比較級的句型，表更
> 有建設性用 more constructive than，表更沒有建設性用 less
> constructive than，所以答案選 (B)。

10. You had better drive _____ on icy roads.

(A) as careful as possible

(B) as carefulness as possible

(C) as carefully as possible

(D) more carefully as possible

10. 在結冰的路面上開車你最好要盡可能小心。

正確答案：(C)

> ：本題考句型 as ～ as one can = as ～ as possible 表「盡可
> 能地 ...」；另外因為空格前方的 drive 為動詞，要用副詞修飾，
> 所以答案選 (C)。

11. I have to acknowledge the fact that you are _____ at programming software than I.

(A) good

(B) better

(C) well

(D) more good

11. 我得承認在軟體設計上你比我厲害。

正確答案：(B)

: 從空格後方出現的 than 可以得知本題考比較級的句型，good 或 well 的比較級都是 better，所以答案選 (B)。

12. In order to support your methodology, you need to compile _____.
    (A) as many evidence as possible
    (B) more evidence as you can
    (C) as much evidence as possible
    (D) as much evidence as you are

12. 你必須匯集盡可能多的證據來支持你的方法論。
    正確答案：(C)

: 本題考句型 as ～ as one can = as ～ as possible 表「盡可能地 ...」；另外因為 evidence(證據) 為不可數名詞，所以前面要加上 much，因此答案選 (C)。

13. The user interface of our new software is not _____ to navigate as our old versions.
    (A) as easy
    (B) as easily
    (C) more easily
    (D) easier

13. 我們新軟體的使用者介面沒有像我們舊版的一樣容易瀏覽。
    正確答案：(A)

: 從題目中的 as our old versions 可以得知本題考原級的句型，另外因為空格前方的動詞是 be 動詞，因此要用形容詞的原級，所以答案選 (A)。

14. Emma Johnson, _____ of the two candidates, has a better chance of landing this secretarial job.
    (A) younger
    (B) youngest
    (C) the younger
    (D) the youngest

14. 這兩位候選人中較年輕的 Emma Johnson 較有可能得到這個秘書工作。
    正確答案：(C)

 ：從句中的 of the two candidates 可以判斷出要搭配「the + 比較級」表「兩者中較 ... 的」，所以答案選 (C)。

---

15. This smartphone is _____ as that robot.
    (A) twice as expensive
    (B) twice more expensive
    (C) as expensive twice
    (D) as twice expensive

15. 這隻智慧型手機的價錢是那個機器人的兩倍高。
    正確答案：(A)

 ：本題考倍數句型「倍數詞 + as 原級 as」或「倍數詞 + 比較級 + than」，所以答案選 (A)。

♛ Unit 11

1. The phone has been ringing nonstop _____ this morning.
   (A) since
   (B) from
   (C) on
   (D) at

1. 電話從早上就一直響到現在沒停過。

   正確答案：(A)

   > 🧑 ：從句中動詞用現在完成進行式 (has been ringing) 可以得知要選「since + 過去時間點」表從過去一直持續到現在的動作或狀態，所以答案選 (A)。

2. The unpopular policy of employees having only fifteen minutes for lunch has been continued by management, _____ the outcries from staff members.
   (A) against
   (B) except
   (C) besides
   (D) despite

2. 儘管員工有所不滿，管理階層還是要繼續執行令人痛恨的員工午餐時間只有十五分鐘的政策。

   正確答案：(D)

   > 🧑 ：本題四個選項皆為介系詞，因此從語意選出答案為 (D) 儘管。

3. The bicycle path runs _____ the banks of the Meyers River.
   (A) against
   (B) in
   (C) at
   (D) along

3. 自行車道沿著 Meyers 河的河岸穿行。

正確答案：(D)

：本題四個選項皆為介系詞，因此從語意選出答案為 (D) 沿著。

---

4. The veteran soldier succeeded _____ all odds by getting a law degree and becoming a famous lawyer.
   (A) despite
   (B) amid
   (C) against
   (D) except

4. 這個退伍軍人克服一切困難成功地取得法學學位並成為了一位有名的律師。

正確答案：(C)

：本題考固定用語 against all odds 表「儘管困難重重」，因此選出答案為 (C)。

---

5. _____ (for) Greg, none of the nurses on staff have received training on how to use the new X-ray machine.
   (A) Except
   (B) Despite
   (C) Besides
   (D) Following

5. 除了 Greg 之外，這些護士中沒有人受過如何操作這台新 X 光機的訓練。

正確答案：(A)

：從句中的 none of the nurses 可以得知 Greg 是例外，因此選出答案為 (A)。

6. In order to keep fit, I make it a rule to jog from my house _____ the park in the suburbs every day.
(A) at
(B) to
(C) over
(D) under

6. 為了保持健康，我養成習慣每天從我家慢跑到郊區的公園。
正確答案：(B)

> 👩 ：表「從 ... 到 ...」用 from ~ to ~，因此選出答案為 (B)。

7. _____ the violent earthquake, many houses were reduced to rubble.
(A) Throughout
(B) Following
(C) Behind
(D) Beside

7. 在強烈的地震之後，很多房子被夷為平地。
正確答案：(B)

> 👩 ：從語意可以得知房子被夷為平地應是在地震過後，所以答案選 (B) following 表「在 ... 之後」。

8. The EU summit this year will be held _____ Greece.
(A) at
(B) along
(C) in
(D) below

8. 今年的歐盟高峰會將在希臘舉行。
正確答案：(C)

> 👩 ：Greece(希臘) 是國家名稱，前方介系詞要用 in，所以答案選 (C)。

9. The new property we are thinking about purchasing is _____ Franklin Avenue.
   (A) on
   (B) in
   (C) beneath
   (D) through

9. 我們正考慮要購買的新地產位在 Franklin 大道上。
   正確答案：(A)

> ：街道名稱前面的介系詞要用 on，所以答案選 (A)。

....

10. Cameron works _____ dawn every day, coming home only to sleep.
    (A) in
    (B) under
    (C) till
    (D) around

10. Cameron 每天工作到清晨，回家就只是睡覺而已。
    正確答案：(C)

> ：till 表「直到」，等同 until，till dawn 表直到清晨，所以答案選 (C)。

👑 Unit 12

1. We _____ lose this client if we can't provide what he needs.
   (A) might
   (B) should
   (C) need
   (D) dare

1. 如果我們不能給客戶所需要的，我們就有可能會失去他。
   正確答案：(A)

：從空格後方接動詞原形 (lose) 可以得知要放助動詞，(C)(D) 當助動詞時要用於否定句或疑問句，所以不考慮。最後從語意選出答案為 (A) 可能。

---

2. High employee turnover _____ lead to a drop in productivity.
   (A) dare
   (B) needn't
   (C) may
   (D) should

2. 員工替換率太高有可能導致生產力的下降。
   正確答案：(C)

：從空格後方接動詞原形 (lead) 可以得知要放助動詞，(A) 當助動詞時要用於否定句或疑問句。(B) 表「不必」，(C) 表「可能」，(D) 表「應該」，因此從語意選出答案為 (C) 最適合。

---

3. You _____ such sensitive customer data on your desk last night.
   (A) should leave
   (B) shouldn't have left
   (C) should have left
   (D) shouldn't leave

3. 你昨晚不該將這麼敏感的客戶資料放在桌上。
   正確答案：(B)

：因為時間副詞為過去時間 (last night)，(A) 和 (D) 用於現在或未來，所以不符合文法結構。最後再從語意選出答案為 (B)。

4. The recent downturn in the economy _____ be the reason why our product sales have sharply decreased.
   (A) need
   (B) dare
   (C) ought
   (D) could

4. 最近的經濟不景氣有可能是導致我們產品銷售急遽下降的原因。
   正確答案：(D)

：從空格後方接動詞原形 (be) 可以得知要放助動詞，(A)(B) 當助動詞時要用於否定句或疑問句，所以不考慮。(C) 後方要接上 to 才能再接動詞原形，所以最後選出答案為 (D) 可能。

5. The bug in our computer software _____ delay our ability to process orders.
   (A) could
   (B) should
   (C) need
   (D) ought

5. 我們電腦軟體的缺陷有可能造成訂單處理的延宕。
   正確答案：(A)

：從空格後方接動詞原形 (delay) 可以得知要放助動詞，(C) 當助動詞時要用於否定句或疑問句，所以不考慮。(D) 後方要接上 to 才能再接動詞原形，最後從語意選出答案為 (A) 可能。

6. Completing several simple tasks successfully _____ boost the students' confidence.
   (A) should have
   (B) might
   (C) needn't
   (D) ought

6. 成功地完成幾個簡單的任務可能會提升學生們的信心。

   正確答案：(B)

   > 👩：從空格後方接動詞原形 (boost) 可以得知要放助動詞，(A) should have 後方不可接動詞原形，所以不考慮。(D) 後方要接上 to 才能再接動詞原形，最後從語意選出答案為 (B) 可能。

7. _____ you please stay on a few weeks longer until we get someone trained to do your job?
   (A) Should
   (B) Must
   (C) Would
   (D) Need

7. 在我們找到人接替你的工作前，可以請你再多待幾個星期嗎？

   正確答案：(C)

   > 👩：Would you please~? 是表客氣的請求，所以答案選 (C)。

8. In order to make good time, you _____ take the tunnel and not local roads.
   (A) must
   (B) ought
   (C) shouldn't have
   (D) need

8. 為了要快速抵達，你必須走隧道不要走地方道路。

   正確答案：(A)

: 從空格後方接動詞原形 (take) 可以得知要放助動詞。(B) 後方要接上 to 才能再接動詞原形，(C) shouldn't have 後方要接過去分詞。(D) 當助動詞時要用於否定句或疑問句，所以不考慮。所以答案選 (A) 必須。

---

9. Tom _____ the reports last night instead of attending the party.
   (A) should type
   (B) shouldn't type
   (C) shouldn't have typed
   (D) should have typed

9. Tom 昨晚應該要打好報告而不是去參加派對的。

　　正確答案：(D)

 : 因為時間副詞為過去時間 (last night)，(A) 和 (B) 用於現在或未來，所以不符合文法結構。最後再從語意選出答案為 (D)。

---

10. It is hard to say how much the uptick in the economy _____ impact us.
    (A) ought
    (B) will
    (C) should have
    (D) need

10. 經濟的復甦對我們的影響會有多大還說不準。

　　正確答案：(B)

 : 從句中的 It is hard to say~ 可以得知是在敍述未來事件，所以助動詞用 (B) will。

👑 Unit 13

1. _____ the merger, everyone in our department was laid off.
   (A) As a result of
   (B) Along with
   (C) Except for
   (D) Instead of

1. 因為合併的關係，我們部門的每個人都被裁員了。
   正確答案：(A)

   ：(A) 因為；(B) 連同；(C) 將 … 除外；(D) 而不是。

---

2. _____ you follow the office guidelines, you will have no problem getting a raise at your performance review.
   (A) Regardless of
   (B) Now that
   (C) As a result
   (D) As long as

2. 只要你遵守辦公室準則，你想要在績效評估時獲得加薪是不會有問題的。
   正確答案：(D)

   ：(A) 不管；(B) 既然；(C) 因此；(D) 只要。

---

3. My supervisor discussed the new business opportunity _____, detailing the role I might play in it.
   (A) at will
   (B) at length
   (C) at random
   (D) at once

3. 我的主管詳細地闡述了新的生意機會，詳細地說明我可能會扮演的角色。
   正確答案：(B)

: (A) 隨心所欲地；(B) 詳細地；(C) 隨機地；(D) 立刻。

---

4. Our entire team _____ Anna's story that she had not been manipulating our financials.
   (A) backed up
   (B) applied for
   (C) appealed to
   (D) accounted for

4. 我們全部的人都相信 Anna 並沒有操弄公司財務。
   正確答案：(A)

 : (A) 支持；(B) 申請；(C) 吸引；(D) 解釋；佔 (比例)。

---

5. This company _____ providing great customer service along with competitive prices.
   (A) is keen on
   (B) is known for
   (C) is involved in
   (D) is equipped with

5. 這家公司以提供良好的客戶服務以及有競爭力的價格而聞名。
   正確答案：(B)

 : (A) 喜歡；對 ... 熱中；(B) 以 ... 聞名；(C) 涉及；參與；(D) 有 ... 配備。

---

6. Mike _____ his own firing when he sent out an inflammatory email about the boss.
   (A) called for
   (B) approved of
   (C) carried out
   (D) brought about

6. Mike 因為寄出一封電子郵件言語攻擊老闆而遭到開除。
   正確答案：(D)

 ：(A) 需要 ...；呼籲 ...；要求 ...；(B) 贊成；(C) 實現 ...；執行 ...；
(D) 導致。

---

7. The company president insisted that all departments _____ one
   another better to increase efficiency and decrease mistakes.
   (A) comment on
   (B) come across
   (C) comply with
   (D) communicate with

7. 公司總裁堅持所有部門都要互相有更好的溝通以提升效率並減少錯誤。
   正確答案：(D)

 ：(A) 評論；(B) 偶然遇見或發現；(C) 遵守；(D) 和 ... 溝通。

---

8. Our supervisor always knows that he can _____ Kevin to work
   overtime whenever a deadline is approaching.
   (A) count on
   (B) contribute to
   (C) conform to
   (D) compete with

8. 我們主管知道當截止期限快到時，他總是可以仰賴 Kevin 加班以完成工作。
   正確答案：(A)

 ：(A) 依靠；(B) 貢獻 ...；促成 ...；為 ... 寫稿；(C) 順從 ...；遵
照 ...；(D) 和 ... 競爭。

9. Tom has _____ one of the foremost experts in software development.
   (A) drew up
   (B) developed into
   (C) come with
   (D) coincided with

9. Tom 已經成為軟體開發最頂尖的專家之一了。

正確答案：(B)

> : (A) 籌備 (計畫)；草擬；(B) 發展成 …；(C) 具備 …；
> (D) 與 … 同時發生。

- -

10. The reporter let the politician know _____ about the tough questions he would be asking.
   (A) in comparison
   (B) in all
   (C) in advance
   (D) in person

10. 記者讓這位政治人物事先知道他會提問的困難問題。

正確答案：(C)

> : (A) 相比之下；(B) 總計；(C) 事先；(D) 親自。

- -

11. _____ the university, we have devised an internship program to recruit future employees.
   (A) In conjunction with
   (B) In contrast to
   (C) In favor of
   (D) In reference to

11. 我們和這所大學合作設計了一套實習生方案以招募未來的員工。

正確答案：(A)

> 🧑: (A) 與 ... 聯合；(B) 和 ... 對比之下；(C) 贊成 ...；(D) 關於 ...。

12. _____ the scandal your company is associated with, we will take our business elsewhere.
    (A) In the event of
    (B) In light of
    (C) In case of
    (D) In place of

12. 有鑑於貴公司所涉及的醜聞，我們將和其他公司合作。
    正確答案：(B)

> 🧑: (A) 假如 ...；(B) 有鑑於 ...；(C) 假如 ...；(D) 取代 ...。

13. This email is to inform you that I am _____ your refund check for the malfunctioning camera you sent me.
    (A) in honor of
    (B) in response to
    (C) in receipt of
    (D) in order of

13. 這封電子郵件的目的是要通知您我已經收到了您所寄的有問題相機的退款支票。
    正確答案：(C)

> 🧑: (A) 向 ... 致敬；(B) 回應 ...；(C) 收到了 ...；(D) 按照 ... 順序。

14. The bug in our software is _____ being fixed.
    (A) in the face of
    (B) in terms of
    (C) in search of
    (D) in the process of

14. 我們軟體的問題正在修理階段。
    正確答案：(D)

：(A) 不顧 (困難等)；(B) 從 … 角度來看；(C) 尋找 …；
(D) 在 … 的過程中。

---

15. I expect you to _____ our contractor to make sure they are staying on schedule with the project.
    (A) kick out
    (B) inquire about
    (C) keep in touch with
    (D) kick off

15. 我希望你可以和我們承包商保持聯繫以確定案子的進度正常進行。
    正確答案：(C)

     ：(A) 開除；(B) 詢問；(C) 和 … 保持聯繫；(D) 開始；(足球比賽) 開球。

---

16. Steve _____ finish all the coding after two straight days of sitting in front of his computer.
    (A) objected to
    (B) felt free to
    (C) managed to
    (D) contributed to

16. 坐在電腦前整整兩天後，Steve 終於完成了所有的編碼。
    正確答案：(C)

     ：(A) 反對；(B) 隨意；(C) 做成某事；(D) 貢獻 …；促成 …；為 … 寫稿。

---

17. I called the restaurant _____ to order enough food for 50 people and was told it could not be ready so quickly.
    (A) on impulse
    (B) on short notice
    (C) on loan
    (D) on leave

17. 我打電話給餐廳希望能短時間之內準備夠五十人吃的食物,但是他們告訴我不可能在這麼短的時間內準備好。

正確答案:(B)

:(A) 一時衝動之下;(B) 倉促通知;(C) 借來的;(D) 在休假中。

---

18. We are _____ signing a deal that would lead to the opening of our first chain store in the suburbs.
   (A) on the basis of
   (B) on behalf of
   (C) in accordance with
   (D) on the edge of

18. 我們快要簽署一份讓我們可以在郊區開設第一家連鎖店的協議。

正確答案:(D)

:(A) 依據;(B) 代表;(C) 依照 … ;與 … 一致;(D) 在 … 邊緣。

---

19. _____ the reason, you have been late to work five times this month, and you will lose one vacation day for it.
   (A) Regardless of
   (B) Rather than
   (C) On the verge of
   (D) On behalf of

19. 不管你的理由是什麼,你這個月已經上班遲到五次了,為此你會被扣掉一天的休假。

正確答案:(A)

:(A) 不管;(B) 而不是;(C) 接近於 … ;幾乎要 … ;(D) 代表。

20. Bob has _____ our beloved mayor for eight years, and now he thinks it's time for him to step down.
    (A) set about
    (B) served as
    (C) registered for
    (D) referred to

20. Bob 擔任我們所敬愛的市長已經八年了，現在他覺得該是下台的時候了。
    正確答案：(B)

> 😊：(A) 開始做 ... ; (B) 擔任 ; (C) 註冊 ... ; 登記 ... ; (D) 提及 ; 參考。

21. Anyone who did not _____ early for the seminar will need to pay the full price of $US 70.
    (A) sit in
    (B) single out
    (C) sign up
    (D) set up

21. 沒有提早報名參加研討會的人都得付全額美金七十元。
    正確答案：(C)

> 😊：(A) 旁聽 ; 列席 ; (B) 挑出 ... ; (C) 登記 ; 報名 ; (D) 設立 ... ; 安排 ...。

22. Ken always _____ all the details, which is what separates him from average employees.
    (A) takes notice of
    (B) takes over
    (C) stands for
    (D) shops for

22. Ken 總是會注意到細節，這也就是他和一般員工不一樣的地方。
    正確答案：(A)

: (A) 注意 …；留心 …；(B) 接手；接管；(C) 代表；(D) 購買 …。

---

23. _____ the new models, the old models received much wider acceptance.
    (A) On the contrary
    (B) In accordance with
    (C) By contrast
    (D) In contrast to

23. 和新的款式比起來，舊款式的接受度比較高。

正確答案：(D)

: (A) 相反地；(B) 依照 …；與 … 一致；(C) 對比之下；
(D) 和 … 對比之下。

---

24. I'll call him back in a minute. There are _____ things I have to do first.
    (A) a handful of
    (B) a variety of
    (C) a couple of
    (D) a great deal of

24. 我等一下就會回電話給他。我還有一些事要先處理。

正確答案：(C)

: (A) 少數；(B) 各式各樣的；(C) 一些 …；零星的 …；(D) 很多。

---

25. The committee was entirely _____ specialists.
    (A) consist of
    (B) composed of
    (C) made of
    (D) inundated with

25. 這個委員會全是由專家所組成。

正確答案：(B)

：(A) 由 … 組成；(B) 由 … 組成；(C) 由 … 製成；(D) 充斥著 …。consist 本身即為動詞，本句前方已有 be 動詞 was，所以不可選 (A)。

♕ Unit 14

1. Our company _____ the real estate deal when we discovered the unscrupulous nature of the seller.
   (A) benefited from
   (B) brought about
   (C) backed out of
   (D) backed up

1. 我們公司退出了這樁地產交易是因為發現了賣方不誠信。
   正確答案：(C)

   > 👩：(A) 從 ... 中獲益；(B) 導致；(C) 退出；(D) 支持。

2. The smartphone _____ the idea that all our personal information could be stored on a mobile device.
   (A) gave out
   (B) gave in
   (C) gave birth to
   (D) got rid of

2. 智慧型手機催生了所有個人資訊都可以儲存在手機裡的想法。
   正確答案：(C)

   > 👩：(A) 發放 ... ；公布 ... ；(B) 屈服；(C) 生 (小孩)；(D) 擺脫 ... ；清除 ... ；丟棄 ... ；處理掉 ... ；賣掉 ... 。

3. My boss and I _____ the key points of the presentation before finalizing it.
   (A) went by
   (B) went after
   (C) got over
   (D) went over

3. 在拍板定案前，老闆和我從頭到尾看了簡報的主要重點。
   正確答案：(D)

: (A) 根據 ... 判斷;(B) 爭取 ...;(C) 克服 ...;恢復;(D) 從頭到尾看過 ...;審查 ...。

---

4. Tom's assistant _____ a copy of the meeting agenda to every person who was crammed into the small conference room.
   (A) handed out
   (B) handed in
   (C) went through
   (D) focused on

4. Tom 的助理發給每位擠在狹小會議室的人一份會議議程。

正確答案:(A)

: (A) 分發 ...;(B) 提交 ...;(C) 瀏覽 ...;徹底檢查;(法律) 被通過;熬過 (困境);從頭到尾練習;(D) 將焦點著重於 ...。

---

5. To quickly master the new programming language, I _____ some great tutorial web sites.
   (A) turned down
   (B) testified to
   (C) took in
   (D) turned to

5. 為了能快速熟悉新的程式語言,我向一些教學網站求助。

正確答案:(D)

: (A) 拒絕;調低 (音量);(B) 證明;(C) 包含;理解;欺騙;攝取;觀賞;(D) 求助於 ...。

---

6. To keep our factory workers from getting _____, it is mandatory that they take two 30-minute breaks per day.
   (A) worn off
   (B) worn out
   (C) wiped out
   (D) worked on

6. 為了不讓我們工廠員工太累，讓他們每天有兩次休息三十分鐘的時間是必要的。

正確答案：(B)

> :(A) 慢慢消失 (效果)；(B) 使 ... 筋疲力盡；(C) 消除 ...；(D) 修理；改善；從事。

---

7. The company sold off a number of their assets to _____ their considerable debt.

(A) give way to

(B) pay off

(C) hear about

(D) hold on to

7. 這家公司賣出部分資產以清償高額債務。

正確答案：(B)

> :(A) 屈服於；(B) 清償；(C) 聽說 ...；(D) 緊握 ...；堅持 ...。

---

8. If you don't _____ your side of the bargain, our contract will be void.

(A) log onto

(B) live up to

(C) look down on

(D) look into

8. 如果你無法遵守協議中你該遵守的部分，那麼我們的合約就是無效的。

正確答案：(B)

> :(A) 登錄；(B) 符合 (期望)；遵循 ...；(C) 輕視 ...；(D) 調查 ...。

9. Employers are seeking employees with the ability to _____ changes.
   (A) apply to
   (B) adapt to
   (C) cling to
   (D) refer to

9. 老闆正在找有能力適應改變的員工。

正確答案：(B)

> :(A) 適用於 ... ; (B) 適應 ... ; (C) 堅持 ... ; 忠實於 ... ; (D) 提及 ... ; 參考 ... 。

10. We'll _____ a proposal, including detailed costings, free of charge.
    (A) put together
    (B) put up with
    (C) put away
    (D) put in

10. 我們會免費完成一份包含詳細成本計算的企劃書。

正確答案：(A)

> :(A) 完成 ... ; 匯整 ... ; 組合 ... ; (B) 忍受 ; (C) 將 ... 放回原處 ; 存錢 ; (D) 花費 (時間)。

11. I'll _____ for her until she gets back from her spring break.
    (A) get over
    (B) get on
    (C) take over
    (D) take on

11. 我們會接管她的工作直到她放完春假回來。

正確答案：(C)

> :(A) 克服 ... ; 恢復 ; (B) 繼續 (做某事) ; (C) 接手 ... ; 接管 ... ; (D) 承擔 (責任)。

12. Whether we will have to cut down on the budget _____ the sales performance this quarter.
    (A) lies in
    (B) counts on
    (C) depends on
    (D) comes with

12. 我們是否得削減預算取決於本季的銷售表現。
    正確答案：(C)

> 😊：(A) 在於 … ；(B) 依靠… ；(C) 取決於 … ；依靠… ；信任… ；(D) 具備 …。

---

13. Please _____ the handrail so that you won't fall.
    (A) hold on to
    (B) hold on
    (C) stop by
    (D) stand by

13. 請緊握扶手以免跌倒。
    正確答案：(A)

> 😊：(A) 緊握 … ；堅持 … ；(B) 等一下 ；(C) 經過 ；順道來訪 ；(D) 支持 ；待命。

---

14. The company offered some special discounts _____ the customer complaints.
    (A) in place of
    (B) in order to
    (C) in the face of
    (D) in response to

14. 該公司提供一些特別折扣以回應顧客們的抱怨。
    正確答案：(D)

> 😊：(A) 取代 … ；(B) 為了要 … ；(C) 不顧 (困難等) ；(D) 回應 …。

15. Mr. Cliff has _____ a conference call for Wednesday afternoon.
   (A) set up
   (B) picked up
   (C) made up
   (D) looked up

15. Cliff 先生週三下午已安排要開會。

正確答案：(A)

 ：(A) 設立 …；安排 …；(B) 撿起 …；學會 …；搭載某人；(C) 編造；
和好；組成；化妝；補足或湊齊；(D) 好轉或改善；抬起頭來；
查閱。

國家圖書館出版品預行編目（CIP）資料

徐薇教你懂新多益文法 / 徐薇編著． --臺北市：
碩英，2015.09
面；　公分 .--（新多益系列；3）
ISBN 978-986-90662-3-5(平裝附光碟片)
1. 多益測驗 2. 語法
805.1895　　　　　　　　　　　　　　104018611

徐薇教你懂新多益文法

發行人：江正明

發行公司：碩英出版社

編著者：徐薇

責任編輯：賴依寬、王歆、黃怡欣、黃思瑜

美術編輯：蔡佳容

錄音製作：風華錄音室

地址：106 台北市大安區安和路二段 70 號 2 樓之 3

電話：02-2708-5508

傳真：02-2707-1669

出版日期：2015 年 9 月

定價：NT$ 450

＜本書若有缺頁、破損或倒裝等問題，請電 (02)2708-5508，
我們將儘速為您服務＞